SUBWAY SLAYINGS

MEMENTO MORI: BOOK TWO

C.S. POE

Subway Slayings
Copyright © 2022 by C.S. Poe

Published by Emporium Press
https://www.cspoe.com
contact@cspoe.com

Cover Art by Reese Dante
Cover content is for illustrative purposes only and any person depicted on the cover is a model.

Edited by Tricia Kristufek
Copyedited by Andrea Zimmerman
Proofread by Lyrical Lines

Published 2022.
Printed in the United States of America

Trade Paperback ISBN: 978-1-952133-41-1

Digital eBook ISBN: 978-1-952133-40-4

For Kale.
Thank you for elevating this series to something more.

AUTHOR'S NOTE

Detective Neil Millett hails from the Snow & Winter series. The Memento Mori series can be read without any prior knowledge, but for his character origin, begin with Book 1, *The Mystery of Nevermore*.

MEMENTO MORI

Remember that you must die.

CHAPTER ONE

It was Tuesday, May 19, 4:57 p.m., and there was a body in a blue IKEA tote bag.

A uniformed officer lifted the crime scene tape cordoning off the stairs to the Fifty-Seventh Street platform, and Detective Everett Larkin ducked underneath. The subway system was over a century old, carved into the ancient bedrock that Manhattan sat upon long before climate control was ever a factor, and the passive ventilation offered little reprieve after an abnormally hot stint for early summer. Coupled with the heat thrown off by 85,000 pounds of steel speeding into the station nearly 200 times a day, and the platform was about as comfortable as a moist blanket.

Larkin had left his gray, glen plaid suit coat in the Audi, a verdict he'd gone back and forth on exactly five times, because the gold pocket square was what really brought the burgundy tie and mint-green derbies together, and without it, Larkin felt his aesthetic was markedly lacking. But the prickle of perspiration already starting under his arms was confirmation he'd made the right decision. After all, he'd just had his dry cleaning done over the weekend in preparation of being given the go-ahead to return to active duty once he'd followed up with his orthopedist that morning, and Larkin had been extremely dissatisfied with the services provided by Carol's Wash and Tailor. He'd need time to properly research other cleaners in the Village—price not being a factor so much as quality of care. Because if Larkin was going to drop a grand on custom-tailored slim-cut suits due to unabashed vanity and a distinct lack of hobbies in which to otherwise invest in, he certainly didn't expect some sort of rust stain on the lapels when they returned from the cleaner. He tugged his phone free, opened the calendar, and quickly added a personal reminder about the dry-cleaning situation before returning the cell to his pocket.

Larkin walked along the stretch of platform devoid of evening rush-hour straphangers, crossed the digital information center, which read *Service Alert: Uptown and downtown F trains bypass 57 St. due to police activity*, and approached the throng of officers and MTA employees hovering around a pair of open double doors slapped with a too-thick and glossy black paint at the opposite end from where he entered. An uptown F train thundered into the station, brakes screeching as it turned too sharply, the faces of overcrowded passengers a kaleidoscopic blur of color as the train didn't slow, didn't stop. Hot air gusted toward Larkin in its wake, and with it the summer aromas of garbage and body odor, and along with those, the unmistakable stench of decomp.

He paused midstride.

August 28, 2011, a wellness check on Herbert Langston found him five days dead from a massive heart attack, naked in his recliner, the television on an adult pay-per-view channel. Herbert still had his dick in his hand. Larkin had been a rookie officer, only one year under his belt of walking the beat, and he'd thrown up in the apartment stairwell.

July 2, 2015, Larissa Brown and her two baby daughters were discovered stuffed inside an oil drum out in the Pine

Barrens of New Jersey almost two months after they'd been reported missing. Her husband had wanted a divorce and didn't want to be stuck paying child support. Larkin had cried in the shower until the water ran cold, because he couldn't seem to scrub the stink of their death from his skin. His tenacity and persistence on that case, one Larkin's own sergeant had told him to set aside numerous times, had garnered the interest of Lieutenant Connor and earned him a promotion into the elite Cold Case Squad.

April 1, 2020, Beatrice Regmore had been found beaten to death by her son and left to rot in the bathtub for two days. Her skull had been caved in, blood crusted her paisley nightgown; her fingers were curled from arthritis, skin like wrinkled tissue paper. And then there'd been an animalistic roar, the collision of bodies, and Harry Regmore had raised a baseball bat in both hands—

"*Grim!*"

The disparaging moniker shook the associations, the memories, like a house of cards falling apart and every face was the ace of spades.

Larkin took a breath. He could taste death on the back of his throat, like fermented green meat and rotten eggs, shit and stale piss, trash left to bake in the heat and humidity.

He reached the end of the platform where Ray O'Halloran stood, a Homicide detective Larkin had had more than his fair share of interactions with throughout the years. It'd been O'Halloran's own reluctance to be saddled with the "loser" case of Andrew Gorman that'd slingshotted Larkin into this holding pattern, this void, this drug-induced composure that wore off every eight to twelve hours and tore his stitching apart so that *emptiness*, that *hollowness* in his chest, wept like a fatal wound.

In Nietzsche's preface to *On the Genealogy of Morals*, he stated: *We are strangers to ourselves, we perceivers. We have never sought for ourselves—how, then, could it happen, that some day we* should find *ourselves?*

Everett Larkin had incredible perception. He never forgot a face; could recite any conversation upon request. He read nonverbal cues with textbook precision and broke down the psychology of place without a roadmap. But when he turned that incredible skill—that incredible guilt—unto himself, there was nothing to see. Nothing to find.

Because Everett Larkin was a nobody.

And nothings and nobodies were gray, and no matter how much color was added, once mixed together, it *always* turned gray. Like summer thunderstorms. Like stainless steel mortuary tables. Like the faces of the forgotten.

Rightly has it been said: "Where your treasure is, there will your heart be also."

But it was impossible to see, to perceive, what that treasure may be when it lay beyond the veil.

O'Halloran wore an N95 mask. He slapped one against Larkin's chest and said, "Welcome back. You'll need this. If you have to puke, puke on the tracks."

Larkin caught the mask. He glanced toward the double doors a second time and watched two individuals in full PPE and respirators move about in what he surmised was some kind of utility closet. "My lieutenant said this was a matter for Cold Cases."

O'Halloran nodded.

Larkin put the N95 on, adjusted the nose piece, then said, "Human bodies begin the decomposition process roughly four minutes after the time of death, and in an ideal setting, the timeline is consistent from rigor mortis to bloat to active decay. But in a hot and humid environment, the progression is often accelerated. In summer of 2018, the Regional Plan Association took the temperature in sixteen of New York's busiest subway stations. They confirmed that twelve of the sixteen reached over ninety degrees by late morning, making these platforms hotter than the ambient temperature outside, which was eighty-six degrees. And while Fifty-Seventh Street was not among the record breakers—the 4, 5, 6 at Union Square was one-hundred-four, and the uptown 1 at Columbus Circle was one-hundred-one—I cite these examples to emphasize how heat down here will compromise time of death estimations, and that what smells like human soup served up in a large-size, polypropylene IKEA shopping bag, available for ninety-nine cents and owned by just about every New Yorker, making it untraceable, has likely been deceased a week or less. Therefore, this murder—I assume murder, as the individual likely did not lock themselves in a utility closet, crawl into a reusable Swedish tote, and expire of their own volition—is firmly Camp Homicide, not Cold Cases."

After a moment, O'Halloran shook his head, muttered, "Jesus Christ," then walked toward the double doors.

Larkin reluctantly followed, the stench permeating his mask the closer they got, and he was forced to take shallow breaths through his mouth instead of his nose. Both detectives stood in the doorway, watching as one of the techs collected maggot samples from the mass writhing on the bloated and partially melted body.

"You fuckers done playing with bugs yet?" O'Halloran asked.

"All bugs are insects," the tech answered as he screwed a cap onto the vial in his hand. "But not all insects are bugs."

The dry and sardonic delivery, the upward lilt in his voice—Larkin's mental Rolodex spun to March 30, to the morning thunderstorm, the uprooted crabapple, the crate, the CSU detective waist-deep in mud as he'd suggested, "*That* is a death mask."—Neil Millett.

Larkin inclined his head politely, saying, "Millett."

"We meet again, Everett Larkin," Millett answered, voice slightly muffled by the respirator mask. "Sorry it's under such conditions."

"When I'm asked to resume active duty fifteen hours earlier than what is explicitly noted by my surgeon on the physician's release form and called to the scene of a homicide, I don't expect the presence of a Crime Scene detective to bring particularly favorable conditions," Larkin answered in his usual modulated tone.

The second man, who had been crouched on his haunches beside the IKEA bag during the verbal ping-pong, rose. He was shorter than Millett, but other than his height and the general impression of a slim build, any defining characteristics were hidden by the bodysuit and mask. "Everett Larkin, Cold Case Squad," the man echoed, his voice not particularly deep, but smooth, laid-back—a sense of well-placed confidence without an overt suggestion of egotism. "If I'd known you'd be here, I'd have worn my fancy respirator." He looked down at Millett, who was labeling the container of maggots suspended in a clear solution, and asked, "Did I tell you about the time he called my office, picked a fight with Joyce, then asked me on a date in return for making him a skull casting?"

At that comment, Millett raised his head.

"Dr. Baxter," Larkin said, addressing the medical examiner who, prior to this moment, he'd only had the briefest of encounters with over the phone. "Pleasure to meet you in person. That's not what happened."

"That's what I remember."

"No. Your mortuary technician wasn't versed in the methodology of facial reconstruction, nor the authority and responsibilities of the OCME, which specifically notes in its mission statement: investigating all deaths of persons in New York City, which includes in any unusual or suspicious manner. My victim was found buried in a crate in Madison

Square Park, and while I don't like assigning labels to the crimes I investigate, the death of Andrew Gorman qualified as both unusual and suspicious. In conclusion, I did not 'pick a fight' with that woman. I merely reminded her of her civic duties."

"And was the offer of a date part of *your* civic duties?" Baxter countered rather coyly.

"There was no offer of a date," Larkin corrected. "Merely a poorly worded compliment I've regretted since that day."

Millett rose, and while pointing his pen at the good doctor, said, "He's messing with you, Larkin."

"I'm not messing with him. I'm *flirting* with him, thank you."

"Dipshits—" O'Halloran tried.

Millett raised a gloved hand and began counting points on his fingers, addressing Baxter. "One, no flirting in the general vicinity of dead bodies."

"Have you forgotten what I do for a living?"

"Two, if you're wearing a respirator, it's too much PPE for flirting."

"That's debatable."

"Three, and I feel like I remind you of this one weekly, don't flirt with married men."

"Oh, he's not married," Baxter said, looking toward Larkin.

Larkin frowned from behind his own mask and slid both hands into his trouser pockets.

"See?" Baxter looked up at Millett and snapped his fingers, the latex cracking loudly. "Keep up, Neil—you work in evidence collection."

A moment passed before Millett looked at Larkin, said, "Dr. Baxter is single, if you're looking," then bent down and busied himself with his kit.

"*Shut the fuck up,*" O'Halloran barked. "Holy Mary, Mother of Christ, what're the odds of me ending up in a room with you homos?"

"One in eleven," Larkin said in a monotone, although he'd been studying the IKEA bag as he spoke. Turning his reaper-gray eyes back on O'Halloran, Larkin's stare bore into the Homicide detective as he continued. "The population of New York City is just over eight million, of which nine percent openly identify as LGBT. Therefore, you have a one-in-eleven chance of being in a room with us. Of course, ratios do vary the more we break down the acronym, but that's not really the point here, seeing as your comment was meant to imply something negative about the competent and professional company you're currently in the presence of. I suggest therapy as a means of addressing your homophobia, as a team of Australian scientists recently conducted a study on the correlation between prejudice against same-sex couples and low cognitive ability. The results did indeed indicate a distinct parallel, with emphasis on this pattern being even more pronounced for verbal ability measures, which is a very scientific way of saying you sound like an idiot and an asshole when you speak."

For a singular second, the subway was silent. There was no screech of trains rolling through the station, no echo of voices from outside the utility room, not even the shift of the PPE bodysuits whispering on the stale air.

And then Baxter let out a long sigh, asking in a dreamy voice, "Are you available, Larkin? Like, emotionally?"

"No."

"Such a shame." Baxter met Millett's *what gives?* hand gesture and laughed, "*What?*"

O'Halloran, whose usual ruddy complexion was well on its way to turning the color of pinot noir, pointed a finger at Larkin. "Listen to me, you sonofa—"

"I have thirty-seven open cases, O'Halloran. I don't intend on adding this one to my stack until it falls within the purview of my job description—namely, when detectives have exhausted all investigative leads."

O'Halloran squared his shoulders and barked, "Show Grim the goddamn photo."

Larkin's gaze cut toward Millett, and he watched the CSU detective begrudgingly acknowledge the demand by retrieving a clear plastic bag, standing, and holding it out. Larkin accepted it and studied the contents: a 4x6 photograph, like something cheaply and hastily developed at any drugstore photo lab across America throughout the '80s and '90s. The snapshot was vertical, of what appeared to be a teenage girl slouched—asleep, drunk, or stoned, it was difficult to say—on one of the infamous oak benches scattered throughout the platforms of the subway system. The white tile wall behind her offered no suggestion as to her location, other than one of the underground stations, and any other details to be gleaned wouldn't be possible in the photo's current state, as it was heavily smeared and discolored with human fluids.

"It was in John Doe's pocket," Millett said before adding, "look at the back."

Larkin turned the bag around. Written across the back of the photograph in a shaky and slanted hand was *Deliver me to Detective Larkin!*

Larkin looked up.

O'Halloran gave him a mocking salute, said, "Mazel tov, motherfucker," and walked out of the utility room.

"You know," Millett stated after O'Halloran had departed, "there's a forensic document examiner at the lab in Queens—"

"Blue ballpoint pen," Larkin interrupted, studying the message again. "Cheap, disposable, probably Bic, which is the world's most popular pen brand, selling an average of fifty-seven units a second. So, untraceable. The handwriting itself is disguised, below the individual's baseline skill level." He studied the evidence for one, two, three more seconds, before concluding, "Right-handed, but they switched as a means of concealment." Larkin raised his head.

Millett's expression around the respirator was pinched. "How do you know that?"

"Ambidextrous by nurture, not nature," Larkin answered, pointing to himself. "Although I still favor my left for shooting and writing. Without practice, penmanship in the nondominant hand has a distinct tremor and slant, as the individual lacks the fine control and muscle memory found in the dominant hand. And because ninety percent of American citizens are right-handed, it is highly likely the individual is masking their identity by simply switching to the left hand."

"How did I not see that?" Millett murmured with a distinct, cynical tone.

"My observation skills and recall are considered to be quite exceptional."

"And so modest too."

"I have neither the time nor inclination to take fragile egos under consideration while doing my job, Detective," Larkin answered. He held up the evidence bag and asked, voice lacking that natural upward inflection found in English, "May I keep this."

"By all means," Millett concluded with an absent wave of his hand.

"You sound like your blood sugar is dipping," Baxter said to Larkin. "Prolonged exposure to heat can do that."

"The brain utilizes one half of the body's glucose, and with a drop in fuel levels, individuals have been known to exhibit an array of negative behavior, leading to the growing body of scientific research behind the term *hangry*. Thank you, Doctor. If you'll be so kind as to update me on the state of the victim."

Baxter didn't sound nearly as perturbed as Millett had been when he replied, "Victim is male. Middle age, at least." He pointed to the IKEA bag and added, "But I won't be able to get you anything more exact until I get this soup back to the OCME."

"Cause of death," Larkin asked.

"I can't say until after a thorough autopsy. All I know is an MTA track worker found him about two hours ago. O'Halloran probably has interview notes for you."

"How long has the victim been deceased."

"Are you asking or telling me?" Baxter countered.

"I'm asking."

"Oh. Eight—*nine days*—maximum." Baxter squatted beside the bag and indicated several clusters of wriggling maggots. "These are blowfly larvae, which show up on the scene of a dead body within minutes to lay their eggs. These larvae are third instar—you can even see a few pupae in the folds of the shirt," he continued, raising a bit of fabric to show Larkin. "They'd emerge as adult flies in about… six days, assuming the body was kept at this level of heat and humidity for the rest of the week."

"Putting time of death between Sunday, May 10—"

—thunder like the howls of a banshee on the prowl, wails of warning, a reminder that everyone must die, and Larkin was no exception. He was a psychopomp of flesh and blood, and some nights, when the rain fell and thunder crashed, and Patrick was brutally murdered over and over and over again, Larkin was so tired that he'd curl up in the tub with too many Xanax and bide his time until the day he'd be nothing more than a DD5 lost in the stacks of another Cold Case detective.

No progress to report.

But the apartment door had banged against the exposed

brick wall, soles of wet shoes squeaked against the wood floor, a bag dropped with a loud thud, *and a voice usually whiskey-smooth had been replaced with visceral panic as he'd called,* "Evie?"—

Larkin closed his eyes, took a breath through his nose, instantly regretted it, and forced himself to swallow the bile licking at the back of his throat. Looking at Baxter again, he reiterated, "Time of death is between Sunday, May 10, and Monday, May 11."

"I concur. Are you okay?"

"Yes," Larkin lied. He looked down at the IKEA bag—at the remains of a lost soul the city had chewed up and spit out—and asked, "Was there anything else on the body."

"Just a business card," Baxter answered. "Neil?"

Larkin turned as Millett offered him a second evidence bag. The cheap cardstock was more heavily damaged than the photograph—soggy and discolored from decomposition. But Larkin studied what print was still legible and made out: S UD M SSI N. Larkin gave his mental Rolodex another hard spin as he studied the fragmented words, but it only took a few seconds to place the organization. "St. Jude's Mission."

—*in sickness and in health, to love and to cherish, 'til death do us part.—*

"I think you should give *Wheel of Fortune* a go," Baxter said bemusedly.

Larkin blinked, shook his head, returned the card to Millett, and addressed both men. "Please email me the crime scene photos and autopsy report as soon as possible." He stepped out of the utility room, tugged the N95 mask off, breathed in damp sour air.

It didn't help.

Larkin was choking, gasping, as death, as expectation, as guilt crushed him, forcing his head under the black currents of the River Styx, and not even Charon crossed those waters without a ferry. Indeed, Larkin was a psychopomp. He knew the names of the now 9,019 victims that time had forgotten—*abandoned*—and one by one, he shuttled them toward justice—toward *respite*. The downtrodden, the nobodies, the wretches whose only misstep was to be murdered in a world too busy and too wary to respect their deaths—Larkin would never forget any of them. Every day was an anniversary of tragedy, his calendar a memento mori, and his weary soul a band of black to mark his mourning.

But Larkin was still a man.

His HSAM allowed him to never forget the forgotten, but he also never forgot the wounds inflicted on his own life. And there were so many arrows in his back, so much bleeding out because he couldn't—*literally couldn't*—let those memories fade into obscurity, some days he wondered how he was expected to go on, how he was expected to function when that footage and those soundbites ran on a broken loop set off by something as inconsequential as a date, a sound.

Larkin pushed through the mingling cops and MTA employees still on the platform, shot up the stairs two at a time, and rushed through the recently renovated entrance, with its tiled floors and mediocre art on the walls, before climbing the next set of stairs to the street. Larkin waited at the curb until there was a break in traffic before crossing Sixth Avenue. His black Audi was parked behind an HVAC repair truck and soccer-mom minivan alongside the bike lane. Circling around the front, Larkin tapped his key fob, opened the driver's door, and got inside. It was too closed up, but the discomfort barely registered as Larkin tossed the evidence bag onto the passenger seat, yanked open the center console, dug out a small, 2x3 hidden envelope, and shook out two Xanax into the palm of his hand. Larkin dry-swallowed the pills before leaning back in the seat.

He counted to sixty before putting the key in the ignition, turning on the engine, and tapping the AC button. The initial gust of warm air quickly cooled, and the sweat slicking his skin began to dry. Larkin rubbed his palms against his thighs and let out a slow breath as the sick sensation that warned of imminent heaves gradually dissipated.

After another sixty count, Larkin glanced at the sodden photograph in its plastic bag. He shifted, pulled his cell from his pocket, and tapped a name in his contacts. On the third ring, the call picked up, and Larkin said, "Hi. Are you busy."

CHAPTER TWO

At 6:32 p.m., Larkin was walking down the fifth-floor hallway of One Police Plaza, the hideous turd of Brutalism architecture that was the new headquarters of the NYPD. Nestled among the Civic Center neighborhood, with Chinatown to the north and the Financial District to the south, 1PP (as it was colloquially known) was home to not only the police commissioner, but detectives considered to be the "big guns" on the force: Major Cases and Real Time Crime. Hardly anyone—civilian administrator, beat cop, or detective alike—was aware that the three-man Forensic Artists Unit was also on location.

Larkin came to a stop outside a partially closed office door. He'd been inside before, on March 31, but it felt wrong to assume he could invite himself in after only a single visit forty-nine days ago. So he knocked. It was quiet around him. Not empty; Larkin could hear life from behind other closed doors on either side of the hall—a desk phone that wouldn't stop ringing, the mechanical whine of a personal printer on its last leg, a muffled, one-sided conversation made up of no less than a dozen incredibly unique variations on *fuck*. The tired overhead lights that never saw rest had an almost subaudible hum to them in the evening hours, and the AC-cooled air was still circulating the scent of someone's late lunch—microwaved ramen and boiled eggs, Larkin suspected.

The door opened and Detective Ira Doyle stood in the threshold. He was lean and slender, with a build similar to Larkin's, if not for the extra half a foot in height. His appearance tended to run the gamut of disheveled, unkempt, and lax, with his five-o'clock shadow at any time of day, the loosened tie, rolled-back sleeves, and more often than not, an absent suit coat. His chocolate-brown hair was constantly a mess, not because it was done on purpose, but because Doyle was a habitual finger-comber.

For all the visual cues that'd led to Doyle's professionalism being called into question, though, Larkin had been the first to admit how wrong he'd been in his initial assessment. Doyle was a gifted artist and a skilled investigator, with seemingly unlimited patience, and a heart no one was good enough for, Larkin included. But when Doyle smiled with his entire body, when those flecks of pyrite in his brown eyes caught the light just right, when he still smelled of neroli and sandalwood and cardamon after a long day, when he said, "Evie," in that smoky voice, that was when Larkin began wishing he was something more.

Something *better*.

Larkin raised the jug of water he held in one hand. "Distilled."

"Perfect." Doyle stepped back, holding the door. "Come in."

Larkin moved into the office. A closed 11x24 sketch pad sat atop the white drafting table on the left side of the room. A steel mesh trash can held several crumpled pages of the thick, high-quality paper and a scattering of candy wrappings—lemon drops. Larkin recognized the Clancy's Candy Counter brand these days, even from afar. The shelves behind Doyle's chair were still crowded with a ridiculous amount of art supplies, tools, and binders of six-packs. Opposite was the worktable Doyle had sat at March 31, hunched over the bust of the person who they'd come to know as Andrew Gorman. Today, the table was clear but for two plastic trays that looked like those used for photo development, a roll of paper towels, a few brushes, and a squat bottle of an unknown substance with a dropper applicator.

Doyle had accepted the gallon jug from Larkin and said while closing the door, "Don't trust the lab to do this?"

"New York has one of the top-performing forensic crime labs in the country," Larkin answered. "They'd do a perfectly adequate job at collecting any trace evidence. Scientists want facts, after all. But artists want stories." Larkin watched Doyle set the jug on the table before pulling on an apron in a midnight-blue hue. "When it comes to understanding the human element in a murder, your skill set far outweighs the lab's."

Doyle was smiling as he crossed the ties once around his front before tying them at the back. "So I guess the check-up with your orthopedist went well."

"Yes. I return to active duty tomorrow," Larkin said dryly. He gave the mesh trash can a second consideration before stating, "You had a bad day."

Doyle wasn't messy, per se. He was one of those people who dispersed belongings as he went—a suit coat shoved onto the ladder rung instead of being hung up in the closet, because the ladder was closer, for example—but he was mindful of actual trash and probably didn't realize that the crumpled mess was atypical of his character and, therefore, credible evidence as to the limit his patience had been pushed that day. He corrected in that usual warm baritone, "A little tedious, is all."

Moving toward Larkin, Doyle stopped to stand before

him. *Close.* Always so close. Separated by a baby's breath. But Doyle was acutely aware of the fact that Larkin shied away from, was even repulsed by, physicality from the wrong person or when he might not have been in a good headspace.

So they'd developed a workaround. Something unique to them. A nonverbal approach to checking in, to asking permission, because Larkin had been hurt for too long by meaningless platitudes and guilted too long into speaking a love language profoundly foreign to him.

"People don't want to know. But I do."

"On August 2, 2002, I was struck in the head with a baseball bat."

Doyle reached down, his hands big and capable, and gave the black hair tie around Larkin's left wrist a tug.

No, Larkin wasn't okay. He was still raw, over an hour after walking out of the Fifty-Seventh Street station. Walking? Try *running*. He hadn't even spoken to the MTA employee responsible for calling in John Doe. How ridiculous. How unprofessional. Larkin could lie. Say that after forty-eight days of medical leave, he was rusty, misread the scenario, had *forgotten*. Except that Larkin forgot to load the wash into the dryer. He forgot where he'd taken off his red derbies. He forgot the grocery list but didn't notice until he was already at the store and nearly melted down in the dairy aisle. Larkin forgot the unscheduled events, the impromptu errands. He *didn't* forget to interview witnesses, because that was routine, and routine was what kept him breathing.

It'd been the two associations while in the utility room.

One right after the other, like he'd been KO'd and then punched in the head a second time, just for good measure.

In the beginning, Larkin had thought the growing distance and dissatisfaction between him and Noah had been the motivation to reach out for pharmaceutical aid. But now he was realizing he couldn't do this anymore—

couldn't *live*, couldn't *work*, without medication. And when one pill hadn't been enough, had barely supplied a sense of calm, of normalcy to his fucked-up neural pathways, Larkin took a second. A third. The prescription didn't stop the associations—memories of the best and worst days of his life right there, as if they'd only happened seconds ago—but the euphoria sure helped Larkin care a whole lot less.

He wished he'd grabbed a third pill before coming upstairs.

Larkin swallowed, cleared his throat, and said, "I—I could use a hug."

Without hesitating, Doyle wrapped his arms around Larkin's shoulders. Larkin slid his own under Doyle's to grip the back of his shirt, and they stood flush against each other—immovable and resilient and quiet. After a moment, when Doyle shifted, Larkin held on just a little longer, a little tighter, because sometimes it felt as if the only thing keeping him standing on his own two feet was *this*.

But eventually Larkin let go. He nodded once and said, "Thank you."

"You're welcome," Doyle answered. His expression was that of a man watching a trainwreck occur in slow motion, who knew Larkin was *not* okay, but who was also aware that asking "Want to talk about it?" before Larkin was ready, would only make everything so much worse. So all he said was "Tell me about this John Doe."

Larkin quickly said, "Victim was an adult male, found in the utility closet at the south end of the Fifty-Seventh Street F train platform." He moved to the worktable and leaned one hip against it. "He was stuffed into a reusable IKEA tote, but advanced decay has currently hindered any further conclusions without an autopsy."

Doyle joined him, his thick and expressive brows furrowed. "How long was he in there?"

"The heat and humidity sped up the decomposition process, but based on insect activity—" Larkin paused as Doyle shuddered reactively, involuntarily, at the mere mention of creepy-crawlies. "Are you—"

Doyle motioned with one hand for Larkin to continue.

"Blowfly lifecycle indicates time of death is between Sunday, May 10, and Monday, May 11."

Doyle glanced sideways at the dates mentioned.

He wasn't the fool he played.

Larkin could see Doyle snapping the clues in place, completing the mental jigsaw puzzle that explained Larkin's immediate need for physical comfort upon arrival.

It's an association. Sounds, typically, are what do it for me, but dates too.

"You're making a compelling case for Homicide taking point," Doyle said.

Larkin reached into his inner suit coat pocket and retrieved the plastic evidence bag. He offered it, saying, "My presence appears to have been requested."

Doyle took the bag, studied the scrawled note on the back of the photograph, then murmured, "The NYPD is allowing suspects in a murder investigation to pick and choose their lead detective?"

"I haven't spoken with Lieutenant Connor and gotten his explanation behind this decision yet," Larkin answered. "But you make an assumption that this note was left by the individual responsible for the death of John Doe."

"It's a pretty sound assumption. What was this photograph sitting in?"

"Decomp."

"Jesus." Doyle dropped it on the tabletop. He popped the cap off the jug of distilled water Larkin had picked up on his way downtown, and poured the contents into both pans before reaching for a pair of latex gloves.

On April 1, after the subsequent brawl and arrest of Harry Regmore at his mother's apartment in the Bronx, Larkin had been whisked to the hospital for surgery to correct a broken arm. It'd been a rather incredible injury in the grand scheme of events. Because Larkin had frozen. He should have died that afternoon. But Doyle had been there, had saved his life. And while Larkin had been alone in the ER, an anonymous letter addressed to him had been delivered to the nurses' station.

HAPPY APRIL FOOLS' DAY, LARKIN

DEATH MASKS ARE "HORRIBLE THINGS"

I HAVE A BETTER MEMENTO FOR YOU

COME FIND ME

Hospital surveillance had only been able to supply law enforcement with a grainy image of a nondescript individual in a dark hoodie, baseball cap, and sunglasses. The nurse who'd accepted the envelope couldn't remember any corroborating details—she'd been nearing the end of a twelve-hour shift, hadn't had a bathroom break in almost as much time, had half a dozen ER patients bleeding, seizing—*no*, she didn't pay any mind to the individual. The contents had been dusted for fingerprints, but all that'd come back were the nurse's and Larkin's own. The incident had been concerning, but with the absence of any evidence to pursue, local precinct detectives who'd caught the investigation had considered it DOA.

But not Larkin.

He had gleaned exactly four clues.

First: The usage of the Parks' Department logo within the cut-and-pasted letters, before Harry's identity had been shared with the public, before he'd even had his mugshot snapped, implied someone internal. Someone with knowledge of who Harry was, what he'd been doing in those parks since 1991, with the suggestion that they could do it all and more.

Second: The quote about death masks had, in fact, been from the third sentence in the introduction of Laurence Hutton's *Portraits in Plaster*, the same book Doyle had mentioned reading while attending art school. The book had been published in 1894 by Harper & Brothers Publishers, now existed within the public domain, and was, as Doyle suggested, not exactly a bestseller. That provided further background into the sort of individual who'd quote such an obscure reference.

Third: The letter had come with an MTA token—the solid quarter-size used throughout the eighties with the iconic Y logo, although lacking its predecessor's cut-out shape. It'd been issued in 1980 when the fare was sixty cents a ride and had lived through two additional price hikes before the style had been discontinued in 1986.

Fourth: This individual had wanted *Larkin's* attention. And now here he was, investigating a curious murder in the depths of the subway system, with his literal name on the only discernable piece of evidence.

Larkin frowned.

Once is chance. Twice is coincidence.

"Evie."

Larkin startled and looked up. Doyle was staring at him. "Hmm?"

Doyle smiled as he repeated, "I asked if you were solving the case without me."

"No. Just thinking."

Doyle didn't know about the April Fools' letter.

Larkin studied Doyle as he carefully removed the stained and damaged photo from the evidence bag, set it in the first pan of water, and began to scrape away human fluids with one of the brushes that'd been laid out on the table. Doyle's actions were attentive, purposeful, gentle.

—Blunt fingertips trailing up every link of Larkin's spine, engrossed in the story of skin and bone, the caress so tender, so heartfelt, Larkin could identify Doyle by the lines and ridges of his fingerprints alone.—

"You look nice," Doyle stated into the quiet. He hadn't glanced up as he transferred the photo to the second bath and rinsed it.

"Yes, thank you. I showered today."

Doyle's sunshiny smile was back and he chuckled under his breath. "Gold compliments you." He set the photograph on a paper towel and began to blot it dry. "It brings out your eyes."

"You've used this line on me before."

"Were you wearing a gold pocket square at the time?"

"Yes."

"Then that's why." Doyle picked up the photo by its edges, studied the image briefly, then said, "That residue came off easier than I expected." He turned it around before adding, "I don't want to use emulsion cleaner too and risk damage to this writing." Setting the photo facedown on a fresh towel, Doyle continued. "I can tell you right off the bat that this print is… maybe thirty… thirty-five years old."

Larkin moved forward, standing shoulder-to-shoulder with Doyle. "How can you tell."

"A few ways." Doyle tapped the gray logo stamped repetitively across the back. "This brand of photo paper was local to the tristate area, but they couldn't compete with the volume produced by companies like Kodak and Agfa. They went out of business, I want to say, just before 1990?" Doyle flipped the photo to show Larkin the now-cleaned-up teenage girl on a bench. "In most cases regarding storage, colored paper won't last even ten years, but this image has no fogging, so it wasn't a recent development with a batch of old, expired paper." He turned it back around a second time.

"And this string of gibberish is data relevant to the minilab that did the printing."

Larkin met Doyle's eyes and asked, "A date. A location."

"Nothing so useful. Part of the information is applicable to the machine itself. Say a small business owned and operated three of them—002 might be the second machine. This number here might imply the job or roll number done that given day. And this section here, I believe, is in regard to any manual color correction done by the operator. In this instance, it looks like a default code, so they probably didn't make any adjustments during printing."

Larkin asked, "Hundreds, if not thousands, of retro family photos in the city might have similar to the exact same code on the back."

"Right."

"Perfect," he muttered.

Doyle chuckled at Larkin's deadpan delivery before saying, "You were right about artists wanting stories, though. In fact, photography is the art of subtle fabrication, of pushing a particular narrative. Susan Sontag wrote, 'The camera's rendering of reality must always hide more than it discloses.' That reality is hidden in the photographer's decisions of not only light and texture, but the actual geometry of the photograph itself."

"It sounds like you're reading from an influencer's vade mecum."

Doyle's head fell forward, as if he were trying to tuck his chin to his chest. "A master's in art history, and he compares it to *The Real Freshman Handbook* for social media bobbleheads."

"I've misspoken."

Doyle raised his head.

After a brief pause, Larkin began to add, "I did not mean

to imply your schooling—" But he stopped abruptly when Doyle smiled—and it wasn't a social or masking expression, but his usual and true, genuine smile—a Duchenne smile, was the technical name.

It was the crow's-feet.

Dead giveaway every time.

"What," Larkin asked.

"You can just say, 'I'm sorry.'"

"I'm sorry."

Doyle picked up the photograph, motioned with a nod of his head for Larkin to follow, and walked to his drafting table. He took a seat, set the photo on the work surface, flicked on the attached desk lamp, and adjusted the magnifying head over the image. "If you had any doubt as to the decade this photo originated, your subject is wearing a polka-dotted shirt, floral-print vest, and acid-wash jeans while sporting perm bangs."

"And these crimes against humanity continued to flourish well into our own childhoods," Larkin replied. He leaned over Doyle's shoulder to stare at the photo. Something about this girl—her expression? her posture?—puzzled him. It was as if she'd failed the uncanny valley test, in that she was *human enough* to provoke a negative reaction in Larkin. It was something in her half-hooded gaze, he decided. Something cold. Something almost lifeless. He stated abruptly, and without hesitation, "She's dead."

Doyle had said in the same breath, his comment overlapping Larkin's, "I think she's dead."

CHAPTER THREE

Industrial disinfectant of an indeterminant citrus scent had been spilled in the women's bathroom of Precinct 19. The door was propped open by a janitorial cart, and Larkin could hear Joseline inside expelling a world-weary sigh as she cleaned the mess. He took the stairs two at a time to the second floor, the bullpen a home away from home for the detectives of the Cold Case Squad. The early mornings and late nights, the twelve-hour shifts, the endless overtime—it could be seen in how ten overworked humans left pieces of themselves behind in a mass-produced American office: a framed photo of a five-year-old black boy wearing his kindergarten finest on Detective Baker's desk, even though her son was now finishing seventh grade; Porter's #1 Husband coffee mug, despite his divorce having settled the year Larkin joined the squad; Miyamoto's Doc Martens that'd been sitting atop a box of files beside her chair for months, because she kept meaning to fix one of the soles with Krazy Glue but never found the time to run out on her lunch break to buy adhesive. It was the accumulation of umbrellas in the stand beside the stairs, the collection of full-sized condiment bottles in the breakroom fridge, the closet beside the copy room overcrowded with coats and sweaters suitable for every season because "it's not like I wear it anywhere else but work" that suggested these unofficial roommates put in more facetime at Sixty-Seventh between Third and Lexington than they ever did in their actual homes.

When Larkin reached the landing, the lemon—possibly orange—cleaner had mingled with fresh toner and coffee that'd been on the warming plate until it overcooked, concocting a stink that he hadn't been subjected to in forty-nine days and so would have to acclimate to all over again. Larkin walked past his desk, noted the cup of pens and Lisa Frank pencils on its spartan top was lacking its usual quantity, and frowned when he counted several pens of his preferred brand on Baker's warzone of a desk. Two were missing the caps.

Larkin continued to Lieutenant Connor's open office door. It was 7:27 p.m. and the imposing Irishman was in the midst of pulling his suit coat on when Larkin knocked on the doorframe. "Sir."

Connor turned, and a smile cut across his freckled face. "Grim!" he greeted him with that usual, booming voice. "Welcome back."

"I need to speak with you."

Connor nodded as he fixed his coat collar. "Sit down."

Larkin took a seat in front of the desk, crossed his legs, and opened his mouth to speak as he raised the evidence bag to eye level.

But Connor asked first, "How's the arm?" He sat and leaned back in the computer chair until it creaked ominously.

"Fine."

"Been doing your PT?"

Larkin's hold on the bag faltered as he answered, "I have stress balls in three different colors, resistance bands, and am particularly adept at the wall push-up now."

"You're a bad patient, aren't you?"

"I'm not a good one," Larkin qualified.

A laugh rumbled from deep within Connor's chest. "I bet your husband is happy to get you out from underfoot, though."

"I'm in the middle of a divorce."

Connor sat up at the comment, his chair screeching again.

Larkin raised the evidence bag a second time and cut off whatever comment Connor was waffling over, because he didn't want pity, he didn't want sympathy, he didn't want to think of Noah, and because refusing to be wholly present to a conversation was what protected Larkin from associations. "CSU found this photograph in John Doe's pocket." He leveled Connor with what he thought of as his "professional expression," although Larkin had been told that particular look was about as monotone in facial grammar as his speech tended to be, and only one step above the manner in which he scrutinized witnesses and analyzed suspects.

Everett Larkin was the star detective of the Cold Case Squad, but he was an aloof personality. He should have been promoted half a dozen times, but he didn't seem to grasp the concept of small talk. He could have been the youngest inspector in the department's history, but he refused to schmooze with his higher-ups. He was distant, calculating, brutal in his honesty and unnerving in his intensity. He spoke strangely. He had compulsive habits. He was queer in a career that used him as a poster child for inclusivity while those same people called him a faggot to his face.

Everett Larkin was odd.

And no one had ever wanted to know why.

Connor accepted the bag and studied the scrawled writing on the back of the photograph. "This is what O'Halloran phoned me bitching about, right?"

"Correct."

Connor grunted.

"Why did you request control of the case," Larkin asked next. "According to the ME, the victim has been dead no more than nine days. It hardly falls within our purview."

"Why do you think?"

"The one viable clue is addressed to me, allegedly by a person of interest in the investigation."

"And?" Connor pressed.

Once is chance. Twice is coincidence.

"Any correlation with the April Fools' letter is entirely coincidental at this moment in time," Larkin answered.

"I don't believe in coincidences," Connor said. "And once you've been doing this for as long as me, neither will you."

"The probability of a coincidence can be calculated by looking at the base rate of two independent events. In this case, that would be the act of myself receiving an invitation to locate an unknown individual, as well as the act of an individual perpetrating a murder within the confines of the subway. The NYPD employs 35,000 uniformed officers, of which I am one, making the probability of me, specifically, garnering this person's interest 1 in 35,000. In 2019, the Mayor's Office reported three murders in the subway system, making the second event a 1 in 3. Together, the data would suggest a coincidence of… 0.0006."

"Seems impossible to me."

"Improbable, but not impossible."

Connor wasn't smiling, but there was a glint in his eyes that suggested amusement. "It hasn't been the same around here without you."

"I think it was a premature decision. I have thirty-seven open cases that haven't seen attention in forty-nine days, and Ray O'Halloran, basic manners aside, is a decent cop."

Connor waved the evidence bag idly. "The fact that your name is on a piece of evidence doesn't intrigue you?"

"I didn't say that. It *is* curious. But I'm being pragmatic."

Connor was nodding in that way people did when they'd already come to a decision and were simply listening for their chance to speak. "I want you to take lead on the subway slaying. If it's related to the April Fools' letter, you've got a better chance of cracking it before those boys in the Bronx can even find the case number in their stacks. One of their own be damned—they're up to their nuts in robberies and felony assaults, and that letter didn't have a suggestion of violence against you that'd otherwise make it a priority."

"The Theater District's crime rate is worse than any neighborhood in the Bronx."

"Tourists are dumbasses, Grim. Don't use technicalities with me."

"Yes, sir."

"If the events are unrelated, okay, but you'll satisfy both our curiosities as to why this"—he raised the photo in its plastic sleeve again—"has your name on it. Now, bring me up to speed."

"The victim was an adult male, badly decomposed from heat and humidity. No wallet or ID, but there was a partially destroyed business card for St. Jude's Mission on his person—I'll speak with them once the ME has completed an autopsy—and of course, that photo was in his pocket."

"Was it cleaned up?"

"Yes. By Detective Doyle of the Forensic Artists Unit. He's logged the procedure."

"Who? Oh right. Jackson Pollock at 1PP."

Larkin frowned but said, "Doyle works primarily in illustration, but he's a very competent visual artist and is knowledgeable on painting, sculpture, and photography.

Based on the brand of photo paper and the printed code on the back, he estimates this picture was taken between 1985 and 1990. Her clothing would suggest Doyle's evaluation to be accurate." Larkin planted both feet on the floor before leaning forward to tap the evidence. "She's also dead."

Connor blinked owlishly. He looked at the photograph. "Are you sure?"

"Yes."

Low and gravelly, Connor murmured, "It's *Inception*, but with death instead of dreams…." He raised his head and stared at Larkin. "What train was this off of? The Q?"

"The F," Larkin corrected. "Fifty-Seventh—" He stopped abruptly, pushed to his feet, and left the office without further word.

"Grim?" Connor called after him.

Larkin removed a ring of keys from his pocket as he approached his desk. He chose a small office key, stuck it in the lock on the second drawer, then jerked it open. Larkin was poring over the precisely aligned and organized accordion files of his active cases when slow, heavy steps on the stairs to his right indicated that Detective Jim Porter was pulling a late night. The crinkle of a plastic bag further suggested that he'd been out picking up something to eat.

"Hey, Grim," Porter said from the landing. "You on duty?"

"Tomorrow," Larkin replied without looking up. He yanked a depressingly slim file free, then shut and locked the drawer.

"Welcome back," Porter answered absently. He set his takeout on the desk in front of Larkin's. The aroma from the bag suggested the meal was Porter's usual go-to: breakfast for dinner.

"There's over a thousand calories in just two of those cheesecake pancakes alone," Larkin said, already on his way back to Connor's office.

"Yeah, well, fuck you too," Porter called without malice.

Larkin stopped in the threshold of the office, unbound the file, and held up a yellowed report as he said to Connor, "On May 19, 1997, Marco Garcia was pushed in front of an incoming Q train."

"At what stop?" Connor asked, his brow furrowed as he struggled to catch up to whatever connection Larkin had already made.

"Fifty-Seventh Street. The Q used to run what is now the F line during the '90s." Larkin studied the printout he'd adopted from Homicide Detective Wally Kent upon his retirement, and said, "Today is the twenty-third anniversary of Marco's death. Once is chance. Twice is coincidence." Larkin looked up and finished with "Three time's a pattern."

CHAPTER FOUR

The arrival of an early summer was already wreaking havoc on those who called walkups in the city home, and Larkin wasn't surprised that the window unit of 4A was on as he opened the apartment door. The hundred-year-old Village tenement, with its fire-engine red façade, was poorly insulated against heat and acted a bit like a poor man's sauna. Despite the sun having set half an hour ago, the unit would be chugging in the kitchen window most of the night as it combatted the effects of a house closed-up for twelve hours.

The television against the bare brick wall was tuned to a Mets game, the volume dialed down low. The fairy lights strung throughout the studio were giving off that ever-welcoming sepia glow. And Doyle stood barefoot at the kitchen counter, wearing a pair of old Levi's with the pant legs cuffed and a white T-shirt with the iconic stencil art of Banksy's Flower Thrower. He was pulling takeout containers from a paper bag as he looked toward Larkin in the doorway.

"Perfect timing," he said, his smile so warm, it made Larkin feel as if he'd been drinking on an empty stomach. "Tonight's dining experience will include spinach salad with blue cheese—not goat, I know you don't like it—walnuts, apples, and a vinaigrette dressing." Doyle raised a white cardboard container and shook it. "Also an order of waffle fries, because who can resist?"

Larkin turned, quietly shut the door, and threw the deadbolt.

"And I made mocktails," Doyle continued as he finished with the takeout containers and threw the bag into the recycling bin. "It's lemonade with raspberries, cucumber, and mint."

Larkin wedged a finger behind the knot of his tie, tugged it free from his neck, and turned right toward the open french doors of the room just big enough for a bed, dresser, and closet.

"Hey."

Larkin looked over his shoulder.

Doyle held a fork in one hand and motioned toward the brick wall.

Larkin reached into his trouser pocket, removed the keyring, and hung it on the hook by the door. He was still getting used to new patterns and routines at Doyle's apartment and didn't mind the occasional prompt, mostly because the way in which Doyle went about it made him feel a little less like a dysfunctional and neurotic mess.

The bedroom was dark, but the reflective glimmer of the fairy lights on the glass doors was enough to see by, and Larkin put his wallet, phone, and cuff links on the nightstand already crowded with Doyle's own wallet, phone, a book entitled *Masterpiece or Master Forgery?: The Geniuses Behind the Lies*, and a photo of his late daughter, Abigail. She was four in that snapshot, sitting on a stoop beside a much younger and clean-shaven Doyle, both of them blowing bubbles from little plastic wands. Larkin returned his tie to the rack in the closet, removed his pocket square, hung up his suit coat, then sat on the foot of the bed and let out a breath he felt like he'd been holding the entire drive home.

According to Marco's scant file, twenty-three years ago, the last thing Camila Garcia ever said to her baby had been: Take the trash on your way out.

Larkin knew she regretted those words, was haunted by them. Because no one ever expected tragedy. That happened to *other* people—strangers, whose universes never overlapped with your own. For you, there would always be a tomorrow. There would always be another opportunity to say the important words, the meaningful words—a hundred more "have a good days" and a thousand more "I love yous."

—woodsmoke in his hair, lips sticky from marshmallows, throat burning from too much whiskey, and that laugh, stuck in limbo between adolescence and adulthood, left behind as Larkin grew old without him, "You're such a lightweight."

"I won't puke."—

No one ever expected tragedy.

Larkin leaned forward, elbows on his knees, and closed his eyes. May 19 was the worst day of Camila Garcia's life, and someone had made a mockery of her loss by presenting Larkin with this challenge, like death was some silly after-school game to be played. A photograph of an unknown dead girl, found on the body of a dead man discovered on the same date, and in the same location, as Marco Garcia's gruesome murder in 1997….

This case was meant for Larkin all right.

—"I won't puke."—

Larkin got up, dropping his pocket square as he left the bedroom in a rush. He slammed open the bathroom door, squatted, and was sick into the toilet.

Doyle owned a couch.

It was a comfortable couch.

There was nothing wrong with the couch.

And yet, he had a propensity for sitting on the floor.

So Larkin was on the floor too, his head in Doyle's lap, feet pointed toward the bedroom, hands folded on his stomach. He stared at the glowing arcs and halos the lights cast on the ceiling, and listened to the low murmur of the announcers on the television discuss the Mets being down two against the Phillies, but there was still plenty of time to turn this game around in favor of the home team.

Doyle had eaten his salad. Larkin had declined his. Once, while Doyle sipped his lemonade, a bead of condensation rolled off the base and splashed Larkin's forehead. Doyle had wiped the wet away with the pad of his thumb before planting his big hand on Larkin's chest, and like an anchor, kept him from being swept away in a current of nausea and survivor's guilt without maybe realizing just how badly Larkin had needed it.

It was the start of the fifth inning when Doyle finally moved his hand, his warmth imprinted on Larkin's skin like a fever. Doyle set the cardboard takeout of waffle fries on Larkin's chest.

Larkin refocused his stare from the ceiling to Doyle's brown eyes.

"Have something to eat."

"French fries."

"Sure. Potato and grease will settle your stomach."

"That sounds like bad medical advice lifted from a mommy blog."

Doyle laughed. "Your parents never gave you fries or plain potato chips when you had an upset stomach as a kid?"

"No. They sent me to the Hamptons for a weekend detox."

Doyle said, "Grandma's budget was skewed more toward Lay's."

Larkin fished a few waffle fries from the container and ate.

Unprompted, Doyle said, "There was a robbery in the Diamond District today."

Larkin turned his head back toward Doyle, who was still staring down at him. "Okay."

"I had to do a sketch of the suspect."

Belatedly, Larkin realized, "I didn't ask how your day was."

Doyle smiled softly and stroked Larkin's head, combing strands of ash-blond hair back into place. "I just want to get you out of your own head for a few minutes."

Larkin held the container and sat up. He set it on the floor, turned his back to the television, and crossed his legs. "Tell me about it."

Larkin had struggled with polite small talk his entire adulthood. It was only another form of sensory stimulation, another conversation he'd automatically catalogue, memorize, another opportunity to be hurt by words that'd be with him forever, like a wound that never scabbed over. And what made it worse was knowing he missed the subtle cues the rest of polite society picked up on without needing a nudge in the right direction. Larkin could remember the sensation of this process before August 2, 2002—it'd been so natural and so seamless. But now, it was like watching old home footage of his younger self speaking in tongues and Larkin simply couldn't interpret those well-mannered speech patterns his parents had once been so proud of.

His brusqueness was part of an uncontrollable defense mechanism. And sometimes, after a difficult day, it was triggered by even the most well-meaning of people in Larkin's life. Like Noah. Noah had always taken it personally. That

Larkin must have forgotten to ask how his day was because he didn't care to know, or was unpleasantly direct merely to get the niceties over with. And that hadn't been true. Of course Larkin had cared to know about Noah's day. They'd been married. They'd been in love.

Larkin might have had irreversible brain trauma, but it didn't make him stupid.

And after spending the last fifty-one days in the company of Ira Doyle, he was beginning to find the words to describe how Noah had made him feel for the last year of their relationship.

One of them was *small*.

"I'm not clear on the specifics of what exactly was stolen," Doyle began. "But I know the security footage at the diamond store was corrupted."

"Inside job," Larkin answered.

Doyle laughed but held a hand out. "Let me finish the story. Major Cases pulled footage from the subway entrance at Rockefeller Center and got a few guys who vaguely fit the description of the suspect—"

"But they called you," Larkin interrupted. "Which means something about the witness's story didn't look right. So instead of blasting the faces of most likely innocent people who, let me guess, were described as dark-skinned and wearing a hoodie, someone opted to pull their head out of their ass and employ in-house support first."

"That'd be Detective Weaver."

Larkin spun his Rolodex and stopped on Weaver, Erik. His memory had bullet pointed: foul-mouthed Ryan Gosling look-alike who'd provided Larkin's card to his own CI last October—an equally foul-mouthed redhead who'd been trying to light a fire under the cold case of his mother's murder. "He's decent," Larkin admitted.

"And smart," Doyle confirmed. "He brought in the vic to

sit for a composite sketch. Even with recent trauma taken into account, the process is usually two or three hours."

Larkin thought of the wastebasket full of discarded pages from Doyle's sketch pad, frustration seeping out from the crumpled contours of expensive paper.

"But I sat with her for nearly five hours," Doyle continued, "and couldn't get her to settle on any one sketch."

Larkin cocked his head slightly and asked, his voice inflecting, "What'd you do?"

Doyle smiled, responding to Larkin's noted interest with "I added a mole."

"What."

"I excused myself to the bathroom and texted Weaver that I intended to add an unremarkable detail to the sketch," Doyle explained. "It was a predetermined fabrication to see if she'd agree to its accuracy."

Larkin felt something in his shoulders begin to loosen. "And if she did, you'd know you were dealing with a false witness." When Doyle nodded, Larkin added, "You are a very competent detective."

"Thank you."

"It was an inside job."

Doyle laughed again and said teasingly, "All right, Mr. Holmes."

Larkin shrugged.

"What about you? Was Connor available to speak with?"

"Yes. He wants me on the case because—" And then Larkin realized what Doyle had done. Again and again, he had this way of engaging Larkin in simple discussion that would draw him away from the distress that was causing an internal spiral. Doyle could lower Larkin's heart rate and soothe the itch that made him grab for Xanax with something as simple as a conversation about a goddamn mole. In fact, he lowered Larkin's defenses so easily this time that Larkin nearly let slip the relation between the anonymous letter and the subway incidents.

But he caught himself with a literal bite of his tongue.

Because Doyle didn't know about the April Fools' letter.

Doyle raised a thick eyebrow and prompted, "Because?"

"Just—my name was on the photograph," Larkin concluded.

"Oh."

Larkin looked away, picking at the cold waffle fries. "I suspect this investigation might be related to another cold case of mine."

"Really?"

"Marco Garcia was pushed in front of a Q train at Fifty-Seventh Street on this date, twenty-three years ago. He was eighteen years old."

Doyle said, "That's a hell of a coincidence."

"One worth looking into," Larkin answered. "I have to try his mother tomorrow."

"You don't sound happy about that."

"I don't sound any way," Larkin corrected. "I speak in a monotone."

"You're not as monotone as you'd like to think."

Larkin looked up, studied Doyle intently, then said, "Please expound."

Doyle shifted, crossing one leg and bringing the other up so as to rest an elbow on his knee. He leaned forward, threaded fingers through Larkin's hair a second time, and gently held the back of his head. "You don't exist in the binary, Evie. You're part of the human condition too. Just because you express that experience differently from the majority doesn't mean you don't feel the same ways. Anyone who thinks you're monotone isn't actually listening when you speak."

Larkin's skin tingled, like from a little static shock, as Doyle drew his fingers along Larkin's throat. He latched onto that sensation, that reminder he was still alive, even when the drugs made him feel like he wasn't, shifted onto his knees so that he was taller than Doyle, and took his face into both hands. Larkin rubbed the pads of his thumbs against the grain of Doyle's stubble, leaned down, and kissed him. With a tender mouth and lips still tart from lemonade, Doyle's kiss was live and in full technicolor. Larkin allowed Doyle to wrap his arms around his waist, allowed himself to be drawn close enough to straddle one leg, allowed the unhurried and curious exploration of tongues.

Doyle had selflessly opened his home and his heart to Larkin, with the expectation of nothing in return. He'd given Larkin a copy of his key. He'd made room for Larkin's belongings. He kissed Larkin like this—like he was *everything*.

What kind of man did that?

A good one.

Larkin broke the kiss. His breath was a little unsteady.

Doyle stared at him, his face a mess of hopeful uncertainty.

All Larkin had to do was say *yes*.

Abruptly, Larkin said, "I'm going to go to bed."

Doyle's expression flickered, like an old television caught between channels, but then he nodded and smiled softly, lowered his hands from Larkin's waist, said, "Sure."

Larkin got to his feet. "Goodnight, Ira."

"Sleep well, Evie."

But even with twice the recommended dosage of ZzzQuil rushing through his veins, Larkin lay wide awake in the dark bedroom, his back to the french doors. He listened to every minute sound Doyle made on the other side of the glass—the shift of jean-clad legs on the hardwood floor, the low murmur of the television cutting off when the game finally ended, the collection of takeout containers, the thump of the garbage bin lid, kitchen sink, bathroom door. Doyle entered the bedroom a few minutes later, quiet but for the rustle of undressing and pulling on a pair of pajama pants. The twinkle of fairy lights that'd reached all the way into the room, their glow like fireflies in a mason jar, clicked off, and the studio was swallowed whole by New York City darkness. The mattress dipped, and Larkin rolled onto his back. He might have still been working to establish new habitual routines, but this one had been easy, had been welcomed. Larkin stretched an arm out and Doyle accepted the invitation, drawing up against him and pillowing his head on Larkin's chest.

Because even though Larkin wasn't certain what they were together, what they were hoping to become, he at least knew that Doyle was his friend.

And sometimes, a hug from a friend was the only drug that helped him sleep at night.

It was 6:58 a.m. and Larkin stood in the bedroom, knotting his red floral-pattern tie and adjusting the collar of his crisp white shirt in the mirror hanging above the dresser. He tested the way the SIG P226 sat under his right arm in its shoulder holster, a weight he'd worn as a detective for seven years and that had long since become a part of him, before reaching for his charcoal-gray suit coat. He gave a black, white, and red houndstooth pocket square a quick Dunaway fold, tucked it into his breast pocket, and twisted it a few times to sit more artfully. Larkin had chosen green derbies with an elongated toe in a shade he'd thought to himself as split pea soup, until Doyle had made a passing comment one day about liking "those chartreuse shoes," because of course the artist would say *chartreuse* in an everyday conversation without any trace of sarcasm.

Stepping out of the bedroom, Larkin studied Doyle seated at the kitchen table.

It'd turned out he wasn't the only one with a routine.

Every morning—*every single morning*—Doyle took a run, returned home and practiced yoga, showered, dressed, made breakfast (he was partial to yogurt with granola and fruit), and then worked on his sudoku puzzles until it was time to head to 1PP.

Erroneously, Larkin had suspected Doyle was one of those chipper early-risers, much like Noah, and had braced for conversation before coffee stabilized his mood. But much to his surprise and delight, Doyle was rather quiet. Reflective, almost. For the first few days, Larkin had actually felt as if he'd intruded on something personal, intimate, and had stayed in the bedroom until Doyle left for work. Doyle had caught on, of course, and said he'd be only more than happy to see Larkin's smile in the mornings, which was presumptuous of Doyle, except that he'd been able to coax one out of Larkin forty days running so far.

At the sound of Larkin's heels on hardwood, Doyle raised his head and looked across the studio. His face had this way of lighting up whenever Larkin walked into a room, like the first rays of sunshine to reach over the horizon at dawn, that always made Larkin want to check over his shoulder, because no one had ever stared at him quite like that before.

"Good morning," Doyle said in that soft, whiskey voice. He wore a dark teal three-piece suit with a very subtle windowpane pattern, the coat thrown over the back of his chair, white shirt with the cuffs rolled back, and a simple black tie. The blue flattered his skin tone and dark eyes and always had a way of making Larkin feel short of breath.

"Morning," Larkin answered. He got himself a cup of coffee from the counter, a protein bar from the cupboard, and took a seat across from Doyle. He wrapped his hands around the mug and studied the lazy, counterclockwise spiral from stirring in cream for approximately twenty-three seconds before Larkin heard Doyle set aside his pen. He glanced at it. Like others scattered around the home, this pen cap had been chewed. Larkin looked up.

Doyle had one eyebrow raised in question.

"I feel like I should apologize to you," Larkin stated.

"For what?"

"For… leading you on. Last night."

Doyle folded his hands on the tabletop.

"It's not that I'm not interested," Larkin continued.

—but when you look at me….

"I'm just trying to make sense of my life."

—how do I say yes….

"And I don't know how long it will take."

—when you're nothing but a mystery?

Doyle reached a hand across the table and pulled one of Larkin's away from his mug. It was dry, warm, his calluses familiar. "More than anything, I want to be your friend."

Larkin whispered, "You are."

A car alarm chirped from the street below.

The window unit one floor above them kicked on with a worrying grind.

Doyle squeezed Larkin's hand, smiled. "Don't apologize." He let go, pushed his chair back, and stood. "How about something more substantial for breakfast?"

Larkin slid his fingers over the tabletop, lingering on the spot still warm from Doyle's hands. He swallowed, imagining the lump in his throat to be the split pit of a peach, mold infecting him all the way down, rotting him from the inside out. Larkin quickly passed his other hand across his face and dabbed at his nose before noticing that Doyle had left the sudoku puzzle half-finished and had instead been drawing in the bottom righthand corner when he'd entered the room. Larkin reached, turned the book around, and was met with a startling, realistic execution of himself in ballpoint pen. He was in profile, seemingly studying himself in the mirror, and adjusting his tie in the reflection. Larkin looked over his shoulder at the direct view of the french doors and into the bedroom beyond.

He glanced at Doyle.

The other man stood sideways at the counter, holding a bowl and studying Larkin in return.

Pulling back the right sleeve of his suit coat to check his watch, Larkin stood and said, "I have to go." He pocketed the protein bar and moved away from the table.

Doyle set the bowl down with a clatter and—*gently*—took Larkin by the elbow, stopping him. He asked, "The mother you're going to speak to… she's the same woman who called during the Gorman case, isn't she?"

"Yes."

Doyle was contemplative, silent for eight seconds that could have been eight years, the gravity around him was so great. Finally, he smiled, but for the first time since they'd met, Larkin saw the crack, the crumble, the broken inner self reflected back, like viewing Doyle through a funhouse mirror. And it wasn't like he'd been privy to an audience from the "real Doyle," because the real Doyle *was* the man standing right there.

It was more like, for a split second, Larkin had simply seen more—the part of himself that Doyle buried deep down underneath the light and sunshine and fool's gold personality.

"My son was a victim of homicide too, Detective."

The pat, *pat*, pat *of rain on the windshield.*

"I self-medicated after losing Abigail."

"Be gentle," Doyle suggested. "And… listen to her."

CHAPTER FIVE

In Larkin's five years on the Cold Case Squad, he'd solved seventy-four cases. He averaged three times the closure rate than his fellow detectives. He garnered the squad positive press with the public and much-needed funding from the department. Judges rarely denied him a warrant.

He didn't like to consider any of that a success, though.

How could he, when his victims were still dead and had been forgotten by everyone?

Justice was bitter when it came at the cost of someone's mother, someone's lover, someone's best friend, and rain or shine, Larkin would visit their place of rest after he'd shelved the finished investigation and say their name, because you were only truly dead if there was no one left to mourn you.

And remembrance was the greatest act of love there was.

But there were times when a case was dropped on Larkin's desk that still had someone else clinging to the dead. Those were the most difficult investigations—the ones where Larkin had to connect with another human. Because grief was complex and frightening and *never* went away. No one person handled loss the same way either, although Larkin

47

had become adept at predicting reactions with a fair degree of accuracy, based on the relationship dynamics.

Except one.

Only one had thrown a metaphorical curveball right at his face.

On March 31, 8:36 p.m., Camila Garcia had said: Marco is always with me. My heart is always broken.

At 11:08 that same night, Doyle had said: I'm okay.

He wasn't, though. He couldn't be.

Because even though Doyle had insisted he could talk about Abigail, he never did. If Larkin caught Doyle studying one of Abigail's photos, he'd smile that sunshiny smile and talk about something else. He was always busy, stimulated with some activity, like he didn't want to be left to his own thoughts. Doyle never admitted to having a broken heart, but Larkin could now see, with a frightening sense of clarity, how just like Camila he was. And it was only because Doyle embodied the philosophical concept of "jubilant up to heaven" and "depression unto death" that Larkin had missed the initial mourning signs he knew so well.

Signs like lying.

Because Larkin, too, knew loss, he understood that propensity. The need to keep that grief tucked away, because it made people uncomfortable and they *didn't want to know*. They'd asked Larkin to stop talking.

Please stop talking.

Stop talking.

Shut up.

Shut up, Everett.

When the verbal abuse became too much, when *why can't you get over it* made a mockery of those memories, lying was the only way to keep new hurts from becoming permanent. Because if they asked, "Are you okay?" and he said, "Yes," no one told him to shut up.

But what Doyle had said that morning—*listen*—it'd been profound and perhaps more insight into Doyle's hurt than he'd intended to put on display. When Abigail had passed and Doyle's sorrow became all-encompassing, had they told him to stop talking, or had they simply stopped *listening*?

Contemporary society had a chilly and misguided view on death culture, this Larkin was hyperaware of. But regarding the death of children in particular—this was a discomfort they outright refused to be a part of. They'd hold their own to their bosom and cover their eyes, as if looking at mortal remains was a danger akin to meeting Medusa. When they'd all turned their backs, because a child's wake was too much to see, a father's cries too difficult to hear, there'd been no one left to listen.

The funeral pall had been draped.

The mourning veil lowered.

And Ira Doyle had become… a mystery.

Camila Garcia lived in the most northern neighborhood of Manhattan—Inwood—on tree-lined 204th Street between Sherman and Post Avenues. Larkin parked his black Audi on the corner at 8:10 a.m., climbed out, and tapped the lock on his key fob. He put his hands in his pockets and started east, walking past a bodega that doubled as the neighborhood hangout, if the plastic lawn chairs under the awning and grandfather-aged men populating them was anything to judge by. Larkin also passed a hair-and-nail salon, what he suspected was an employment office, although the sign was in Spanish and his parents had insisted he study French growing up, and then a Latina woman pushing a cart toward Sherman, laden with whole and sliced mangoes and shakers of lemon juice, salt, and chili powder.

Larkin's stomach growled. He stopped, reached into his suit coat for his wallet to buy a bag of the sweet and spicy fruit, but found the forgotten protein bar he'd pocketed on his way out the door. Not nearly as satisfying, but it was certainly less messy, so he begrudgingly ate it in three bites before arriving at the front of an H-shaped apartment building. Larkin approached the front door as it banged open and a boy and girl—siblings—barreled outside.

"We're gonna be late!" the brother shouted.

"My backpack's unzipped!" the sister protested.

Larkin grabbed the door before it could fall shut and automatically lock. He looked over his shoulder, watched the older boy stop to zip the backpack his sister wore, then grab her hand again before they ran to the sidewalk and disappeared around the corner of the building. Larkin stepped inside. His derbies *tip-tap*ped across the tile floor of the lobby, up the stairs, and down the fifth-floor hall before he came to a stop at 5D. Larkin had been here before, but Camila hadn't opened the door for him. He had slipped his business card under the door and she had, weeks later, called.

Then he'd failed her.

Larkin quietly knocked.

The shuffle of flip-flops approached the door, the deadbolt was turned, and the door was opened as far as the chain lock would allow. Camila Garcia was a short, petite woman in her sixties, with salt-and-pepper hair and pronounced frown lines around her mouth. She wore a pair of black-framed glasses, a gold cross on a delicate chain around her neck, and a white top with an abstract floral pattern.

"Mrs. Garcia." Larkin removed his badge and flashed his ID. "I'm Everett Larkin with the Cold Case—"

Camila shut the door and threw the deadbolt.

Larkin let out a breath as he pocketed his badge. He knocked a second time, but the home's silence was his only response. "Mrs. Garcia," he called, attempting to soften his modulated tone. "I won't lie—I want to ask questions. I'm a detective. But I'm here to listen to you. And I'll wait until you're ready. As long as I have to." With that, Larkin moved to the wall opposite the door, leaned back, slid down to the floor, and began counting.

He'd reached thirty-eight long minutes when his phone buzzed with an incoming call. Larkin shifted to one side, winced as a zing of discomfort shot from his tailbone and up his spine, and collected the phone from his pocket. The name on the screen caused his heart to miss a beat, and the sensation was like the first drop on a rollercoaster. Larkin's grip on the phone case tightened until the plastic protested. He answered with a crisp "What."

"Good morning," Noah said.

Larkin glanced at the door to 5D. He could hear no movement on the other side. Keeping his voice low, Larkin said, "I'm at work."

"Oh. So… everything went well at the doctor's, then?"

"We're not supposed to be speaking without a lawyer present."

"I know." But then Noah took a breath that sounded shaky and unsure.

"That was at your request, Noah."

"I know, I know," he repeated. "Sorry. I'm fine."

"You don't sound fine." Larkin cradled the phone between his ear and shoulder, checked his watch, and asked, "Shouldn't you be in class."

"The kids are at the library. I have to pick them up in a few minutes. Listen, Everett…."

Larkin let the abrupt silence linger until he was certain that Noah was waiting for a cue. Reluctantly, he said, "I'm listening."

"Can we talk? I mean, in person. Just us. No lawyers." Noah took another breath, this one wetter.

And Larkin could imagine him, sitting in an empty classroom wallpapered in brightly colored construction paper, overlaid with 123s and ABCs, mentally preparing to pick up a group of twenty six- and-seven-year-olds who would all be asking Mr. Rider why his face was so red. Larkin closed his eyes, pinched the bridge of his nose. "Fine."

"Really?" Noah sounded hopeful—happy, even. "How about Skylight Lounge? Where we went for our anniversary. I can get a table for 6:30."

The deadbolt of 5D was thrown. The chain lock slid free.

Larkin raised his head as the door opened.

Camila studied him from the threshold. She asked suddenly, curtly, "Are you going to sit on that dirty floor in your nice suit all day?"

Larkin hesitated a fraction of a second before he said into the phone, "Goodbye, Noah," hung up, and climbed to his feet.

Camila's gesture was irritated as she asked, "*Well*? Are you coming in?"

"Yes. Thank you, ma'am." Larkin stepped through the doorway and into an immaculate front room that doubled as both living and dining room.

A plump tan couch was pushed up against the far wall with a knockoff Queen Anne oval coffee table set before it and a matching tan recliner to the right. White lace curtains in the open window to the left billowed in the morning breeze. Sunshine bounced off the glass of dozens of family photos displayed on the wall above the couch—Camila in a wedding dress alongside a big-shouldered, thick-necked man with a mustache who Larkin had to only assume was Mr. Garcia, but mostly, they were school photos of Marco. His lifetime on full display, from that gleeful kindergartener, the self-conscious elementary boy who'd lost all his front teeth at the same time, to the handsome teen on the verge of manhood in a snapshot from prom with a banner proclaiming the night's theme to be Enchanted Forest.

Whatever that meant.

A television sat dark across from the couch, and the dining table near the front door was spotless—not even a placemat sat on its surface. A hall with an open doorway on the left, the scent of Fabuloso wafting out, marked it as probably being the kitchen. The closed doors beyond were likely bedrooms and the bathroom.

"Please sit," Camila said with another wave, this time in the direction of the couch. "I'll make coffee."

"That's not necessary."

She said nothing to that and walked into the kitchen.

Larkin moved to the mantelpiece under the window, considered the carefully arranged religious talismans, before crouching to read the spines of books on the shelf below, only to realize they were actually all photo albums. Larkin gently tugged one free, its plastic-covered pages peeling apart like the loud crack of chewing gum. Big glasses and bigger hair overlain with distinct yellowing and discoloration marked their origins as the '70s and '80s. Lots of big family gatherings. Lots of smiling faces. So many photos of Marco.

"I wanted to be a photographer."

Larkin abruptly stood and turned, still holding the album.

Camila studied his face a moment before setting a tray on the coffee table. She poured black coffee into a tiny teacup. "See the world, you know? I got pregnant instead. I was nineteen. I didn't know how to say 'I don't want this life,'" she continued, pointing at the wedding photo on the wall without looking at it. "Moved from California because *his* family lived here." Camila studied Larkin a second time. "I don't speak ill of the dead, Detective, because I believe in

Jesus. But I think even the Blessed Mother breathed a sigh of relief when Oscar choked to death on a bucket of KFC, December 12, 1985."

Larkin returned the album to the shelf without a word, moved around the table, and took a seat on the couch.

Camila poured milk into Larkin's coffee until the ratio was in favor of dairy, then made herself a cup and sat in the recliner. "We'd tried for more children, but Marco was my miracle. He was six when his papá passed. I could have gone home. My whole family still lived in California. But we'd managed to carve out a life here and… I don't know. Maybe I wanted to prove something."

Larkin took a polite sip of the milky coffee. His fingers were too big to properly hold the cup by its handle.

Camila studied her own drink. She spoke without glancing up. "I took so many pictures because I wanted to be a photographer…. I never thought they'd one day become my only connection to Marco." She raised her head. "It's getting more difficult to remember his voice. Sometimes, I wake in the middle of the night, sweating and crying. I come in here, in the dark, and go through the albums by the glow of city lights, and it's almost like I can hear an echo of that exact moment when the shutter clicked. And then Marco is still alive."

"Echoic memory," Larkin said.

"What's that?"

"Sensory memory," he answered. "Specifically, how we remember what we hear. It's very brief. Only a few seconds. Afterward, it moves into our short-term memory, where our brain can interpret sounds, such as syllables, into words and meanings and we can converse. It takes a considerable amount of impactful associations for that sort of memory to become housed in the long-term. Which is why their voice fades away and maybe you can only recall it when focusing on a specific moment, like studying a photograph. A majority of people experience sensory memory loss of a loved one. It's not you—it's biology."

Camila leaned forward, set her cup on the coffee table, and stared at her hands, which she clasped in her lap. "It doesn't seem fair."

"I know."

"A mother shouldn't be able to forget her child's voice." She raised her head. Her expression was tired. Grief had aged her in a way that time could never. "You told me, when I called that first time, you knew loss. What was their name again?"

Larkin set down his own cup, swallowed roughly, said, "Patrick."

"That's right…." Camila nodded slowly. "Have you forgotten Patrick's voice?"

—*"No, no, no, please! Don't—!" His ear-piercing scream abruptly silenced, like Patrick had been swallowed by a vacuum.*

Thunder boom*ed overhead.*

Heavy-soled shoes squish*ed in the thick mud.*

And then Everett Larkin heard his own skull crack.—

Larkin rocked back in his seat, the memory so violent, it was like he'd been struck in the head all over again. The stunned reaction quickly gave way to panic, animalistic fear, the instinctive necessity to protect his face, his head, because Larkin couldn't—*he just couldn't*—survive the pain of a crushed skull a second time. His eyes stung and he was barely able to speak around the sickening rush of unwanted adrenaline. "May I use your bathroom?"

Camila saw the memories play out. There was no way she could have missed them. She pointed down the hall and said, "First door on the right."

Larkin stood, took long, quick strides out of the room, pushed the door open, and closed it too loudly behind him. His vision was black around the edges, like he wasn't getting any air. He knocked something from the counter as he hastily turned on the cold water, cupped it in his hands, and splashed his face. A second time. Third. Then he drank a mouthful and spit it out, because he could taste blood and mud on the back of his throat.

Larkin blindly turned the faucet off before hunching over even farther, forearms resting on the sink as his knees shook like Jell-O in an earthquake. His hot exhales bounced off the shallow bowl of the sink and hit him in the face. He couldn't excuse himself to go retrieve the Xanax from the Audi. Not only was Larkin certain he wouldn't make the short walk, but he'd already disrupted the moment between them too much. He needed positive associations in order to collect himself. His Rolodex spun haphazardly, and it felt as if the mental cards were spilling every which way.

Another *deeper* breath.

May 20, 2007, Larkin had finished college with a double major in psychology and criminology. It wasn't without a healthy dose of irony that Dr. Katz of Larkin's Advanced Cognitive Neuroscience Theories course couldn't understand his perfect score and so had concluded that Larkin must have been cheating. Larkin had successfully disputed the claim before the chair of the department and graduated summa cum laude.

May 20, 2011, he had been driving in the late hours—something about New York at night settled Larkin's restless mind—and had come upon a woman contemplating suicide from the Manhattan Bridge. He'd pulled over, asked if he could call for help, then talked with her for an hour while EMTs waited at a distance that wouldn't provoke her. The conversation wasn't a pleasant recollection by any means, but when she'd stepped away from the edge and taken Larkin's hand, it had reinforced his desire to be a cop, when only hours earlier, he had been questioning whether to turn his badge in.

May 20, 2013, Larkin went on his second date with Noah. It had been a Monday night, and the Peruvian restaurant hadn't been busy. They'd sat in a quiet corner for hours, drinking several rounds of Pilsen Callao, talking about their respective childhoods and careers and lamenting the challenges of dating seriously in a city hellbent on only hookups, and no matter what Larkin felt for Noah now, that night had been one of the best he'd had in a long, long time.

Larkin raised his head, grabbed a few tissues from the dispenser on the back of the toilet, and dabbed his face dry. He stared at his reflection. He was still a bit flushed, his eyes red-rimmed, but he'd managed to collect his wobbling pieces and adjust how they precariously balanced before he'd fallen apart. He threw the sodden tissues into the garbage, opened the door, and returned to the front room.

Camila looked up at the sound of Larkin's heels on hardwood. "Are you okay, Detective?"

Larkin took his seat and said, "I do remember Patrick's voice. Sometimes I wish I didn't."

Camila considered Larkin, considered his honesty, for a long minute. Without prompting, she said, "Marco had a part-time job his senior year. He'd been accepted into CUNY for an art therapy program and didn't want to depend on his mother financially. He was a good boy."

"Yes, ma'am."

"He worked as a youth mentor at an after-school program. He grew up with a lot of at-risk kids, you understand. He wanted to help. And this Center offered students an alternative to an unsafe home or the streets. There were tutors to help with schoolwork, counselors on-call to help with troubled kids, and they even had a lawyer on retainer. There was a kitchen—Marco said some of them got their only meal of the day at the Center. They offered lessons in art and cooking and physical fitness… that's what Marco did. He helped teach classes. He loved it."

"What was the name of this Center."

"New York Youth Empowerment Center. All the kids called it, The *YEC*. Youth Empowerment Center."

"I understand."

Camila nodded. She was clutching her hands together, her knuckles white from the pressure. "This was when the MTA still issued student passes for the subway. Do you remember those?"

Larkin did, not that he'd ridden the subway alone to and from school. That was far too pedestrian for his parents. "1997 was the year the MTA rolled out MetroCards for students."

"Only the students who took the bus had the new cards. The ones who rode the subway didn't get theirs until the fall," Camila corrected. "You're wondering why I remember this."

Larkin waited.

"The student-issued MetroCard worked until 8:30 p.m. But the *passes* were only good until seven o'clock. The Center closed at 8:00 p.m., so the final duty of the mentors was to walk the students to the nearby stations and get the kids through the turnstile. The Center was preparing to save a lot of money come fall, since students would be able to get home on their free cards. But a lot of mentors—Marco included—worried that the time discrepancy would encourage those boys and girls to cruise the system and not go home."

"Where is the Center located."

Camila replied, "It's long gone. It had donors, but mostly it was subsidized by the city. And in 2007, the city wanted to save money. It didn't survive the recession." She added after a breath, "Fifty-Fifth, between Eighth and Ninth."

"And which station did Marco walk his students to in the

evening."

Camila raised a penciled-in eyebrow. That singular shift in her expression suggested satisfaction, *approval*, in the direction of Larkin's thought process. "Fifty-Seventh Street. When it was the Q. The kids took it into Brooklyn."

Larkin laid out a mental map of the current subway system, then overlaid it with his best approximation of how it stood in 1997, although he was aware there was room for error, as this was five years before HSAM changed everything he knew and understood about his own memory. Larkin asked, "Marco grew up in this apartment."

"Yes, sir."

"He would have taken the A home after work."

"That's right," Camila answered. "He'd see the kids to Fifty-Seventh and then walk to the A at Columbus Circle. He rode it to 207th Street."

"It wasn't the responsibility of mentors to wait on the platform with students," Larkin asked.

Camila shook her head curtly.

"And so why was Marco pushed in front of an uptown Q when his students rode the downtown and he took a different train located five blocks away."

"That's a good question, Detective," Camila said neutrally. "One that I've been asking for twenty-three years."

CHAPTER SIX

Larkin stood in the open doorway of the bedroom at the end of the hall, his gloved hand still resting on the tarnished doorknob.

He had been in homes like this, in rooms like this.

A tomb, a sepulcher, a mausoleum for the dead, cared for and protected by those they had left behind too soon.

"Please, Detective," Camila murmured from his side. She beckoned Larkin to enter Marco's bedroom.

Larkin squared his shoulders and took a step back in time. The floor *pop*ped under his steps, and it smelled a bit closed-up. There was a bed, desk, and dresser—a matching set in pine—their design clunky and overwhelming in the small bedroom. The comforter was a floral pastel pattern, something Camila had likely purchased from a department store as far back as the '90s, with a matching dust ruffle. It looked recently made—an impression of a hand still lingered near the foot where Camila would have leaned over to tuck a corner in.

Childhood keepsakes and relics of a bygone era littered the top of the dresser: an unplugged lava lamp, two Trolls—

green and blue hair, respectively—a handheld Tiger-brand *Batman* video game, a plastic character cup likely from a fast-food restaurant half-full of loose change, four AA batteries, half a dozen home VHS tapes with penned titles such as: *Dragon Ball Z*, *Super Mario Bros.*, and *A Nightmare on Elm Street*, the last of which had been crossed out and looked to have been recorded over with *The Last Unicorn*.

"Marco liked cartoons," Camila stated. "The other boys all watched those horror movies where the psycho kills a bunch of teenagers."

Larkin nodded, moving to the opposite side of the room toward the desk.

No computer, but then again, this room was a time capsule. Less than 40 percent of American households owned a computer in the late '90s, and most kids weren't so lucky as to horde those behemoth towers and monitors in their rooms. Instead, there was a stack of books: *To Kill a Mockingbird*, *The Great Gatsby*, *Go Ask Alice*. Assigned reading, Larkin concluded. He drew his gloved finger along the spines. Laminated stickers marked them as library editions. Only twenty-three years past due. There was a two-inch, three-ring binder that looked like Marco had had friends doodle all over, based on the differing penmanship. Larkin lifted the top. A half-finished report on the unreliability of Hamlet as a narrator for Mr. Reynold's fourth-period World Literature class. It was the go-to topic for any high school senior hellbent on wrapping their English class with a passing grade. A desktop lamp and a stuffed bear with texture like the Velveteen Rabbit completed Marco's setup.

Larkin turned to Camila in the doorway. "May I take a more thorough look."

She hesitated, glancing from one side of the room to the other, as if searching for a reason to deny the request.

"I'll return everything to its rightful place," Larkin

promised.

Reluctantly, Camila said, "I suppose." She took a step back into the hall, told Larkin she would be in the kitchen, then departed.

Larkin removed his suit coat, folded it, and set it on the seat of the desk chair. He began his search in the desk drawers, confirming that highlighters were nothing but dried-out nibs and not impromptu storage devices for something else. Detective Kent had bet all his money on a horse named Drugs, but Camila had been adamant Marco wasn't involved in the stuff. While parents could often be blind to the reality, Larkin agreed with her. Marco's story, as he understood it, didn't lend itself to the theory of a drug deal gone wrong, but still, he was obligated to be as thorough as possible. And because Larkin had once been a teenager—albeit he'd coveted copies of *XY* and *Blueboy* magazines, back when he'd been straddling that line of wanting to understand what it meant to be a queer boy at the turn of the century and simply wanting to see an absolutely *hung* man—he understood the necessity to hide secrets.

In the bottom drawer, which seemed to have been relegated to mostly junk, Larkin found a few well-read manga volumes of titles that had seen a surge in popularity outside of Japan in the '90s and had been undergoing translation into English. Larkin shut the drawer, put his hands on his hips, and gave the desktop a second once-over. Then, clear as day, the discrepancy made itself known.

"Hamlet," he murmured.

Marco had been writing a report on *Hamlet*, but there was no copy of the play in his stack of books. So where was it? Larkin scanned his surroundings, turning in a slow circle as he did. The room was limited in both furniture and hideaway options, but there'd been one place Larkin had used with relative success as a boy, considering his parents had been positively sidelined when he'd come out to them, and that was under the bed. Specifically, in between the slats and mattress—where a magazine or two could fit—because even the eyes of prying parents rarely remembered to look *up* while looking *under*. He pulled out his phone as he got on his knees, turned the flashlight app on, and belly to the floor, Larkin crawled partially under the bed. There were some dust bunnies that had avoided Camila's cleaning habits, as well as plastic storage bags of what looked like linens, but otherwise, it was empty. Larkin shifted enough that he could crane his neck, and there in the far right corner at the front of the bed against the wall—where you'd never feel a lump because who laid their head on the edge—was a paperback wedged into the slats. Larkin slid along the floor sideways until he could reach the book, carefully tugged it from its hiding place, and then pushed himself free.

Larkin sat on his knees and studied the 9x11 book, far thinner than the mass market editions more often purchased by public schools. It was the right size to hide, since anything thicker would have caused an obvious lump in the mattress. He noted the library sticker on the spine, checked the pocket glued to the inside front cover, and the due date card still inside, stamped in a cracked black ink: MAY 23 1997. Larkin opened the book and let the pages fall where they wanted. Something slipped from Act II and dropped into his lap. He picked it up, recognized the printed string of gibberish on the backside, and held his breath as he prepared himself for the kind of photograph a teenage boy wanted to hide.

Larkin turned it around. The snapshot was a medium wide angle on a black boy, maybe junior-high age or maybe a late bloomer, slouched to one side on a subway bench, his head lolled back against the tile wall.

The boy was unequivocally dead.

Larkin raised his head and looked around the bedroom—a shrine to an only child who loved his mother, did his schoolwork, and enjoyed mediocre cartoons enough to tape them off television. There were absolutely zero indicators that Marco had sadistic, psychopathic, or God forbid, necrophilic tendencies.

And yet, the photo….

Larkin reached into his suit coat and removed the evidence bag with the first photograph. He'd stopped by his precinct that morning to pick it up with the intention of asking Camila if she recognized the girl, and he held the two side-by-side. The odds of two separate individuals taking photos of dead teenagers in the subway were so astronomically slim that Larkin didn't even entertain the probability. But it wasn't a statistical likelihood that brought him to the conclusion that this was the same artist—for lack of better description. It was the—how did Doyle put it?—the geometry of the space. The storytelling of the image.

It was a fingerprint. A signature.

Larkin grabbed his phone from beside him on the floor and chose a name in his contacts.

On the third ring, Doyle picked up and said, "Hey," in his smoky baritone.

"Hi. Are you busy."

"Busy is relative. What's up?"

"How would you feel if I were to speak with Lieutenant Connor and request you be brought onto this case in an official capacity."

"Which case are you referring to—yesterday's subway murder or the twenty-year-old subway murder?"

"Twenty-three years," Larkin corrected. "And both. I now have tangible evidence the two deaths are related, and I believe your unique expertise would be beneficial to my investigation." In the background of the call, Larkin could hear the legs of a chair scrape the floor, and then pages in a book, binder—no, planner—being turned.

"The way you flirt with me...."

"You're very funny," Larkin said.

Doyle chuckled before saying, "I don't have any composite sketches on the schedule today, so I could be in your neck of the woods... in about an hour?"

"That's fine. I'm still in Inwood."

"Ouch. All right. I'll see you soon, partner." Doyle hung up.

Larkin lowered the cell from his ear and smiled as the screen went black.

Larkin usually got what he wanted—professionally speaking, that was—and while his request to partner with Doyle a second time had come as a mild surprise to Connor, his lieutenant promised to make it happen. Larkin returned to searching the bedroom after his two calls, but after thirty-seven minutes, he found nothing more problematic than that Marco's ideal woman seemed to have been an even split between Daria and Kate Moss, and Larkin wasn't certain which Marco would have had a better chance with. He collected the copy of *Hamlet* before exiting the room, and after twenty-three years of the photograph being wedged against the spine, it allowed for the pages to fall open to the exact hiding spot again and again. Scene ii—Polonius's conversation with Hamlet.

"Though this be madness, yet there is method in't."

Larkin grunted, snapped the book shut, and walked down the hall. He stopped in the open doorway of the kitchen and said, "Mrs. Garcia, if I may have a moment."

Camila paused from scrubbing the already-sparkling countertop. She projected an air of casualness, nonchalance, but the lie was in the way her face hardened. "Yes?"

Larkin offered the evidence bag. "Do you recognize this girl. We believe this was taken between 1985 and 1990."

The creases around Camila's mouth and forehead smoothed as whatever she'd been braced for gave way to curiosity. She took the photo and studied it for a moment. "No, I don't think so. Why?"

"Did Marco have female friends."

"A few, when he was younger. You know high school boys… they can get so shy around girls."

"Did he have a girlfriend."

"One or two. Nothing serious." Camila gave the photo a shake before staring at the image a second time. "Not her, though. Marco wouldn't have even been in junior high yet—way too young for a girlfriend."

"Infatuation among preteens and teenagers rarely includes logic," Larkin replied. "The human brain isn't fully developed until our midtwenties, and with the onset of puberty, rising levels of testosterone and estrogen collide with the concept, or idea, of what love is—it's been described as a high not unlike what you'd experience with cocaine.

"I estimate that girl's age to be thirteen, perhaps fourteen, which, when you consult the United States Census, age differences between couples in a heterosexual relationship were reported to be an average of three years. Of course, the census has only just this year agreed to include data on LGBT couples, although it is sorely lacking in many significant ways, so an insightful study was done based on public Facebook data that determined LGBT couples are far more likely to be part of a more significant age gap relationship, with an average of seven years. It's an interesting subject when you consider the biological imperative to produce offspring versus—" Larkin paused, recalibrated. "My apologies. I've gotten off topic."

Camila said, after a considerable span of silence, "You're not like any cop I've met before." She glanced at the picture a final time and added, "I don't know her, Detective." She started to hand it back but paused, brought it closer, and asked, "Is she sleeping?"

Larkin gently plucked the bag from Camila's hand. He held up, but didn't extend, the photo he'd uncovered in Marco's room. "Do you recognize this child."

Camila considered the picture, and then her eyes darted to the book in Larkin's hand. She asked, "Did—was that in Marco's room? Where was it?"

"Mrs. Garcia."

She bristled. "No, I don't know them. Where did you find it?"

Larkin exchanged the photo for the copy of *Hamlet*. "Inside this book, under the mattress."

"Under the—but I make that bed. How did I not notice it?"

"People don't see what they don't expect to find. You had no reason to suspect Marco hid anything from you."

She looked distraught and chafed her arms.

"Was Marco interested in photography."

"*What?*"

"Did he ever borrow your camera equipment."

"No, no, no, Marco did not take those—those creepy pictures."

"What about the art classes he assisted with at the Center," Larkin asked next. "Were any of them photography."

"Detective!"

"Mrs. Garcia, my asking as to Marco's access to camera equipment isn't meant to implicate him in any nefarious activities. It helps me construct a complete picture in my mind of the time and setting and people he interacted with. Investigating a murder isn't like walking a straight line. It splinters, the way that glass cracks. Focusing on only one direction is what led us to where we are today."

The color was high in Camila's cheeks as she answered roughly, "My son assisted with lots of different classes. He painted murals with the kids, helped them build portfolios for college… and one weekend a month they took field trips to city parks to practice photography."

CHAPTER SEVEN

It was 10:55 a.m. as Larkin took the stairs two at a time to the second-floor bullpen of Precinct 19, carrying *Hamlet* and the second, unidentified photo in a Ziploc bag Camila had provided on his way out. Larkin heard Doyle before he saw him—heard the heat and smoke that'd make someone a millionaire, if only they could figure out a way to bottle and sell that voice—and when he rounded the first landing and hiked the final steps, there was Doyle. He was leaning against the front of Larkin's desk, assuming that habitual pose of long legs stretched out and big hands planted on the edge of the furniture. He'd inclined forward to speak with Porter, who'd spun around to face Doyle as they chatted.

At the sound of Larkin's heels, Porter glanced toward the stairs and said, "Hey, Grim, look who dropped by to say hello."

"Detective Doyle didn't drive eighty-four blocks out of his way to simply say hello to me, Porter."

"You? Who said anything about you? I was talking about me."

Doyle twisted to catch Larkin's eye. He wore a flirty smile as he asked, "Eighty-four blocks?"

"Approximately."

"Uh-huh."

"It can be difficult to account for all the blocks with the chaotic, nongrid pattern of the Lower East Side," Larkin continued, taking in Doyle's disheveled state of loosened tie and rolled-back sleeves. He noted one of the molded plastic chairs that was always being punted around the bullpen had been dragged up along the right side of his desk, and Doyle's suit coat was tossed over the back, his portfolio bag wedged between its leg and the furniture.

"'By miles' would probably be easier," Doyle suggested.

"That's the least common measurement of distance in the city," Larkin answered.

Doyle continued, unfazed, "It was four and a half miles."

"If we're not using blocks, time taken is the second most utilized method of gauging distance. Although not an actual measurement of physical space, it is more typical of walking than driving, and fairly useless when taking rush hour into— 1PP is six miles via the FDR."

"I didn't take the FDR."

"Why."

Doyle glanced over his shoulder at the desktop, reached, and nudged a small takeout box stamped with Krispy Kreme's logo. He looked at Larkin again.

Larkin moved to the desk and flipped the lid on the box. The corner of his mouth tugged into a shy smile. He handed Doyle the evidence bags, took a seat, and removed a cake-batter-filled donut coated in yellow frosting and sprinkles. He took a big bite, caught a blob of filling on his thumb as it oozed free, and sucked it clean.

"That's it?" Porter asked, and when Larkin looked up, the older detective was motioning at him while addressing Doyle. "One donut and he shuts up?"

"It's three donuts," Doyle corrected, rising from the desktop in that lazy, catlike way he had of moving, while studying the contents of the Ziploc bag. "Even geniuses get cranky when their blood sugar's low. This is out-in-the-field rule two, Porter: If being hangry can be avoided—avoid it."

"So what do I have to do to get donut deliveries?" Porter continued. "How many other artists are in your unit?"

"Two." Doyle plopped down into the seat beside Larkin. He added, almost like an afterthought, "But I don't think you're their type."

"What about you, then?" Porter spun in his chair, grabbed a thick accordion file, then held it up, saying, "Want a big, juicy, double homicide? Twelve years cold, gang hit—"

Larkin pointed his half-eaten donut at Porter and interrupted, "I found him first."

Doyle murmured, "That was hot."

"Stop it."

"No, no, I like that I honestly can't tell if the territoriality is because of the art or the donuts."

"Don't be ridiculous."

"You're right. It's the donuts."

Larkin all but rolled his eyes before taking another bite.

"Why don't you two just get married while you're at it?" Porter suggested.

"Oh, we already are," Doyle answered.

"No, we're not," Larkin hastily said around the last bite of dough and cream.

"Work husbands for life," Doyle concluded before winking at Porter.

Larkin turned in the chair, his knee knocking Doyle's. He took Doyle by the tie and tugged forward. "I'm going to eat a second donut."

"And what am I going to do?"

"You're going to tell me everything that isn't obvious about that photo," Larkin said with a nod of his head at the Ziploc bag.

"You might want to let go of my tie before I develop a kink." Doyle smiled when Larkin quickly released him. He patted Larkin's thigh twice, the touch more than friends but less than lovers, then leaned back into a slouch. "What's the book for?"

Larkin plucked the second donut from the box. "I found it wedged between the mattress and bed slats. The photo fell out of Act II, scene ii."

"Is that a relevant detail?"

"Only ironically."

Doyle hummed absently, held the bag up toward the awful fluorescent overheads, then said, "Ah… this boy appears to be deceased."

"Yes, I gathered that much on my own."

"Okay… well, track pants and a baggy hoodie would suggest death occurred at a cooler time of year, but I'm not comfortable with the way the pants have been tugged so low… almost like… for titillation purposes. There's the oak bench and white tile wall, which would make this a subway, but with no other environmental details…."

Larkin turned his attention on Doyle and caught how his expression was in the midst of drifting from curiosity to thoughtfulness to recognition—so much character in those thick brows of his. "What is it?"

And Doyle must have heard the inflection in Larkin's voice, because he looked up. "The boy is holding one of his shoes in his lap."

Larkin set the half-eaten donut in the box, closed the lid, then pushed against the floor with his heels, directing the wheeled chair to bump up against Doyle's so he could study the evidence too. "Yes. A dirty sneaker. Counterfeit Nikes, by the looks of it."

"It's not the shoe itself that's important."

"I don't understand."

Doyle lowered the bag. His face was stoic as he asked, "How much do you know about postmortem photography?"

Larkin blinked. "The nineteenth-century mourning phenomenon?"

Doyle nodded.

"Photographs were taken of family who'd passed away. It fell out of favor after the turn of the century."

"By the 1920s," Doyle confirmed. "As death was removed from the home in favor of mortuaries, society's attitude toward mortality began taking a dramatic shift, until it's become what it is today."

"Taboo," Larkin answered.

"Taboo," Doyle echoed in agreement. "But in the mid to late 1800s, whether the photograph was of a loved one on their deathbed, someone who'd already passed, or an image of those *in* mourning, it was meant to be a token of remembrance. For some families, it was the only visual of who'd they'd lost."

Larkin said, "A memento mori."

"Come with me."

Larkin got to his feet and followed Doyle across the bullpen, down the hall, and into the former-office-turned-junk-room—where everything broken or obsolete was left to die—fondly referred to by the squad as the Fuck It. Larkin shut the door behind himself, leaned back against it, and watched as Doyle turned, one hand still holding the bags, the other resting on his hip.

"Last month," Doyle began, "you were involved in

tracking down a serial killer who created replica nineteenth-century death masks with his victims' likeness."

"We both were," Larkin corrected.

Doyle ignored that interjection as he continued. "Now there's evidence in an all-new case, addressed *specifically* to you, that appears to be recreations of nineteenth-century postmortem photography."

Larkin didn't reply.

"Is there something going on you haven't told me?"

"Why would you ask that."

"Because this is really weird, Evie," Doyle said, shaking the evidence bags for emphasis.

"I agree."

Doyle frowned, his brows knitted together. "Has anyone checked on Harry Regmore recently?"

"He's not involved."

"Inmates always find a way to get messages to the outside, even those in a maximum security prison. We should ask about any correspondence, any phone calls—"

"These are two completely different psychologies at work."

"Sure, but whoever is on the outside, they're naturally going to add their own spin—"

"*No,*" Larkin snapped.

Doyle fell silent.

Quieter, Larkin said, "The fact is, Marco Garcia was killed during Regmore's golden years, when he was hyperfocused on women on the fringes of society and creating 'art' that is unlike the methodology of photography. *This* perpetrator stalks a different environment and victim type entirely, with the only similarities being time period of activity and its general relation to outdated Western mourning practices. And even if this was not the case, if this was some kind of attempt at having Regmore's art continue from behind bars, he would seek a submissive personality—someone he could control, treat like an apprentice—to ensure *his* vision is what survived. What we're dealing with is another master. For lack of better description."

Doyle's voice was subdued as he asked, "You're confident Marco's case is tied to yesterday's John Doe?"

Larkin pointed at the evidence bags and asked, "In your professional opinion, are these the works of the same person."

Doyle reluctantly turned his gaze downward and studied the two photos side-by-side in his hold. He said, on a gentle exhale of breath, "Both appear to exclusively utilize the ambient light of the subway. Harsh highlights and saturated shadows. The compositions are distinctly that of portraits— full face and what would essentially be direct eye contact, if the subjects were alive, that is."

"Is that typical of mourning photography," Larkin asked.

"So little could be controlled by photographers at the time, what with bulky equipment and a time-consuming process, but one element they strived to use artistically was the composition of the deceased. The images were meant to be sympathetic, after all. But I've seen a few, mostly of young children propped in chairs, that are comparable to this raw… almost aggressive emotion felt in the framing." Doyle looked up before finishing, "I'd consider the style in both of these photographs to be exceptional enough that it could be one artist's signature."

Larkin's thoughts immediately spiraled outward, like from the hub of a spider's web. He could confirm both photographs were developed prior to Marco's death, could even confirm Marco's tenuous connection to yesterday's DB through the existence of the pictures themselves, but what Larkin *wasn't* yet confident in was the *motive* for Marco's death. The photographs were relevant, of that he was absolutely certain, but to what degree? Had Marco stumbled across someone's dark, vile secret and so had to be killed to keep the truth from coming out? Or had Marco somehow been more intimately involved in the creation of these photos? Because as much as Larkin didn't want to even consider it, the truth was, Marco had worked with children and taught them a number of different artistic disciplines—including photography. But that sat in Larkin's gut like bad takeout.

There was also the matter of John Doe. What was his relationship to Marco and the photographs? Had he known Marco when the teen was alive? Had he been involved in the picture-taking process? Or was he nothing more than an unfortunate bystander, stuffed into a cheap bag like dirty laundry, meant to be a means in which to garner Larkin's attention?

No. That didn't make sense.

Because the first detective on the scene had been O'Halloran. And O'Halloran was with Homicide. If someone had wanted Larkin to come into custody of the photo, they could have just as easily had it anonymously delivered to the precinct through the US postal service. John Doe had a more immediate and relevant connection, although Larkin wasn't yet in a position to say what that was, specifically.

And then there'd been the April Fools' letter....

Had the perpetrator of these long-ago murders been the one to reach out on April 1?

They'd goaded Larkin with the promise of a "better memento." They'd seemed to prey on a sect of society entirely forgettable to the public—*at-risk youth*—just like Harry Regmore had done with his exotic dancers. But if that was the case, why, after comfortably living in the shadows and delighting in the deaths of God only knew how many children, had the perp decided to take such a profound chance and step into the light?

It certainly had nothing to do with guilt or remorse for those murders committed.

This person was an artist.

They were proud of their work.

Perhaps they wanted somebody worthy to sit up and take notice.

Then along came Everett Larkin.

The perp saw their first real challenge in nearly thirty-five years.

And they were *excited*.

"There's the possibility you've gained the attention of someone unstable," Doyle said, his voice pulling Larkin free from the mess of webs anchored by half-formed truths.

Larkin scrubbed his face with one hand. "What do you mean."

"You were in the news after we apprehended Harry Regmore," Doyle answered. "All anyone had to do was google your name and they'd pull up a lot of successes and little failures."

"Perhaps," Larkin answered absently, because he knew that the perp had been aware of him and his powers of deduction *before* mainstream media had latched onto the Death Mask Murders. And he was now certain of two possibilities: that this suspect was either watching Regmore's movements throughout the '90s (perchance they were aware of *each other*, although there was no evidence the relationship went both ways), or that this death portrait photographer was most definitely someone on the inside.

But Larkin still hadn't told Doyle about the letter, and now he wasn't sure how.

Larkin continued, "I'd been investigating Marco's murder a month before Andrew Gorman was discovered."

Doyle asked thoughtfully, "So we should do a double-check on who you've already interviewed regarding Marco?"

"I've only spoken with Camila Garcia, Marco's mother. Of her own volition, she admitted to a background and interest in photography, but there is absolutely no way she was involved in Marco's death. Not only did she have an alibi for the time of death, confirmed by Kent, the original detective, but her grief is sincere. And she couldn't have been involved with yesterday's DB either. Camila is five feet tall and a hundred pounds soaking wet. She doesn't possess the necessary physical strength to stuff a full-grown man into an IKEA tote bag."

"Then what do you suggest?"

"What was the importance of the shoe," Larkin asked, sliding a hand into his trouser pocket.

The uneasiness in Doyle's stance had dissipated some, but there was still a jagged edge to the line of his shoulders. "The shoe was a popular symbol in postmortem, used to signify a childhood cut short." He held up the photo of the unknown girl. "Yesterday, I just thought she had a flower or even some kind of debris tucked behind her ear, but the presence of the shoe motif is making me think someone put an acanthus leaf in her hair."

"Why."

"It's more mourning imagery. Some of the oldest, in fact." Doyle paused a beat before adding in a lighter tone, like he was trying to alleviate the remaining tension, "I like that look you have."

Larkin met his eyes. "What look."

"The one that says you're thinking all those great big Holmesian thoughts."

Larkin realized he'd been tapping his chin with his index finger in an offbeat rhythm. He stopped, asked, "Where's your notepad."

Doyle made a vague motion that suggested Larkin's desk.

Larkin turned, opened the door, and left the Fuck It. As he entered the bullpen from the hall, Detective Byron Ulmer, tall and broad, with a dark complexion, shaved head, and goatee, was entering from the staircase at the opposite end.

"Well, well, well, look who's finally—"

Larkin sidestepped Ulmer without a word, ignored the indignant protest, circled his desk, and grabbed Doyle's suit coat from the back of his chair. He reached into a front pocket and found a handful of lemon candy.

Ulmer asked from behind Larkin but seemed to be addressing someone else, "The fuck you doing here?"

And it was Doyle, smooth and unperturbed, who replied. "Working a case with Larkin."

"*Again?*"

"Inner pocket, Larkin," Doyle called.

Larkin shoved the hard candies back and reached around the lapel. "Ulmer," he stated, tugging the small, bent notepad free from the breast pocket before turning around. Ulmer stood parallel in the aisle between desks, not so subtly sizing Doyle up. He glanced toward Larkin as he continued, "I'd like to begin my first day back with a set of new and well-thought-out regulations for you to adhere to. One: Stay away from me. Two: Stay away from my partner. Three: Stay away from this case and every other case that lands on my desk—from now until whichever of us dies first. Because if I find out you've so much as read a notation in the margins of my paperwork, breathed a word of my investigative process, had so much as a *single thought* about being some talking head's inside source, I will make it both my professional responsibility to see you shitcanned and my personal pleasure to ensure you can't even get a part-time security gig at Target. Have I made myself clear."

Ulmer snapped, "What the fuck are you talking about?"

"It's a simple yes-or-no question."

Ulmer snorted loudly and shook his head in disgust. "You think you can just waltz back in here, throwing your dick around like the goddamn commissioner? Fuck you, Grim."

Larkin took several steps forward, breaking through Ulmer's boundary of personal space that was considered, by Americans, to be a suitable distance in which to keep professional relationships, and pressed right into Ulmer's intimate circle, the eighteen inches or fewer reserved specifically for romantic partners, family, and only the closest of friends. It caused Ulmer to visibly recoil, his upper body bending away from Larkin in an attempt to recover the security inherent in distance, while simultaneously maintaining his ground against a threat.

"Get away from me, faggot," Ulmer growled.

Looking up at Ulmer, his face a careful expression of indifference, Larkin said, "In this context, 'yes' is a function word used to express assent or agreement. It's very simple. Only three letters. So when I ask if I have made myself clear, you reply—"

"Fuck you, you pompous dickbag," Ulmer all but shouted before he turned on one heel and stomped toward the opposite end of the bullpen.

Unperturbed, Larkin offered Doyle the notepad. "Would you mind taking notes."

"You should report him," Doyle said.

"It's not worth dealing with HR."

Larkin moved to the banister behind his desk, set his hands on the railing, and studied the ground floor. Officer Miller was pretending to draft another incident report for Mr. Cunningham, a man of eighty-seven years who'd been coming to the precinct at least twice a week for the last three months to file grievances against his neighbor, who in fact, did not exist. Multiple units in his apartment building were undergoing renovation, and Mr. Cunningham continuously mistook the sound of hammers, electric drills, and saws as some kind of "midnight disco party," despite the construction taking place well within the confines of 7:00 a.m. and 6:00 p.m. He was the elderly sort who'd immediately jumped to phoning the police instead of his landlord, and simply did not understand why his calls were being ignored, so here he was, making his complaint in person. Larkin heard Doyle take a seat in the computer chair, heard the squeak of the casters, the shift and slide of Doyle's shoes against the linoleum.

Larkin turned to face Doyle before saying, "We have two murders separated by twenty-three years, with Victim Two discovered on the anniversary of Victim One's death." He watched Doyle draw a line down the middle of the paper. "We've connected the victims via the possession of photographs depicting suspicious deaths of two children—"

"Janie and Johnny Doe," Doyle interrupted. "For convenience's sake."

"That's adequate."

"Have you gotten an ID on IKEA-John Doe?"

Larkin stepped forward, reached over Doyle's shoulder, and pressed the power button on the small computer tower that sat on the lefthand side of his desk. He turned the monitor on next, then returned to his position against the banister as he answered, "I haven't checked my email yet."

Doyle nodded and scribbled in each column on his notepad. "In the meantime, causes of death were different, but both vics died at the Fifty-Seventh Street station."

"Presumably," Larkin said. "It is highly unlikely that IKEA-John was killed elsewhere, carried down two flights of stairs, across an island platform, and then discarded in a utility room without at least one person noticing, but I should have a more definitive answer once I get the autopsy report from the ME and scene report from CSU."

Doyle was smiling to himself as he drew a little asterisk

beside the note in the second column. "We'll circle back on that. Janie and Johnny were both photographed relatively soon after their deaths—"

"Rigor mortis would have made it impossible to pose them."

Doyle hummed in agreement. "Exactly. So no later than six hours after death, but it's far more likely the photographing took place within the first hour, not only to avoid rigor in the face, but time would have been of the essence." He looked up and pointed his pen at Larkin. "It would be impossible to say when IKEA-John came into possession of Janie's photo, prior to obtaining an ID on him and understanding where he fits in this story, but can we estimate when Marco may have come into custody of Johnny's?"

"Marco was writing a report on *Hamlet*," Larkin answered. "The play was checked out from his high school library with a due date of May 23, 1997. This date is before my time, of course, so no party trick."

Doyle leaned to one side, removed his cell from his pocket, tapped the screen a few times, then said, "Friday."

Larkin nodded and continued. "High school libraries typically have a two-week checkout period. So that would mean the earliest date was… twenty-three… sixteen… May 9. Marco could have had the photograph in his safekeeping for longer, of course, but it's far more likely he grabbed the first thing he had on-hand in order to hide it. The report was half-finished and probably due the same week."

Doyle quickly jotted down a few bullet points before asking, "And Marco was killed Monday the 19th, right?"

"Correct. He had a part-time job as a mentor and teaching assistant at the now-defunct New York Youth Empowerment Center. It was an after-school program for—"

"At-risk kids?" Doyle asked, but he was nodding knowingly. "Yeah. I spent more than a few summer vacations enrolled in those programs."

Larkin cocked his head to one side. "Really?"

Doyle leaned back in the computer chair, now rolling the pen between his thumb and index finger. "I was a bit of a hellraiser."

"I find that difficult to believe."

"Daddy's mellowed out in his old age."

"I *never* called you 'Daddy.'"

Doyle's laugh was low, rumbling in his chest like a cat's purr. "So you're saying that Marco was killed after work?"

"Yes," Larkin said with a curt nod. "Part of his duties included walking students to the subway and paying their fare, since the center closed at eight o'clock and this was after-hours for the student passes."

"The Q doesn't go to Inwood," Doyle pointed out.

"No. Marco rode the A home."

"So why...." Doyle trailed off when Larkin held his hands out, his palms up. "That's the mystery. Got it. And we know for certain he didn't fall onto the tracks, right?"

Larkin collected an accordion file from his desk drawer. He removed a slim folder, flipped through the years and years of DD5s to the original report, and read, "Brian Hoffman, fifty-three, CPA with Harold, Hirth & Goldman in Midtown, asserted he was waiting on the downtown side, having just missed the Q that, presumably, was carrying Marco's students home. He claimed to be the only straphanger besides Marco, who he noted was standing somewhat closer to the northern mouth of the uptown tunnel, but otherwise he was focused on reading the *New York Times*, which Mr. Hoffman had been unable to read on his morning commute. Quote, 'I thought the kid was talking to himself, but when I heard shouting, I looked up, and there was a second guy. I didn't notice him come down the stairs. They were arguing, but I don't know over what, because the uptown train was approaching. Then the kid was shoved. He went right over the edge. The train laid on the horn, but it had no time to stop.' End quote. Detective Kent asked about the second man, but Mr. Hoffman could only say that he was taller and wore some sort of utility uniform."

"What does that mean?"

"Your guess is as good as mine. Marco was dragged under two of the eight cars before the train was able to come to a full stop. Mr. Hoffman said the second man was long gone by then." Larkin snapped the folder shut.

"Did Kent ask Mr. Hoffman to note where he himself had been standing on the platform?"

"He did not."

Doyle blew out a breath. "Okay, well, I know that entire station has gotten a facelift since the '90s, but the suspect could have run up the stairs nearest the northern mouth of the uptown tunnel and not have been seen, if Mr. Hoffman was standing toward the middle. Alternatively, the suspect could have jumped onto the downtown tracks and hidden in *that* tunnel."

"Unfortunately, we'll never be able to clarify," Larkin said. "I reached out shortly after adopting the case—Mr. Hoffman died of an aneurysm in 2004."

Doyle looked down at his notepad, stuck the end of his pen in his mouth, and chewed absently on the cap. "So we've got no suspects or persons of interest in the murder of Marco Garcia, and even fewer in the case of IKEA-John."

"And that about brings us up to speed," Larkin concluded. He dropped the folder onto the desktop before leaning over Doyle a second time to reach the keyboard. "Can you move."

"I don't mind."

Larkin typed his password and hit Enter.

"You smell nice."

"Don't smell me at work."

"If you didn't want me to smell you at work, you wouldn't wear a very expensive Eau de Toilette that you've now taken to spritzing on both your wrists and neck."

Larkin glanced sideways.

Doyle's smile could have bankrupted even the most moral of men. "You used to only spray your wrists," he clarified.

"Fair enough." Larkin navigated to his inbox, which was clean and orderly, because despite the medical leave, he had refused to return to work with hundreds of unread messages that would only bog him down, and so had diligently tapped out one-handed responses to each new email every morning, but only after Doyle left for his precinct, lest Larkin be called out for working while off the clock.

Doyle turned in the chair and said, "We need to get creative with our approach. What about that *Hamlet* essay? It's likely to have been a final project, because a week later would have been June and—Marco would have been a senior, right?"

"Correct."

"So he'd have had class finals, potentially some AP tests, even Regents, if he hadn't finished fulfilling those requirements. It'd be worth running to ground any of his former teachers and asking if they recall suspicious or concerning behavior during that time. Maybe Marco was being bullied. Maybe he had a bad breakup. I know neither of those circumstances would explain the photos or IKEA-John, but we have to start somewhere."

Larkin briefly looked away from the screen. Doyle was staring at him expectantly. "Camila insisted Marco was well-liked and well-behaved. She said he had one or two girlfriends in high school, but nothing serious enough that she could recall a name."

"Sometimes parental figures are the last to know there's a problem," Doyle replied.

—*"A divorce? Everett, you're being absolutely ridiculous! Noah is perfect for you."*—

Larkin studied Doyle's dark eyes and said, "That's true." He returned his attention to the screen, downloaded an attachment from L. Baxter, MD, and clicked Print. "Marco went to PS 51. Fourth period, World Literature with Mr. Reynold."

"How do you know that?" Doyle called as Larkin walked toward the printer along the wall in between Connor's office and an interview room.

Larkin answered, while collecting the paperwork spitting out at lightning speed, "Marco properly labeled his reports."

"All right. We've got Camila Garcia and Mr. Reynold, so far. Is Dad still in the picture?"

"Dead since 1985," Larkin said upon returning to his desk.

"And what about that youth center?" Doyle continued as he made notations on his pad. "When did it close?"

"Shortly after 2007, I believe. It was a nonprofit that Camila said didn't survive the recession. A subpoena to the Secretary of State's office ought to get us the records we need."

"One of the officers of the nonprofit might remember Marco," Doyle suggested. "Or could at least refer us to other mentors and instructors he worked with."

"And it would be wise to ask the officers if they recognize either Jannie or Johnny as kids once enrolled in their program," Larkin concluded before raising the still-warm papers. "I'm going to read the autopsy report for John Doe. No, don't worry, you can sit there." Larkin moved around the computer chair and unbuttoned his suit coat with one hand while dropping into the molded plastic chair.

"Mind if I take point on Mr. Reynold, then?" Doyle asked.

"9-1 to dial out," Larkin answered. He crossed his legs and settled into the account.

John Doe had been found wearing a pair of Dickies black slacks, white undershirt, and white athletic socks. He wore no shoes, but the balls and heels of his socks showed no signs that he'd been walking on unclean surfaces. No jewelry, wallet, or identification was found on his person, only the aforementioned business card for St. Jude's Mission and the photograph addressed to Larkin.

John Doe was white, between fifty and sixty years of age, five foot ten inches, and 180 pounds at the time of autopsy. It was noted that he had physical wear and tear in his lumbar region and both rotator cuffs, indicative of years of manual labor and not a high intensity sport. Varicose veins in his lower legs suggested a job in which he was on his feet for most of, if not all day. Based on how blood had settled postmortem, Dr. Baxter's professional opinion was that the body had not been moved from one scene to another, and that John Doe had likely been killed in or near the utility room and immediately put into the bag. The cause, however, was more interesting.

Asphyxia due to ligature strangulation.

Not only did the good doctor confirm that John Doe's hyoid bone had been broken, but due to how the body had been contorted and stuffed into the IKEA tote bag, his shoulder had partially protected the side of his neck from insect activity. Dr. Baxter had discovered a large pattern in the skin measuring two inches in height. The design had repetitive rounded shapes with points that had left small punctures in the flesh. It was a curious outline Larkin hadn't seen before.

"John Doe was strangled," Larkin said, not looking

up. "Dr. Baxter confirms that the pattern and dimensions are unlike typical weapons, for example, scarves, rope, wire, chain, or a strip of leather." Larkin studied the second page before adding, "His left shoulder was also dislocated postmortem. Could have been caused by forcing him into the bag…. He was found only wearing slacks, an undershirt, and socks."

"Sounds like he was undressed," Doyle answered as he was busily typing and clicking at the computer. "The perp yanks John Doe's arm back to pull a shirt sleeve off and pops the shoulder."

"I agree," Larkin said. "His clothing likely had some sort of company brand or logo that'd have otherwise made him more easily identifiable. It also appears that due to the state of decomposition, Dr. Baxter was unable to collect fingerprints and so had to utilize thanatopractical processing. That's interesting."

Doyle sighed before saying, "I know I'm going to regret asking what thanato-whatever processing is."

"Thanatopractical. It's a process which involves extracting fluids from the body's tissues, allowing the volume to return to antemortem tenseness. It yields a seventy-five percent accuracy rate with fingerprints applicable for AFIS entry."

"Gross."

"He sent the prints in to be run. Results are pending." Larkin set the report aside, stood, and leaned over the keyboard as Doyle scooted back to make space. He minimized the Google results Doyle had been searching, checked his inbox again, and this time, downloaded and printed a report from Detective Millett.

Doyle, meanwhile, had punched in a number on the desk phone, and receiver to ear, said, "First one to get a lead drives."

"Are you making a bet during a homicide investigation."

"It's only driving."

"No one drives the Audi but me."

"I've driven it," Doyle corrected.

"Extenuating circumstances," Larkin said in a clipped tone.

"Afraid you'll lose?"

"I'm not going to lose—"

Larkin was cut off when Doyle grinned and said into the phone, "Hello, ma'am, my name is Ira Doyle. I'm a detective with the NYPD's Forensic Artists Unit. I'm working in conjunction with the Cold Case Squad and was hoping to speak with Principal Widalski? … That'd be great, thank you."

Larkin didn't run to the printer, but he was very conscious of walking quicker than usual.

CHAPTER EIGHT

"It's illegal to drive and use a cell phone anyway," Larkin was saying from the passenger seat of his Audi while scrolling through his list of contacts.

"And you've got calls to make," Doyle said by way of suggestion.

"Yes," Larkin answered, only a touch defensively. He caught a quick, there-and-gone smile flicker across Doyle's face. "NHTSA no longer recommends hands at the 10 and 2 position."

"No?"

"Due to the dangers certain airbags present, 9 and 3 is now advisable. I bring this up because you currently have only *one* hand on the wheel."

Doyle responded by putting his left hand on the steering wheel as he made the turn onto the FDR, but before he could even straighten out, it had dropped into his lap in what was clearly a subconscious, automatic behavior that would take more than one reminder to correct. The actual aspect that frustrated Larkin was how unreasonably attractive Doyle's cool and calm demeanor was when he drove one-handed.

Larkin wasn't certain why he'd always found competent male drivers to be, if he was being crude, a turn-on, and he'd been unable to find any serious studies on the subject outside of Reddit users asking about the very same phenomenon, so Larkin could only surmise it had something to do with confidence. Doyle struck that golden mean between self-doubt and arrogance in just about every facet of his life, but add 4,300 pounds of machinery into the equation, and it made Larkin's heart beat a little faster.

Larkin put his phone to his ear and said, "Ira."

Doyle glanced away from the road, round tortoiseshell-framed sunglasses meeting Larkin's steady stare.

Larkin felt his skin prickle from a sudden rush of heat, and instead of whatever he'd thought to say, he blurted, "Please use both hands."

"Why the fuck you callin', Grim?" Ray O'Halloran growled over the line.

Larkin redirected his attention to the phone call and replied, deadpan, "I'd like your opinion on Pantone's decision to award Classic Blue as color of the year."

Doyle had to stifle a laugh with the back of his hand.

"Come again?"

"I thought they played it too safe after choosing Living Coral for 2019."

"You're not funny, shithead."

"So no future at the Comedy Cellar," Larkin asked.

"I'm hanging up."

"I need the name of the MTA employee who reported yesterday's DB, as well as their supervisor's contact information."

O'Halloran snorted. "You were supposed to conduct that interview yesterday."

"Just give me the name and phone number."

O'Halloran sighed heavily, dramatically, like there wasn't enough patience in his soul for even one more asshole today, but eventually asked, "Got a pen ready?"

"I'll remember it."

"Uh-huh. You'll transpose a 9 and 8 and end up calling the Pussycat Pleasure Hotline or some such bullshit. Actually, you know what? *That'd* be funny, Grim."

"Yes, a gay man calling a straight sex hotline is very eighth-grade funny, O'Halloran, but at least my sexual partners have never needed to draw me an anatomical map with an X marking the spot that, at best, you only found by accident while you were motorboating her—a tip you probably read about on a wildly hetero blog called something like Manliness 101, where that same expert also said, with absolute conviction, that the alphabet trick works."

The Audi swerved hard to the left and Doyle swore under his breath as he corrected.

"This is why I said to drive with two hands, Doyle," Larkin stated.

"You got some fucking nerve—"

"Name and phone number," Larkin prompted a third time.

O'Halloran snarled like a caged predator before barking the information loudly, and without taking a breath, then hung up.

Larkin lowered the phone and calmly tapped the newly obtained number on the dial pad.

"I can't believe you made a 'where is the clitoris' joke," Doyle said.

Larkin put the phone to his ear a second time, saying, "It's healthy to humble straight men now and then."

After Larkin had spoken with Tanisha Crowley, Station Manager of Fifty-Seventh Street, who agreed to bring

Demetrius Armstrong, the track worker responsible for the 911 call, to meet Larkin at the station by 2:30 p.m., he opened his calendar and inputted the details of the appointment. "PS 51 at one o'clock," Larkin stated. "MTA at 2:30. The kitchen at St. Jude's Mission is open from noon to two o'clock, so we'll speak with the staff and guests tomorrow, at the earliest…." Larkin raised his head. He watched the dark, choppy water of the East River pass in a blur. "I'm forgetting something."

"Professional or personal?" Doyle asked.

"I'm not sure." Larkin stared at the calendar again, scrolled to the beginning of the day, then back to the evening, before letting out a dissatisfied huff and tucking the phone in his pocket. He leaned his elbow against the passenger door and propped his head against his fist. Afternoon light gleamed off the glass and steel of towering skyscrapers. Larkin lowered the visor. A comfortable, companionable silence had settled between them, broken only by the *thrum* of the Audi's tires and the *slide* of Doyle's hand on the steering wheel, when Larkin said suddenly, like he hadn't a chance to process the thought before verbalizing, "I'm very attracted to you. Also, thank you."

"Are you thanking me for being hot?"

"No. I mean—those were two independent and unrelated concepts I thought at the same time, because my brain doesn't turn off. And I attempted to condense them for the sake of efficiency and because my straightforwardness is usually awkward, but… I ended up making it worse." Larkin tugged on his seat belt so he could better study Doyle. "I think you're very striking. When driving, especially. Not specifically."

Doyle's smile exploded like a timelapse blooming rose. "Can this be a new out-in-the-field, rule? The tall and sexy will drive?"

"Don't let one compliment inflate your ego. I bought the Audi for me."

Doyle laughed, and it was like smoke skimming the surface of amber heat. "And what was the thank-you for?"

Larkin slowly leaned back in his seat. He fingered the latch on the center console where he'd hidden the Xanax prescription he'd filled without Doyle's knowledge.

Click.

—dock planks rough and sun-kissed, their toes dipping in and out of the cool lake water as they swung their legs back and forth with the carefreeness of the children they still were, Patrick's fingers working down Larkin's bare arm with the tentativeness and novelty of first love—

Click.

—Doyle crawling into bed when Larkin couldn't get out, pulling the sheet over their heads, his face haloed in white cotton and sunshine, his smile undeniable proof that there was still one thing in this fucking world that was beautiful—

Click.

—"Do you think we'll be together forever, Everett?"—

—"Whenever you're ready, you can talk to me."—

Click. Click.

—"I love you."—

—"People don't want to know. But I do."—

Clickclickclick.

"Hey." Doyle switched hands on the wheel before taking Larkin's into his own and pulling it away from the console. "Evie?"

Larkin blinked, letting out the breath he'd been holding. He stared at Doyle's big hand wrapped around his own, the hair tie on his wrist. "Never mind." He tugged his hand free from Doyle's and turned to watch the sunlight sparkle and glitter atop the dark water until it made his eyes tear.

It was 1:06 p.m. when Doyle parallel parked outside PS 51 in Inwood. He turned off the engine but hadn't opened the driver's side door before Larkin spoke.

"I need a Xanax." Larkin held an expectant hand out. "I haven't had one yet."

Doyle had taken control of Larkin's prescription a little over a week ago. He'd been limiting Larkin to his daily dose while at home, which had been… tolerable, since he'd still been on medical leave and could always depend on ZzzQuil if he needed something a little extra. But Larkin could already tell this new routine would *not* be successful, now that he had returned to active duty. Doyle kept the Xanax well-hidden at home, hence Larkin having to hide a backup prescription, but at least Doyle had taken to carrying two pills on his person at all times, because he'd admitted to not knowing when a panic attack would strike and Larkin would need medication.

Doyle didn't question him, shifting in his seat to retrieve the discreet, daily container from his pocket and dropping one pill into Larkin's palm.

Larkin dry-swallowed the Xanax and then got out of the car. He stepped between bumpers, swiped his keys from Doyle's hand, and led the way across the street toward the five-story high school with a façade reminiscent of medieval castles, like its architect had had an identity crisis during the design phase. Larkin pulled open the bright red front door and was promptly stopped by a uniformed school safety agent.

"Can I help you, sir?" the woman asked, standing from her desk and moving to intercept Larkin's path. Her hair was pulled back in a tight, slick bun.

Larkin reached for his wallet and displayed his shield. "Detective Everett Larkin, Cold Case Squad." He glanced over his shoulder as Doyle entered. "My partner, Ira Doyle. We have an appointment with Principal Widalski."

The safety agent looked at Doyle, waited until he'd flashed his own badge, then returned to the desk and made a call. "Yes, I have two detectives at the front who're here to meet with Principal Widalski? Okay, thank you." She hung up, grabbed a clipboard, and slid it sideways along the countertop above the desk. "She's on her way. Please sign in here."

Larkin scribbled his name, passed Doyle the pen, and couldn't help but notice how chaotic his penmanship looked in contrast to Doyle's—his signature practically artwork.

"Are either of you gentlemen armed?"

Larkin looked up from the form. "Yes." He drew back the right side of his suit coat to reveal the holstered SIG.

The agent nodded. "Keep the safeties on and firearms holstered for the entirety of your appointment."

"Is that really a necessary warning," Larkin asked.

She let out an unprofessional snort and said, "Sir, I've been workin' here a long time. You aren't the first cops to come through those doors. Some of 'em think they got something to prove, if you get my meaning."

"We do," Doyle confirmed. "In fact, I think we work with those guys."

She cracked a smile.

"There's a study that was recently published concerning the Male Warrior Hypothesis," Larkin interjected. "It breaks down the correlation between testosterone and intergroup competition among men and how that particular form of aggression, in fact, promotes a certain type of cooperation against outsiders. It also demonstrates that body musculature plays a critical factor in the amount of aggression presented. For example, two groups with similar abilities will present a higher level of formidability, such as rival sports teams who are on par with each other will present a higher likelihood of violence while on the field. It's an interesting study when viewed against the complexity of today's society as a possible explanation for why men still behave like children at their places of employment."

"In case you wanted a more scientific explanation," Doyle added when the safety agent stared at Larkin like he'd grown a second head.

"Thank you" was all she said.

"Detective Doyle, I'm so sorry to keep you waiting," a woman said, approaching quickly on heels, their *click-clack* reverberating loudly on the high-traffic tiles. She was a robust, middle-aged black woman in a sharp pantsuit, bright purple top, matching colored glasses, with box braids pulled into a beautiful high bun, and a lanyard around her neck with school ID and keys. "I'm Nichole Widalski, principal of PS 51."

Doyle moved around Larkin, close enough that Larkin got a breath of neroli and sandalwood and cardamon. He shook hands with Widalski and made the necessary, polite small talk, before turning to Larkin as a means of inviting him into the conversation.

Larkin offered Widalski a hand. "Everett Larkin, Cold Case Squad. Thank you for taking time to speak with us, ma'am. Regarding Mr. Reynold," he prompted.

Widalski appeared to not be bothered by Larkin's bluntness as she motioned them to follow, taking the lead as they turned down a long, empty hall lined with red lockers on the left and closed classroom doors on the right, the fluorescent lights gleaming off the tile floor. They must have been relatively close to the cafeteria, because Larkin could smell remnants of the day's menu—chicken nuggets and what he thought might have been boiled cauliflower. It mingled with rubber erasers, bleach, and the permanent cloud of young adult odor and store-brand body sprays that were all chemical aggression and no subtleness.

"As I said to Detective Doyle on the phone," Widalski began, "Mr. Reynold is an institution here at PS 51. He's been teaching English since 1995. Well before my time. I'm not sure if he'll remember Marco Garcia—by law we only maintain student records for twenty years—and of course he's had thousands of students in that time."

"Of course," Doyle echoed with the perfect amount of sympathy.

Widalski looked over her shoulder at them both and added, "I went ahead and told him you'd be stopping by, just so he'd have a chance to jog his memory."

They took a flight of stairs at the end of the hall to the second floor.

At the landing, Widalski lingered long enough to ask, "This boy was murdered in the '90s?"

"1997," Larkin answered. "By the time a homicide reaches my desk, all avenues of investigation have been exhausted."

"And you're expected to solve what other cops couldn't?" Widalski questioned.

"I'm very good," Larkin clarified.

Widalski's dubious expression shifted to Doyle. "You said you're with Forensics, though, right?"

"Yes, ma'am, the Forensic Artists Unit," Doyle said.

"Uh-huh. And there's a lot of crossover?"

Larkin looked up at the same moment Doyle looked down. Larkin said to Widalski, "More than you'd expect."

That seemed good enough for Widalski, and she continued walking until about the halfway mark, where she stopped outside a door that looked like every other door and peered through the glass window. Her mouth tugged into a subtle frown before she opened it and stepped into the classroom. The commotion of a dozen different conversations, teenagers laughing, the legs of a chair slamming down on the floor after leaning too far back, all filled the quiet hallway.

Larkin moved into the doorway and studied the room. He'd been inside public schools plenty since his marriage, but was accustomed to the bright colors and homey elements that Noah incorporated into his class layout. In contrast, Mr. Reynold's room was about as friendly as a prison cell: off-white walls, more of the same fluorescent overheads, two large windows with the typical security grating, and a few laminated posters with generic tips and tricks of the English language, as well as one featuring phrases used today that were popularized by Shakespeare, which actually appeared to have been a student project that'd simply outlasted its classmates' longevity on the wall. The whiteboard was a mess of half-erased talking points on two or three different subjects—previous classes, Larkin concluded—and the clunky steel desk on the opposite end of the room, with the filing cabinet to its back, would belong to Mr. Reynold.

"Yo, who's that?" a boy asked.

Larkin glanced at the rows of desks—the sort with the blue seat, metal basket underneath that no one used, and attached arm and desktop—and the thirty-two students inhabiting them. Teenagers sat sideways in order to talk with a friend across the aisle, one sat on the desktop itself, three more heads were down and taking the opportunity to nap.

"He's a cop," another kid answered. "I can tell he's packin'."

"Everyone settle down," Widalski said. "Tyrone, off the desk—this is a classroom, not a jungle gym."

Larkin turned his head enough so he could speak to Doyle standing behind him, but didn't take his eyes off the class. "There are far too many students in here."

"Welcome to an underfunded public school," Doyle murmured.

Widalski waited until the teenagers had settled down before asking, "Where's Mr. Reynold?"

"He weren't here when the bell rang," a girl in the second row said as she ran fingers through the hair pulled over one shoulder.

"Wasn't here," Widalski corrected. "This is AP English, Leslie."

Larkin took a step into the room and asked Widalski, "When did the period begin."

She checked her watch and said, "About ten minutes ago."

Larkin considered the answer, moved around Widalski, and approached Reynold's desk. He scanned the content littering its surface: computer monitor; keyboard; mouse; desk phone; empty water bottle missing the cap; coffee cup repurposed to hold pens, pencils, and a variety of markers; a clipboard with nothing clipped to it; stacks of colored folders stuffed with turned-in homework; a teaching-themed page-a-day calendar that hadn't been torn away since Friday, April 24.

—living room dark but for the fairy lights and harsh flicker of the television, Larkin stretched out on the couch, and Doyle's longer body curled up against him, one leg hanging precariously over the side, the other tangled with Larkin's— his once-partner fast asleep after an exhausting week—

Larkin turned away from the calendar, checked beside the desk, and pulled out the sagging computer chair before determining the teacher's personal effects—bag, phone, keys, anything of that nature—were absent. Larkin focused on a spot near the right edge of the desk that was devoid of the clutter that took up the rest of Reynold's workspace. He pointed to it, looked at the teenagers who were studying him with a combination of curiosity and boredom, and asked, "What usually sits here."

No one replied.

"Something is missing from this desk," Larkin said to the sea of faces. "Pencil sharpener, calculator, Post-its, glasses case—"

"Mr. Reynold doesn't wear glasses," a Latino boy in the front row answered. He had his chin propped up and looked only half-awake.

"What is missing," Larkin repeated, addressing him specifically.

The boy answered on a sigh, "A picture frame."

"Detective?" Widalski asked.

But Larkin ignored her inquiry as he bent at the waist to collect the trash bin pushed into the kneehole of the desk. He reached inside, but the contents only consisted of an empty cup from Dunkin' Donuts and a test page noting a printer was out of cyan ink. Larkin put it back, checked the middle drawer—years of hoarding office supplies, by the looks of it—then opened the three along the lefthand side. The top was a continuation of Reynold's collection of junk: half a dozen power cords, four bags of gummy candy that drugstores kept stocked at the counter for impulse shoppers, scissors, Scotch tape dispenser, a torn mousepad, and a small, half-empty bottle of Tabasco sauce. Larkin shoved it closed and grabbed the middle drawer.

It was locked.

Larkin frowned, checked the bottom drawer, and found it full of hanging folders, binders of what were probably the same lesson plans Reynold had used for the last decade, if not more, and those blue test booklets students wrote their finals in. He shut it and checked for a set of keys in the other drawers, but there wasn't one.

Doyle had joined him by then, whispering, "What are you doing?"

Larkin turned his back to the class and Doyle mimicked

the action. He said quietly, "A picture frame is missing, this drawer is locked, the keys are gone, and Gary Reynold isn't on the premises after being informed we were coming to ask questions about Marco."

Doyle rubbed the stubble on his face before nodding. "Okay. Fair. But you can't just break into his desk."

"No. I don't know how. Do you."

"Larkin—"

Larkin turned toward Widalski, still standing at the front of the class. "Do we have permission to open this locked drawer." He tugged on the handle for emphasis.

"Good God," Doyle muttered, his back still turned.

Widalski considered Larkin's question, hyperaware of the audience before them.

"Twenty-three years, Principal Widalski," Larkin reminded. "He was only eighteen. A student of PS 51."

At that, she pulled her shoulders back, straightened her posture, and said resolutely, "The desk is school property. You have the school's permission."

Doyle pivoted on his heel, ushered Larkin aside with a brush of his hand, and collected a stray paperclip along with the pair of scissors. He squatted, stuck the bottom blade into the lock, wedged the bent tip of the paperclip in, dug at the tumblers for exactly two seconds, and then the drawer popped open.

Larkin met Doyle's expression as he rose to his feet. "Thank you."

"Always happy to be of service."

Larkin plucked a tissue from the box shoved underneath the computer monitor, then carefully pulled the drawer open the rest of the way. If not for the comfort of the Xanax, Larkin would have likely hit stimulation overload already, as this drawer was just as full as the others: fast-food ketchup packets, a dented ping-pong ball, book of stamps, files of loose paperwork, bent, torn, and yellowed around their edges. Larkin removed a flip phone and set it on the desktop.

"That's definitely not a student's confiscated phone," Doyle said, his whiskey voice low, almost intimate. He reached for his own tissue and carefully opened the phone as Larkin kept digging. "Looks like a burner. There's a few texts… all to the same number."

Larkin found the missing frame at the bottom, under the stack of files. It was a tacky thing of faux gold, containing a photo of a man, probably in his fifties, although it was difficult to tell, as he was wearing a ballcap, sunglasses, and waders, proudly displaying a fish for the camera. The location in the backdrop could have been anywhere in upstate New York. "Is this Gary Reynold," Larkin asked, turning the photograph toward Widalski.

She nodded. "Yes, it is. Detective, I really must ask what—"

Doyle interrupted her as he held the burner out for Larkin, still carefully cradled in the tissue. "Look at this."

"F RED HAIR 14"

"got 10"

"2 YOUNG"

"will get back 2 u"

"HELLO?"

"ITS BEEN 2 WKS"

"NVM ILL DO IT MYSELF"

"*Detective*," Widalski tried again, her tone less understanding, more impatient.

Larkin replied, "Principal Widalski, I need to ask that these students leave the classroom."

The teenagers immediately erupted into a chorus, conversations competing to be heard, pitches rising, questions ringing out among laughter, complaints, thirty-two voices pounding away at the fortification the Xanax was busily erecting and drilling into Larkin's long-term memory.

"Mrs. Widalski, where are we supposed to go?"

"Maddie just sent me a pic of her tit from the girl's locker room."

"I gotta take a leak."

"Fuckin' hate this class anyway."

"Mrs. Widalski, I don't think this is legal!"

"Girl, you are *so* thirsty for a cop."

"I'm sorry, but did you *look* at his ass? It's got a damn zip code."

Larkin pressed the knuckles of his right fist against the desktop for grounding, squeezed his eyes shut, and tried to breathe through the commotion of Widalski ushering students to the door with orders to use the rest of the period as a study hall at the library—yes, that includes you, Devon. He pinched the bridge of his nose with his left hand, waited until the noise level in the room dropped, then ceased entirely as the last of the students filtered into the hall. "Jesus Christ," he finally muttered.

"Hey." Doyle tugged on the hair tie around Larkin's wrist. "Do you need me to leave you alone for a minute?"

Larkin considered the offer. He would have appreciated being alone. A few seconds to realign his senses without distraction, a heartbeat to adjust his composure, his stance, his attitude, a minute for them both to read their parts in this play, pretend that everything was okay. But as badly as Larkin wanted that—frankly, needed that—it felt profoundly… like cowardice. Wrong to turn away the one man who never took it personally. Wrong to shut out the one man who understood that Larkin was different, and that different was okay. Wrong to not show himself, the good and bad, the beautiful and ugly, the strong and sick, to the one man who hoped every day that

Larkin would say *yes*.

Larkin lowered his hand from his face and looked up. "You can stay." He cleared his throat and tried to say as casually as his modulated tone would allow, "Sometimes there's so much stimulation to sort and catalogue that even Xanax can't keep up."

"Evie," Doyle said, his voice a whisper.

"I know."

"After last week—"

"I know," Larkin said, his tone more clipped. His chest itched, a panic-induced sweat had broken out, but he ignored it and returned his attention to the gold picture frame. He flipped it around and worked the fastenings free.

"Straight men do love selfies taken with fish," Doyle commented, voice a little rough around the edges. "But a framed photo of *themselves* on their own desk? At minimum, you'd expect whoever snapped the picture to share the moment with Reynold."

"My thoughts as well." Larkin took the cardboard backing off, and with the blunt edge of his fingernail, tugged the photograph free. What came up with the largemouth bass picture were two separate portraits of young white girls— Larkin would estimate they were no older than fourteen or fifteen—each wearing ensembles unique enough that he could roughly identify the '90s in one and the early '00s in the other, although their clothing had been tugged down and hiked up in places to suggest something horribly sexual had taken place.

Both were posed on subway benches, hands delicately folded against their stomachs.

Both were dead.

Larkin said, "Mr. Gary Reynold has been very, very bad…."

CHAPTER NINE

Larkin stared at the disturbing contents recovered from the drawer as Doyle put in a call to have CSU come up and fully process the desk—preferably Detective Neil Millett, if he was available, at Larkin's behest. "Gary Reynold isn't on school property," he stated.

"Have a uniformed officer come along for door duty. … Yeah, school's still in session. … Great. Thanks." Doyle hung up, met Larkin's stare as he tucked the phone into a pocket, and asked, "What was that?"

"You spoke with Principal Widalski at quarter to twelve."

"Roughly."

"She would have likely informed Reynold by noon of our imminent arrival—between periods. He then hid this evidence that incriminates him in a… murder? Underage pornography?… I'm not sure *what* these photographs signify exactly. Then he collected his personal effects and left sometime between 12:00 p.m. and 1:06 p.m. without anyone noticing."

Doyle's thick brows rose, and he said, "Public schools usually have two lunch periods. I'll bet his last class finished just as second lunch began. Widalski would have spoken to him then—probably closer to 12:30. Reynold left on his lunch break and simply didn't come back."

"Why."

"Isn't it obvious?"

"No. The question is, why did he leave and not take these items with him," Larkin corrected, motioning to the pictures and phone.

Doyle hesitated. "Because he didn't expect them to be found? He intends to come back?"

Larkin raised his index finger. "Yes."

"If he planned on returning to work, why run off to begin with?"

"He has evidence elsewhere that's *not* hidden."

"He's disposing of it right now," Doyle said, his voice sinking. "But where—"

"Home," Larkin answered. "He took his keys. He went home." He started for the classroom door just as Widalski reappeared.

"I'm sorry about that," she began.

"Call the office," Larkin interrupted. "Tell them I need Gary Reynold's home address right now."

And then he ran into the hall.

Larkin could hear Doyle's brief instructions to not touch anything and to please wait for responding officers who would be processing the room, and then his partner's steps were pounding the tiles, the soles of their shoes beating in sync as they made for the stairwell. Even with the late start, Doyle had longer legs, and he reached the stairs before Larkin. He put even more distance between them by sliding down the banister, the slap of his oxfords on the floor bouncing off the bare walls and high ceiling. Doyle turned as Larkin jumped the final two steps, caught his hand, and pushed Larkin to take the lead.

Larkin burst through the doorway of the ground floor, dodged a lone janitor in gray coveralls pushing a mop and bucket out of a storage room, and skidded to a stop outside the glass door of the main office located just before the security desk. He threw it open, raised his badge, and said to the receptionist, "Gary Reynold's home address."

She was hardly more than twenty years old and dressed like a fifties housewife in a pastel blue dress, a white sweater that was more for aesthetics than practicality, honest-to-God pearls with matching earrings, and with blond hair done up in what probably took an hour's time and a full can of hairspray each morning. She squeaked as she put the phone receiver down and began clicking feverishly on her computer. "Principal Widalski asked me to print—"

"Just tell it to me," Larkin snapped.

She squeaked again, sounding very much like a dog's chew toy, before turning to the monitor and reading off a full address—state and zip code included.

"Is there an apartment number."

"Um… garden."

"What does Reynold drive."

"I—I—"

A second woman, older, with salt-and-pepper hair and glasses hanging from a chain around her neck, came into view from around the corner. She held a stack of printouts in both hands. "What's the question?"

"He w-wants to know what Gary d-drives," the receptionist stuttered, her voice almost a squeal now.

"He doesn't drive," the second woman said to Larkin. "Gary takes the train."

Larkin let the door slam shut behind him, and he and Doyle left the school. They ran across the street, got into the

Audi, and Larkin peeled onto Broadway as Doyle put in a call requesting uniformed officers at Gary Reynold's home address that he repeated into the phone as Larkin said it aloud for him. When Doyle had hung up, Larkin asked, "Closest subway stop."

"Ah—West 181st Street… let's see. Reynold could take the A or 1. Either one is only two stops from the high school," Doyle answered quickly. "But—God, let me think—his address is on Bennett Avenue. So he'd take the A."

"He'd save at least ten minutes taking the A."

"Yeah. So he's got about a forty-five-minute head start to toss whatever's spooked him."

Larkin floored the gas, laid on the horn, cut around a USPS mail truck, sped through an intersection as the yellow light turned red, and swerved around a guy with a hand truck stacked with bottles of liquor as he crossed the street from his double-parked delivery truck with its hazards on.

"I'd like to get there alive, Larkin," Doyle objected, grabbing the *oh-shit* handle beside his head.

"Reynold's text message."

"*What?*"

Larkin said, with frightening composure for a man doing fifty in a twenty-five zone, "Reynold's text specified that he was looking for a redheaded girl, age fourteen."

"I do recall that."

"He sent that message Tuesday, April 28. He inquired, after two weeks had passed, for an update on Tuesday, May 12, at 4:47 p.m. A second text was date-stamped 6:10 p.m. The last message was delivered Wednesday, May 13, at 7:12 a.m., when Reynold implied he'd find what he was looking for himself." Larkin made a hard right on West 184th Street.

"You think he has a kid at his apartment?" Doyle protested, his voice rising suddenly, uncharacteristically, in volume.

"I think it's been a long time since I've been surprised by the depths human depravity is capable of reaching, and if there's even a remote possibility that it involves a child, I'm willing to break a few rules of the road in order to prevent a tragedy."

The sudden whir of sirens sounded, and red and blue lights spun in Larkin's rearview mirror. He ignored the cruiser attracted by an expensive car they could ticket the hell out of, and turned down the one-way, tree-lined Bennett Avenue. Larkin hit the brakes as they neared West 181st Street, parked in the middle of the road, and climbed out from behind the wheel. He slammed the car door and held his badge in his free hand to the cruiser pulling up hard behind him.

"Detective Everett Larkin, Cold Case Squad," he called as both uniformed officers got out, hands going to their service weapons. He glanced over the roof of the Audi to see Doyle displaying his own identification, and then he approached the officers. "My partner and I are about to enter building 52. We believe there's a person of interest in the garden apartment who is currently destroying evidence in an ongoing murder investigation. There is the possibility of a female minor being held captive on the premises." Larkin tucked his badge away and pointed to the six-story apartment building on his right. "Backup has already been requested, but seeing as you two are especially gung-ho, please take point on the garden's back door."

The female officer who'd been driving, her eyes now as big as saucers, gave Larkin a curt nod and spirited "Yes, sir," before directing her partner to follow.

Larkin and Doyle raced to the front door of the complex, and Larkin began tapping apartment buzzers, waiting for someone who might have been home in the middle of the day to answer. "December 24, 2010, I was responding to a domestic, but the woman had barricaded herself in the bathroom and couldn't buzz me in." Larkin pressed more button combinations after no initial response. "The only tenant to answer told me to 'fuck off, you shit-for-brains, it's Christmas Eve and my fuckin' kid thinks you're fuckin' Santa and won't go back to bed,' so I found the fire escape, hoisted myself up, climbed to the third floor, and got inside through an unlatched living room window just as the boyfriend broke down the bathroom door and took a kitchen knife to the vic."

"'*Ello?*" answered the staticky voice of a dude-bro who sounded higher than a kite.

"NYPD, buzz us inside, sir," Larkin demanded.

The lock unhitched.

"I discharged my weapon for the first time that night," Larkin told Doyle as he grabbed the handle and flung the door open. "Put a bullet in the sonofabitch's kneecap."

They both drew their pistols as they entered the vestibule and stepped through the second set of doors into a lobby the size of an afterthought, its walls a thick, landlord off-white, the tile floors and staircase banister a not-quite-black. To the right were two first-floor apartments; to the left was a partially shut door, no number indicating it was someone's home. Larkin carefully stepped toward the left, moving on the balls of his feet to limit the echo his derby heels usually gave off. He took a quick glance through the crack, then cautiously pulled the door open. The bottom hinge groaned, and then there was enough room to slip down a set of stairs that led to the basement. Larkin took the steps slowly and at an angle, keeping his gun at low-ready while watching the door behind the stairs come into view.

House letters were affixed above the peephole: GDN.

Larkin reached the bottom of the stairs and moved against the wall, training his weapon on the front door as Doyle moved past him to a second door at his back. He was only gone a moment before returning to whisper, "Laundry and utility rooms. All clear."

Larkin nodded, approached the apartment, and banged loudly with the side of his fist. "Gary Reynold, NYPD. I want you to unlock this door, take a step back, and put your hands where I can see them. Do you understand?"

There was a shuffle of movement somewhere inside, a harsh murmur, then a scream that was abruptly cut short.

"Gary!" Larkin shouted as Doyle holstered his weapon and left his side a second time. "I don't want you doing something you'll regret. Let the girl unlock the door and join me in the hallway. Then the two of us can talk."

"Get out of the way." Doyle had returned from the utility room wielding a sledgehammer heavy with cobwebs. He gripped the handle at the end with one hand, the other behind the head, and slammed it down against the lock plate. There was another scream from inside the apartment. Doyle heaved the sledgehammer again, this time breaking the lock. He dropped the hammer to one side, drew his Glock 17, then threw his shoulder against the door, snapping the chain lock free.

Larkin took lead, SIG raised as he entered the apartment. The tile floor of the expansive living room was dull and in desperate need of waxing, and the furniture sparse, even for a bachelor pad of a middle-aged man: a single recliner in the middle of the room; an entertainment stand against the far left wall housing a relatively small flat-screen television, home printer, and a closed laptop—all the cables were in complete disarray. The home had no bookshelves or even displaced books piled on the floor, despite Reynold's entire adult life having been committed to the pursuit and study of the English language. A brief glimpse through an open doorway at the far end of the room showed a mattress on the floor, the bed made up of mismatching sheets. But it was the walls of the apartment that, for one critical second, distracted Larkin.

They were covered in cutouts and printouts of teen girl models. Years and years of *Back-to-School Fashion Tips & Tricks*, *OMG Hair*, *Are You a Flirt?*, and *Get Gorgeous Skin*, all advertised with fresh faces and pert bodies no older than sixteen, with an apparent emphasis on redheaded girls. Mingled among the clothing and hair photoshoots and advertisements for the hottest eye cream of 2003 were paparazzi-esque photos of celebrity teenage couples. The boy in each relationship had been scribbled out with a black marker.

Larkin shook his head, blinked, saw a negative of a sea of smiling faces in his mind's eye, then spun on his heel toward a sound directly behind him. Gary Reynold, tall and rail-thin, with black hair, a receding hairline, and a bushy mustache, shuffled sideways out of a kitchen, his forearm wrapped around the neck of a teen girl with poorly dyed red hair, wearing scuffed and beaten-up pink boots, black jeans torn at the knees with ripped mesh tights showing, along with a white long-sleeve shirt, the wrists frayed, and imprinted with a logo, probably for some obscure band, that looked to have been drawn by hand with a black Sharpie. She was crying, and cheap eye makeup was running down her cheeks.

"Gary—" was all Larkin got out before Reynold let out a panicked yelp, pointed the bright yellow taser he'd been holding to the girl's head, and fired at Larkin.

The darts struck Larkin in the chest and 50,000 volts of electricity immediately locked and paralyzed his muscles. His jaw clenched, he made some kind of pained sound in his throat, and the SIG fell from his hand as he stumbled backward into the wall covered with one man's sick obsession. Larkin knew, logically, that the current of electricity would only last five seconds, but it'd already felt like it'd been five fucking years, and he couldn't react, couldn't move, could only grit his teeth through the hurt.

Doyle was shouting, "Drop the weapon!"

The girl was sobbing louder.

"Drop the goddamn taser!"

Gary warbled something, protested something, screamed something.

Then Larkin was hit with a second round of darts, and he immediately collapsed to the floor.

—*a cannonball off the dock, the lake swallowing him whole, the water growing colder, darker, more and more pressure squeezing his ribs, his lungs, sinking down, down, down—*

"Move out of the way!"

—*Noah standing on the bottom, sand and silt washing through his blond hair, watching with disapproval as Larkin slammed down on the lakebed like a cut anchor, oxygen knocked from his lungs, water filling him, choking him—*

A deafening gunshot in close quarters.

—*thunder crashing overhead, mud sloppy underfoot, Larkin's skull fracturing, a crack so loud that he was deafened by it, and Patrick lay with his own head caved in, green eyes watching Larkin as Noah piled sediment atop his body like a gravedigger at work—*

"Larkin? Evie? *Evie*, can you hear me?"

—*underwater currents twisted Larkin's body, dragged him away from Patrick, from Noah, and he was screaming, but it was only water in his lungs, and then a wave grabbed him up like God's fist, hurled him toward the sun, its reflection like shattered glass seen from the underside, and Doyle was on the dock, calling Larkin's name over and over and over—*

"Rush the bus!" Doyle was shouting, but it sounded distant, muffled, like his voice was inverting on itself.

Then everything went quiet.

And finally… Larkin could rest.

CHAPTER TEN

—*"Do you think we'll be together forever, Everett?"* Patrick asked.

But when Larkin looked at their joined hands resting on the planks of the dock, his silver wedding band glinted in the sunshine. Larkin raised his gaze and Patrick glitched, twitched, his handsome, forever-boyish face suddenly Noah's face. Noah had on the suit he'd worn the day they'd gotten married.

"'Til death do us part," Noah said.—

No, that wasn't how the memory played out.

—*Patrick leaned in and Noah kissed Larkin—*

No.

—*thunder crashed, lightning cast ghostly flickers in the closed up bathroom, and Doyle reached into the water, pulling Larkin—*

No, no, no, there hadn't been water.

—*Doyle hoisted Larkin's limp body from the tub and laid him on his side just as Larkin began to profusely vomit—*

Larkin opened his eyes.

He sat on the edge of a gurney in the ER, his crisp white shirt no longer crisp but wrinkled, unbuttoned, and sporting four small holes where the taser darts had torn through the fabric. His flesh wounds had been properly cleaned and bandaged and were hardly more than a discomfort, whereas all the muscles in his chest and abdomen ached like the worst kind of postworkout hangover imaginable. Larkin's head was pounding, and every time he closed his eyes, unprovoked associations played out of sequence—people and places and times mixed up like someone had taken out every single card from his Rolodex and replaced them at random.

He let out a shallow breath and focused on doing up his shirt, the ambience of the hospital seeping into his concentration: the *whoosh* of the AC, telephones ringing at the nurses' station, medical lingo being punted back and forth between EMTs, nurses, and physicians, the groans, cries, and snores of patients, and somewhere, a faulty machine had been beeping obnoxiously for forty-three seconds straight.

Doyle's deep baritone, tense where it was usually as smooth and smoky as Laphroaig, could be heard moving down the hall and toward the curtained wall that made up Larkin's "room." "—Just want to make sure, because he suffered a traumatic brain injury about eighteen years ago."

"I understand your concern, Mr. Doyle," a tired-sounding but ever-polite doctor answered before drawing back the curtain, the rings jangling. She was about Doyle's age, honey-brown hair drawn back into a no-nonsense ponytail. She wore no makeup, and the shadows under her eyes suggested she was on the latter half of a very long shift. "Mr. Larkin?"

Larkin stopped what he was doing, his gaze shifting to Doyle, who hadn't stepped into the cramped space, then back to the doctor. "Yes."

"Because your partner said you briefly lost consciousness at the scene, we wanted to run a few tests before discharging you." She opened the manila folder she held in one hand, flipped the pages quick enough to scan pertinent details, then said, "Your EKG came back normal, as did your CAT scan."

"I had a CAT scan."

She seemed confused and cocked her head to one side.

"I'm asking," Larkin clarified. "I don't—remember a CAT scan."

"Yes, you did."

"If it came back normal, why don't I remember the process."

"Some people do suffer a more serious, adverse reaction to being tased. It's rare, but it definitely happens. They can experience anxiety, lethargy, brain fog, even a brief lapse in memory within that first initial hour. Studies show that these individuals have a cognitive responsiveness about on par with that of a seventy-nine-year-old."

"But I don't forget," Larkin said. He further emphasized his point by adding, "Anything."

"The events should come back to you over the next few hours," the doctor insisted. She moved to a line of cabinets against the wall, retrieved a few plastic packages, and then offered them to Larkin. "In the meantime, take acetaminophen for any headaches or body aches—no more than the recommended daily dose—and if you don't have any questions, we're ready to discharge you."

Larkin accepted the pain pills and said, "No questions."

She smiled at that and excused herself.

Doyle stepped into the space then, moving to stand before Larkin. His face was drawn and his pyrite eyes too bright—not with his usual sunshine, but unshed tears. His throat worked, Adam's apple bobbing. "Can I hug you?"

Larkin nodded.

Doyle set his large hands on Larkin's knees, pushed his legs apart, and stood between them. He leaned down, wrapped his arms under Larkin's, and buried his face into the crook of Larkin's neck. Very quickly, Larkin realized this embrace was not like Doyle's typical hugs. This was desperate, him needing rather than giving. So Larkin reached his arms up and around Doyle's neck, and despite the angle made more awkward by Doyle's height, he squeezed as tightly as he could.

"You scared the shit out of me," Doyle said as he pulled free but didn't step out of Larkin's space.

"Sorry."

Doyle hastily wiped his still-dry face on the sleeve of his shirt and said, his voice closer to its usual comforting huskiness, "How do you feel?"

"Like a pedophile shot me with 100,000 volts of electricity." Quieter, Larkin admitted, "I have a headache."

Doyle touched Larkin's right temple—unbeknownst to him, it was the exact spot that'd been cracked with a baseball bat—and then moved his hand to card fingers through Larkin's hair.

"I passed out," Larkin asked.

Doyle nodded. "Briefly. They told me you came around in the ambulance."

"I don't remember an ambulance…." Larkin raised his head and asked, "Did you ever watch *The Wizard of Oz*."

"Sure."

"I feel like Dorothy when she wakes at the end of the film and says, 'And you, and you, and you, and you were there.' Old memories are all mixed up."

"The doctor said to give it a few hours."

"I guess."

Doyle reached and finished buttoning Larkin's shirt.

"Tell me what happened at the apartment."

"After the second tase?"

"Hm-hm."

Doyle popped Larkin's collar, slid the floral pattern tie around his neck, and began to knot it. "I shot that sonofabitch in the kneecap."

Larkin laughed suddenly, reflexively at Doyle's echo of his own story. "Did you really."

A reluctant smile tugged at the corner of Doyle's mouth. "Yeah."

"What about the girl."

"She's okay," Doyle confirmed as he set the collar in place and took a step back.

Larkin ignored the look of disapproval as he climbed off the gurney and winced. "Where is she," he asked, tucking his shirt into his trousers.

"Upstairs. She turned down a rape kit test. She's only fourteen and they haven't been able to contact a legal guardian yet, so the hospital counselor is sitting with her."

"When can we speak with her."

"*I'm* going to interview her," Doyle corrected. "You're going home to rest."

"No."

"This isn't up for discussion."

"The hospital gave me three packets of Tylenol, which they will surely charge to my insurance at fifteen dollars a pill, and sent me on my way. I do not need to be on medical leave."

"I'm not suggesting you do," Doyle countered. "But you got tased. *Twice.* Most people would opt for an afternoon nap."

"I need to work," Larkin said. "This is the first break in Marco's case in twenty-three years. I can't do it without you, but I also won't let you do it alone."

Doyle crossed his arms.

Larkin stared, unblinking.

And then Doyle sighed. "We'll go out someday like Butch Cassidy and the Sundance Kid."

"A murder-suicide pact in Bolivia?" Larkin asked with a curious inflection.

Doyle laughed, and the remaining tension in his body seemed to finally relax.

"It's a rather poor comparison for our partners-in-crime relationship," Larkin continued, grabbing his suit coat and throwing it on. "First and foremost being that they were actual criminals and we're lawmen."

"Right."

"And I've no intention of putting you out of your misery, should you suffer mortal wounds in a shootout."

"Why am I the Sundance Kid?" Doyle asked.

"Because Harry Longabaugh was six feet tall and Robert LeRoy Parker was only five foot nine."

"But Longabaugh was involved with Etta Place."

"You're the one who made the comparison. I'm doing my best with the available facts," Larkin answered.

Doyle slid an arm over Larkin's shoulders and said, pulling him into another hug, "It's fine. I always thought they were a little gay for each other, anyway."

It was 3:22 p.m. when Larkin and Doyle reached a patient room on the fourth floor of New York-Presbyterian at Columbia University. A uniformed officer had been assigned to the door, but one look at Doyle and he was ushering the detectives inside. The room was one of those semiprivate layouts, but the second bed was unoccupied, so the curtain separator had been pushed against the far wall to allow afternoon sunlight to filter in. Aesthetically, it looked like any other hospital room: beige walls, beige tiles, drop ceiling, and two uncomfortable-looking chairs in a shit-brown vinyl, which Larkin felt was a misstep in the decorating of a locale known for its dealings with bodily fluids. The room was heavy with the smell of antiseptic, liquid soap sold in those industrial tubs, and lasagna—the last of which made sense when Larkin spotted a food tray on the overbed table, nothing left of the meal except an untouched Red Delicious apple.

Sitting up in the hospital bed and now wearing a shapeless gown was the same redheaded girl from Gary Reynold's apartment. Her face had been scrubbed of makeup, and her hair looked clean too. She seemed younger than Larkin remembered of that split second before Reynold had tried to fry his brain. Young but hard—a child who'd already seen too much of the world and knew it only got worse from here. She was patently ignoring the counselor, an older woman who wore her hair in a poof of gray with a pantsuit to match, seated nearer the windows. The girl was staring at the overhead television playing an edited-for-daytime-TV version of *Don't Tell Mom the Babysitter's Dead*.

The girl shot the door a quick glance before she shoved the blankets back, jumped out of bed, and barreled into Doyle. She had her arms wrapped around his back and face pressed into Doyle's chest as she asked, "What took so long?"

Doyle was smiling as he put a hand on the back of her head, stroking gently. In the second that hung between her question and his response, Doyle had transformed—transcended to a higher existence that Larkin refused to consider as an option in his own life because he wasn't strong enough, brave enough, selfless enough. In that singular moment, Larkin saw in Doyle what he truly was and what had been taken away from him—he saw Doyle as a father.

"I had to check on my partner," Doyle answered. He moved his hands to her shoulders, took a step back, and studied her face. "I told you I'd be back."

Her complexion was tinged with pink, and her blue eyes were a little wet, but when she looked at Larkin, her voice was steady enough as she said, "You're alive."

"Yes."

"Did being tased hurt?"

Again, Larkin said, "Yes."

Doyle inclined his chin. "Why don't you get back in bed?"

She rolled her eyes like every teenager did, but obediently returned. "I wanted a blue Gatorade, but the nurse gave me cherry Pedialyte and it tastes like mouthwash."

"Pedialyte is better for dehydration," Doyle said as he motioned Larkin to take the spare seat. "Megan, this is Everett Larkin. Larkin, this is Megan Flouride."

Larkin sat in the shit-brown chair opposite the counselor, who hadn't said anything, was merely watching the interaction, noted Megan's pink boots beside the bed and the scuffmarks that were actually words written in Sharpie—PUNK'S NOT DEAD—and replied, "Flouride is the stage name of Geoffrey Lyall, the bass player for the Dead Kennedys."

Megan glanced at Doyle.

"I told you he was smart."

Larkin fought down the urge to smile at the compliment. To Megan, he said, "I'd like to ask you some questions, if that's okay."

"About… the dude?" Megan asked.

"Gary Reynold, yes."

"Can Ira stay?" Megan's expression softened when she looked at Doyle a second time, grew both hopeful and timid as she so clearly stood at the crossroads of whether she wanted to view Doyle as a parental figure or as a man her young and clueless heart was smitten with.

"Detective Doyle will stay," Larkin agreed.

Megan must have picked up on the hardening in Larkin's tone, the clear usage of Doyle's title, because her eyes narrowed and she promptly returned her gaze to the television. She studied Christina Applegate's character, overwhelmed as the new executive administration assistant, and asked, "What's a fax machine do, anyway?"

The counselor made a noise of distress at the question.

"Megan," Larkin prompted, "what were you doing in Mr. Reynold's apartment."

She shrugged and, for a long minute, fiddled with the volume on the remote control.

Up three.

Down three.

Up two.

Down four.

"Makin' some cash," she eventually answered.

"How."

Another one-shouldered shrug. "Taking pictures."

Doyle moved to the foot of the bed, took a seat, and studied her. "Megan," he said, his voice like a blanket, fresh and warm from the dryer. "We think that Mr. Reynold might have been involved in hurting some children in the '90s."

"Hurting them?" she echoed.

"Killing them," Larkin clarified.

Megan shot him a startled, terrified expression, that thick-skinned attitude of someone who'd been left to care for themselves too long and at too young an age was briefly overwhelmed with the realization of having gotten away with flirting with death. "Is—is he gonna kill me too?"

"No," Larkin said. "Detective Doyle arrested him."

"That's right," Doyle cut in. "And there's a very nice police officer right outside your door who won't let anyone in. You're completely safe." He shifted, patting Megan's hand a few times. "The thing is, these kids died over twenty years ago, and no one has ever been held accountable."

"But—so you didn't go there looking for me? You didn't even know who I was, or that I was there?" Megan asked, her pitch as erratic as the television's volume.

Doyle said evenly, "Detective Larkin figured out you were there."

She asked defensively, "How?"

Larkin weighed how open, how gentle, he needed to be with her. The clues were abundant as to the sort of victim he was dealing with: Megan had been, or still was, a street kid, and logically, she was toughened to the realities of the adult world in a way she should still be ignorant of. She was still a child, though—barely a teenager—teetering on the age of profound insecurity and stupidity. But it'd been a long goddamn day so far, and Larkin already felt like he'd been hit by a bus. He decided he couldn't lower his defenses any further than he already had. He couldn't emote on the level she needed and still get through the rest of his workday without a second panic attack.

So Larkin laid it all out, cut-and-dry. "Mr. Reynold had been texting another person, identity unknown, asking for a redheaded teenager. When this individual abruptly ceased communication, Mr. Reynold texted that he'd handle the search himself. Myself and Detective Doyle went to PS 51, where he works, but when Mr. Reynold hadn't returned after the lunch period, I surmised it was due to incriminating evidence he was trying to get rid of—more specifically, evidence in his home. His last text had been sent on Wednesday, May 13, which suggested to me that he went in search of a girl last week, had found one, and was potentially still holding her against her will."

Megan made a sound, something between a snort and a

laugh. "I'm really a blond," she whispered.

"Obviously," Larkin answered. "No one can claim to being born with hair color akin to cherry crush."

"Can you tell us what happened?" Doyle asked calmly.

"What's today?"

"Wednesday," he answered.

"Oh…." That seemed to have mildly surprised Megan, as she said next, "I was in his house for almost two days."

Doyle reached into his suit coat and retrieved his mini notepad and pen.

Larkin prompted, "You said you'd gone to Mr. Reynold's to make money—taking pictures."

Megan nodded stiffly. She looked at the television when a commercial for Domino's came on, advertising their mix-and-match deal. "Five hundred bucks if I let him take pictures of me. You know what I could do with that much money?"

"Due to severe inflation and stagnant minimum wage, never mind that we live in the country's most expensive city, almost nothing in the long term can be achieved with five hundred dollars," Larkin replied.

"Gee, I guess my investment portfolio will have to wait," Megan shot back, sounding far older than fourteen at that moment.

Doyle tapped his pen against the spiral spine of the notepad for a minute, then asked, "Where were you going?"

Larkin narrowed his eyes and glanced at Doyle, but Doyle was entirely focused on the girl.

Megan had been picking at the chipped black nail polish on her thumb but stopped at Doyle's question. She looked up. "How'd you know that?"

"Runaways with five hundred in cash tend to either use it on drugs or an escape. You strike me as a girl with a plan," Doyle answered, having made the same deduction as Larkin.

But then Megan leaned forward, like a celestial body caught in Doyle's gravitational pull, and asked the one question Larkin hadn't ever expected, "Did you couch surf too?"

Ira Doyle had been a mystery all this time.

Monday, March 30, sunlight battering the gray clouds, white blossoms carpeting the ground around them at the Arsenal, and Larkin telling Doyle, "We all do it, to an extent. Hide someone. Whether out of shame or safety, we hide who we know in certain situations."

Something in his past had shamed him, traumatized him, and he hid that damage because *we all do it.*

"Stupid, unsupervised kids think they're invincible."

Nonetheless, Doyle had tried to tell Larkin.

"At-risk kids? Yeah. I spent more than a few summer vacations enrolled in those programs."

But Larkin hadn't been listening.

He couldn't breathe. It was like being shot with 100,000 volts of electricity again, and every muscle and organ was seizing, locking up. For being such a decorated officer, Larkin really was a piss-poor detective when it came to understanding the one man, potentially the only man, who'd come to matter. He'd misread Doyle's appearance, personality, grief, and now, his shame. It sent a queasy roll through Larkin's gut, and he gripped the vinyl armrests until the material protested and Doyle looked at him.

And Larkin could see the exact second that Doyle realized—*knew* that Larkin had finally pieced the clues together. There was a microexpression of control that attempted to wrangle his humiliation and keep it from surfacing, since by its very design, humans sought to avoid showcasing shame so as to protect themselves from disgust, rejection. The fact that Doyle's childhood, with circumstances that'd been wholly beyond his control, still affected how he presented himself, so much so that it'd fooled someone as perceptive as Everett Larkin, was tragic.

Doyle looked away first—the floor, his lap, then Megan. "Where were you planning to go?" he asked again.

"Montana. I have an aunt out there. Amtrak has tickets for three hundred."

"But Mr. Reynold didn't pay you, did he?" Doyle concluded, a sort of weary heartbreak in his knowing.

Megan shook her head. "He asked me to dye my hair, so I did that in his bathroom. He gave me a crop top to wear that must'a been from GapKids or something. It was too small, but I guess that's what he liked about it. Do you think I can have a snack? I'm still hungry."

The counselor checked the time on her phone before finally speaking. "Lunch is over, but I'll see what I can get from the cafeteria."

Megan watched the woman leave the room and then she let out a very loud, very teenage huff. "She keeps asking me if that creep touched me and stuff, but he didn't. Not really."

"Not really," Larkin echoed.

"I mean, he touched my hair a few times, and it was definitely gross, but he didn't… you know."

Larkin asked, "He didn't pressure you or force you into a sexual activity of any kind."

"No. I kept telling her that too. I know how to look out for myself. After that… he took the pictures." She met Larkin's steady stare and said, "And I don't fuckin' care what you think of me doing that. I don't care what anyone thinks."

Larkin ignored the attitude. "Can you be more specific. Where in his house did these photos happen. How many did he take. How did he make you pose. Did you see what he did with the camera afterward."

She countered by holding her arms up and moving them

stiffly, saying, "I am a robot."

"Megan," Doyle chastised before Larkin could tell the kid it took a lot more than a mediocre attempt at HAL 9000 to hurt his feelings. "Larkin is one of the smartest detectives in this entire city. You want him on your team. You want him as a friend."

"*Why*?" she protested. "He's weird, and he doesn't understand any of the shit you do. And you arrested the dude anyway, so what's it matter?"

"It matters," Larkin interjected, "because the details make all the difference between Gary Reynold getting a minimum of five years for kidnapping in the second degree, or life without parole for the aggravated murder of victims under the age of fourteen—if we can, in fact, connect any of these twenty-plus-year-old murders to Mr. Reynold with your help. If nothing else, your compliance will help us stick him with a minimum of twenty years for attempted murder in the first degree of an on-duty police officer. Now I ask you, Megan, do you want Mr. Reynold on the street again when he's still physically capable of doing this, or would you rather he die behind bars."

Megan had sort of shrunken inward as Larkin spoke, her shoulders hunched and chin tucked against her chest. "How many other kids?" Her voice was a whisper.

"Five, that we know of," Larkin answered. "One was an eighteen-year-old boy named Marco Garcia. The other four, we don't know their names. One boy and three girls. We estimate they're all between twelve and fifteen years old."

"Were they runaways?"

Doyle answered, "Due to some of the evidence that's arisen, we think there's a high probability they were at-risk youth."

Larkin spread the aforementioned photographs out in his mind, organized them chronologically to the best of his ability, beginning with the girl, whose cryptic message to Larkin was scribbled on the back, then the black boy found inside *Hamlet*, and finally the two girls found hidden in Reynold's picture frame. All of the photos were taken by the same individual, of this both he and Doyle were confident, but the anomaly was the boy.

The girls were all different, sure—the first appeared to be Latina, older than the other two, and *those* girls were both white with red hair—one natural, one from a box. But to avoid being too categorical and developing blinders, the three were teenage girls. End of story.

So why the young boy?

Because he was someone's type.

Just how Reynold had photographs of dead redheaded girls, had saved clippings of female teen models with red hair, had forced Megan to dye her hair for their "photoshoot."

A quality, a characteristic, a feature—there was something about the male victim that someone had desired, craved, *sought*.

Sought like through a text message.

I'm looking for a boy or girl of a certain age.

And the individual on the other end checks their available wares….

Except, for men like Reynold, it wasn't about deviant sexual fantasies that needed to be translated into the real world to satisfy the lust, the hunger. He wasn't looking for a living, breathing child to manipulate and destroy. He was looking to live his fantasies through already-committed acts. Reynold was a collector of content, a closeted pedophile who didn't do the abusing himself, but benefited off the actions perpetrated by another.

Actions taken to the point of murder.

Then staging the body in a provocative pose.

Snapping photos.

And… *selling them*?

With the exception of Marco's death, Larkin had no bodies. He had no witnesses, no stories, not even their names. All he had were photographs. Death portraits of sad children, desperate children, all barely getting by in a rough-and-tumble world and killed so that some sick fuck could rub one off to their likeness night after night.

Those forgotten children had been a commodity, and Gary Reynold had been a repeat customer.

So the new question was, who was the one profiting?

"Reynold didn't kill those kids," Larkin stated.

Doyle's brows knitted together as he shot Larkin a look. "What?"

Larkin stood and walked to the door. "Come with me." He heard Doyle tell Megan he'd be back in a moment, that'd he'd be right outside the door, and then the two detectives stood in the hall, empty but for the uniformed officer and the occasional nurse in scrubs rushing by.

"What's going on?" Doyle asked.

"Gary Reynold's psychology isn't that of a killer."

Doyle settled his hands on his hips. "I want to disagree, but I'll hear you out first."

"Appreciated, thank you. Molesters can be broken into two major categories: situational or preferential. Reynold has made it clear that he has a type and it's consistent, so he can be considered preferential. Megan didn't attend PS 51, and I'd wager none of the other victims did either, ergo he prefers strangers. Reynold kept a collection, and while violent by the very nature of its content—the sitters were all dead—it's fantasy fodder. He prefers not to inflict pain. These are all indicators of an introverted molester personality."

"Larkin," Doyle said with a heavy breath. "How can

you claim he's averse to violence? He kidnapped Megan. He tased you."

"He tased me because he was cornered and panicking. The tase, while it most certainly pissed me off, wasn't lethal. Even more to the point, Reynold had forty-five minutes, if not an hour, head start on us, but he didn't kill Megan, didn't dispose of her as evidence. He couldn't do it because neither homicide, nor sexual homicide, is within his makeup."

"Hang on. *Sexual* homicide? Do you mean—"

"I believe that Gary Reynold is a closet collector—someone who doesn't engage physically with their victims. They use photos or videos to fantasize and that satisfies their urges. But considering the subject matter of his collection, I believe Reynold might also straddle a very rare subcategory of sexual dysfunction, in that he has necrophilic fantasies. This is similar to the closet collector, in that they fantasize without engaging, and in this instance that would be in either necrophilic homicide—murder in which to obtain a corpse—or regular necrophilia—the use of the already dead. He puts in a request, *an order*, and then he's delivered a photograph that aligns with his deviant fantasies."

Doyle had reached up as Larkin spoke, dug his fingers into his thick brown hair, and left them there. "This is sick."

"Yes."

"But then how do you explain Megan? How do you explain his deviation from an established norm?"

"Desperation. An urge that was carefully controlled until it reached its peak, and when this unknown individual he was texting failed to follow up, Reynold tried to quench the thirst himself. But because he's not inherently a murderer—please don't misunderstand me here, Gary Reynold is a disgusting fuck who belongs behind bars for the rest of his life—he tried to replicate his photo collection with a living girl. Mark my words, when we find the photos he took of Megan, they will be posed in such a way as to *suggest* she's dead."

"But if he didn't sexually assault her, why keep her afterward?"

"What else was he to do," Larkin asked. "While we can believe, based on the photos discovered hidden in the frame, that Reynold has been making these purchases for decades, he's never done *this* before. Rookie mistakes from the very beginning. He didn't know what else to do."

Doyle tugged his fingers free from his hair, leaving it in more of a disarray than usual. He watched a nurse scuttle past, her sneakers squeaking on the linoleum floor. Doyle looked back at Larkin. "Since sometime around 1985, someone has been killing at-risk youth and selling death portraits to paying customers. That's what you're suggesting?"

Larkin nodded solemnly.

"This still doesn't explain how Marco fits into the storyline."

"No. Not yet." Larkin reached out and quickly patted down some of Doyle's errant hairs.

"How did you figure this out?"

Larkin's mouth quirked, and while the flat effect of his voice was still present, he quietly sang, "One of these things is not like the others."

"Did you just quote *Sesame Street*?"

"I watched my fair share of children's programming while married to an elementary teacher." And although Larkin was still legally married to said man, he felt it was a technicality not worth bringing into the conversation. "The photograph of the boy that I found in Marco's custody was obviously different from the other victims, but seeing as how the details of the picture itself aligned with the others, I concluded that, much like how Reynold has a penchant for redheaded girls, someone... preferred him."

"I got it."

"I feel the pertinent details to glean from Megan are, one, where did she meet Reynold, two, has she seen any other strange individuals in that area before, and three, everything that Reynold said or did prior to our arrival."

Doyle nodded, scrubbed his face with both hands, and said as he reached for the doorknob, "Let me lead."

"Did you ever watch *The Max Headroom Show*."

"She's a teenager, Evie. Teenagers say stupid, sometimes mean, things." Doyle entered the room, took a seat on the corner of the bed again, and with pen to paper, asked, "Megan, can you tell us everything that happened once Reynold came home? Up 'til when we entered the apartment?"

Larkin returned to the vinyl chair and remained silent.

In their brief absence, Megan had raised the bed to a more comfortable sitting position, found a mindless reality show to watch, and was now leaning her head back on the squishy hospital pillow. "He'd locked me in the bedroom closet when he was at work both days," she murmured. "Said if I made any noise—tried to get a neighbor's attention or something like that—he'd kill them. He said the woman who lived above him was eighty years old and I'd be responsible for someone's dead grandma." The admittance seemed to have sobered Megan's attitude. "So I stayed quiet. He left me food and water, and he hadn't done nothing, so… I don't know. I thought he'd let me go soon. I thought that when he came home in the middle of the day, but then I heard him talking to himself and, like, practically running back and forth from the kitchen to the living room, and I started to think something was really wrong."

"Did you hear what he was saying?"

"Mostly swearing. A lot of 'fucks' and 'shits.'"

"Then what?"

"He unlocked the closet," Megan explained. "Told me that he was gonna get my money and we just had to go to the bank to pick it up."

"Did he tell you what bank? Or where it was located?" Doyle tried, clearly angling for an idea of where Reynold thought he could have possibly run for safety.

Megan shook her head. "He turned away to grab my boots and I saw the taser tucked into the back of his pants and that's when I thought *we aren't going to a bank*. I put the boots on really slow, even though he started yelling at me to hurry the fuck up. I told him I had to pee, that I felt sick, I needed some water… just like… anything to not leave, because I thought he was going to electrocute me and throw me into the back of a car or something. He was all sweaty and shouting, and then you guys were knocking on the door and—and that's about it."

"That was smart thinking," Doyle told her. "Really smart."

Megan smiled, soaking up the praise like a plant left to wilt in a windowsill and it'd finally gotten a gulp of water.

Doyle asked next, "Where did you meet Reynold? The exact place he approached you with the offer of money in exchange for photos."

"Fifty-Seventh Street."

Larkin perked in his seat before leaning forward. "You mean, down in the subway."

Megan glanced at him, shrugged that ambivalent shrug.

"Which Fifty-Seventh Street station," Larkin pressed. "The Q, N, R, or F."

"I can't tell you."

"Why."

"Because if the cops knew, everyone would have to leave."

"Megan," Doyle said, always so gentle at the moment it mattered most. "Detective Larkin is going to figure it out, whether you tell him or not. Remember, we want to keep Reynold from hurting you or any other kid, ever again."

Her still-chubby cheeks grew a rosy pink before she sniffed loudly. "I don't want anyone gettin' in trouble."

"No one's in trouble," Doyle insisted.

"You won't tell them it was me who said something, will you?"

"I promise."

Megan looked down at her hands wringing the blanket on her lap. "The F station. Sometimes… when you got no couch, you can go there for the night."

"Other kids spend the night on the platform?" Doyle asked.

"Not the platform," Megan said with a despondent shake of her head. "In the tunnel. That's where I met Gary… Monday night."

Doyle asked, "Had you seen Gary there before?"

Another small headshake. "No. I think he found out about our hangout from Creepy Dicky."

"Who's Creepy Dicky?" Doyle asked, hastily jotting down everything Megan said.

"He's this old guy. Everyone calls him Dicky. He lives in the tunnel. He's been there since forever, I think. Sometimes he hangs out with us and no one really wants him there because he's always strung out, but he'll bring chips or Gatorade for us, so…. I haven't seen him in a while, though."

"How long is 'a while,'" Larkin butted in.

Megan said, "Last Friday. Maybe he finally OD'd."

Larkin was staring at Doyle as he asked, "Could you describe this man."

"Right down to the last gross little skin tag on his face." Megan made a noise and shivered melodramatically before asking, "Why?"

CHAPTER ELEVEN

It was 4:42 p.m. and Larkin stood outside Megan's hospital room, watching through the window in the door as Doyle sat in the vinyl chair Larkin had previously occupied, the overbed table's height adjusted and situated in front of him, as he worked on a composite sketch of Creepy Dicky. Larkin placed his cell to his ear, watching Megan swing her legs back and forth over the side of the bed while gesturing animatedly with her descriptions. Larkin put in a call to the Major Cases Squad at 1PP and filled the responding detective in on Megan's kidnapping, subsequent rescue as it related to Cold Cases, and relayed her current location in hopes of promptly passing responsibility for her to a more qualified unit in the department. He answered a few questions, confirmed her age, suggested that due to the circumstances of the kidnapping, it wasn't a matter for SVU, but he'd leave that for Major Cases to decide, then hung up.

Larkin asked the uniformed cop, who was still keeping watch, where Gary Reynold was being kept, and the officer said his partner had reported that Reynold was out of surgery and she was on guard in room 512. Larkin took a final look through the window, watched Doyle's progress on the characteristics stage—shaping the face and hair style, defining the linework, turning an unremarkable mess of shapes into a piece of art—and headed for the bank of elevators. Upon reaching the fifth floor, Larkin made a second phone call, this one to MTA Station Manager, Tanisha Crowley.

"Detective Larkin," she said, her voice rich and resonating like the Mother of Blues, Ma Rainey. "How can I help you?"

"My apologies, Ms. Crowley. I wish I had been able to inform you earlier that we will be unable to meet this afternoon."

"I know that."

"You do?" Larkin countered, a rise in his pitch.

"Your partner called me. Almost two hours ago. He said there was an incident and you were delayed at the hospital. I hope it's nothing pertaining to you, specifically?"

Larkin automatically put a hand to his chest, feeling the bandages under his dress shirt. He stopped walking, closed his eyes, clung to the vestiges of the all-but-exhausted Xanax high.

—*Noah slid a silver band over Larkin's finger, the air heavy with the perfume of summer flowers, sun dancing across the water*—

Larkin shook his head and pressed his thumb against his left eye until it hurt.

—*Noah slid a silver band over Larkin's finger, the venue of St. Jude's Church an oppressing and unhappy concession to Larkin's frosty in-laws, and even his willingness to marry in a religious setting, when he himself was not a religious man, had done nothing to garner their respect*—

"No, nothing pertaining to me," Larkin answered.

"Your partner suggested tomorrow. I'm free after twelve."

"Yes, that works. How is three o'clock."

"Perfect. I'll see you then."

"Goodbye, Ms. Crowley." Larkin ended the call, opened his calendar, and amended the date and time of his MTA appointment.

Larkin found room 512, knocked, and entered without waiting for a response. The room was smaller than Megan's, but private, with the same color palette and antiseptic perfume. A uniformed female cop was seated on the farther side of the bed, resting her head against her fist and scrolling on her phone. She glanced up, likely expecting a nurse or doctor, but when Larkin flashed his badge from where he stood in the doorway, she promptly tucked her phone out of view. Larkin studied Gary Reynold—handcuffed to the bed railing and looking sufficiently doped from anesthesia and pain medication.

"Give us a moment," Larkin stated.

"Yes, sir." The officer rose, moved around the foot of the bed, and slipped past Larkin into the hall.

Larkin's step was in-beat with the heart monitor as he reached the bed. He set his hands on the railing. "I thought perhaps Detective Doyle might have been joking," he said, and his voice was like a gunshot in its own right. "But I see he visits the range for more than his twice-a-year recertification." Larkin's gaze shifted from Reynold's heavily bandaged, postsurgery knee, to the man's sunken face. "It's almost a shame he's so competent. It'd have been something else if he missed and shot your nuts off."

Reynold swallowed and made a quiet, whimpering noise. "I-it's *you.*"

"Where would you like to begin," Larkin asked. "With Marco Garcia or Megan Flouride."

"I—I'm sick in the head," Reynold protested with a wheeze, causing his New York accent to distort a bit. "It's not my fault that I'm like this."

Larkin narrowed his eyes. "Marco Garcia, then."

"I don't remember—"

"Sure you do."

Reynold swallowed so hard, he might as well have choked on his own tongue. "He was just a kid in my AP course. I never touched him."

"No. You prefer fourteen-year-old girls," Larkin answered. "Marco Garcia."

"It was a long time ago."

"Marco Garcia."

"What else do you want me to say?"

"Marco Garcia."

"*Stop it*!" Reynold shouted, his voice rising, spittle wetting his bushy mustache.

Unperturbed, Larkin hunched forward to rest his forearms along the handrail. "Marco Garcia was murdered twenty-three years, one day, and—" Larkin consulted his watch. "—about twenty hours ago. But so long as I keep saying his name, Marco Garcia won't actually die, because remembrance is the greatest act of love there is." Leaning forward, unblinking, Larkin asked with a disturbing sense of aloofness, "Do you want to know why the force calls me the Grim Reaper."

Reynold began sobbing. "You're crazy, you know that? Oh God, don't hurt me! I didn't touch him. I swear, I swear, I *swear*."

"I believe I missed the part of your plea that sounded convincing. You see, I think you know exactly what happened to Marco. I think you even had a hand in it. Because I found a photograph in his copy of *Hamlet*—he was writing his final paper on unreliable narrators, do you remember that?—and this picture looks remarkably similar to two I found hidden behind a snapshot of you holding up a largemouth bass."

Reynold was gulping again, the doped-up glaze of his

eyes burned off by fear and adrenaline. His heart monitor was beeping faster than when Larkin had first entered the room. "I just—just—the internet was different back then. The Wild West, you know? And in the forums, someone said the YEC had a contact. A friendly face."

"Another molester, yes, I understand."

Reynold's complexion was steadily going waxy. "I only suggested it to Marco. He was looking for part-time opportunities and—and he could have been my way in."

Larkin asked, "You mean, a foot in the door for you to make contact with this other individual."

Reynold weakly nodded.

"Then what."

"Marco got the job. After school, mostly. He told me how it was going now and then."

"And did you meet your new friend," Larkin asked.

"I mean, not—not really."

"I don't believe you."

"I didn't," Reynold said in another half-sob, half-wheeze. "We never met in-person. None of us in the forums did. Marco's presence was what helped… *facilitate* our business relationship."

"How did you conduct business, if not in person."

"I, um… I mailed cash and then he mailed my… artwork."

Larkin straightened his posture and asked, "You participated in the shipping and receiving of underage, necrophilic pornography through the United States Postal Service."

Reynold barely whispered, "Y-yes…."

"Jesus Christ. What's your pen pal's address."

"It's a ghost address. Totally anonymous. Like a P.O. Box, but you pay in cash and there's no legal information on file."

"Where is it located."

Shriveling under Larkin's unrelenting gray stare, Reynold reluctantly gave him the address of a commercial facility in Bushwick that he mailed payments to, and one in East Harlem where he retrieved his packages. "He went by Archie Bunker."

Larkin rolled his eyes while he pulled the addresses up on his phone to confirm they were legitimate, still-existing locations. "Why did Marco have one of those photos in his possession," he eventually asked.

"I don't know. I have no idea. I swear to God."

"God doesn't give a shit what you say," Larkin stated, tucking his cell back in his pocket. "Did Marco find out about you and your buddy."

"I don't *know*," Reynold repeated. "I found out Marco died the next day, at school, like everyone else."

Larkin felt as if he were running face-first into a wall.

Like the world was hellbent on proving that even a star detective and shepherd of the dead and forgotten couldn't win them all, save them all, or remember them all.

Taking a deep breath and recollecting himself, Larkin reconsidered the clues at present and asked instead, "Who's Creepy Dicky."

Reynold groaned and turned his head away.

Larkin snapped his fingers in front of Reynold's face. "Look at me when I talk to you."

"He's just some homeless schitzo."

"Mr. Reynold," Larkin began with a frown. "Need I remind you, I was tased earlier this afternoon, and suffice it to say, I am not in a particularly amicable mood. So if you bullshit me one more time—"

"He—he was just someone Archie mentioned in the old

141

forums!" Reynold wailed, his mustache quivering so much that it looked like it'd sprout wings and fly away. "After the YEC closed down, I guess Archie kept in touch with Dicky. He'd posted that he had a point of contact who knew the kids, where they went for free meals or what tunnels they slept in. The kids are always changing, like… like a revolving door. But Dicky knows them all."

"And when Archie, whom I presume is the individual you were texting on that burner phone, ceased all communication, did you take it upon yourself to find Dicky and his band of Lost Boys."

Reynold hesitated.

Larkin narrowed his eyes a second time.

"Archie let slip enough details over the years that I was able to piece together the area that Dicky panhandled when above ground. And about a year ago, I saw him waiting in line for lunch at St. Jude's Mission over on the East Side—that's his neighborhood. It's rich, you know? And lots of kids go to St. Jude's, but you can't… you can't approach them there."

"Yes, whatever would Jesus think of you, preying on the weak in his own home," Larkin said. "Why the falling out with Archie after all these years."

"I wish I knew," Reynold answered. "The forums closed years ago. The only regular communication we've had since then is through burner numbers. Do you think he's been hurt?"

"I certainly hope you're not asking a police officer to be concerned about the well-being of your molester bestie."

Reynold clamped his mouth shut.

Larkin laid out the present murder's timeline in his head and then spun the mental Rolodex in reverse, stopping on Sunday, May 10, the estimated date of death for John Doe in the utility closet. He shifted forward again. Three days. "On Wednesday, May 13, at 7:12 in the morning, you texted

Archie a final time, suggesting you'd find a girl on your own. Where were you that night."

"I was at home."

"Mr. Reynold, this is my good cop persona. I have a DB at Fifty-Seventh Street station with a connection to St. Jude's Mission that is painting you in a very bad light."

"W-wait… *what*? I didn't—I mean, holy crap, no. Is Dicky dead? I didn't kill him. I went to St. Jude's last Saturday to see if he was there, to ask about girls he might know, and pay him."

"Pay him in what."

"Uh… Archie said he'd give you whatever you asked for if you offered heroin. And I've been a public school teacher a long time. You learn a thing or two about how to buy drugs."

"Brilliant." Larkin sighed and pressed his thumb against his left eye again—he still had a throbbing headache, despite the Tylenol.

"He wasn't there," Reynold insisted. "And since they're closed on Sundays, I took a chance and followed some of the punk kids who had been eating there."

"Was one of them Megan."

"Yeah," he whispered. "They went down to the Fifty-Seventh Street station—the F. They were down there for hours, so I thought, maybe that was one of their spots. I went back to the subway Monday night."

"And that's when you offered Megan five hundred dollars in exchange for allowing you to take pictures of her in your home."

Reynold licked his chapped lips and nodded.

"So where's Dicky."

"I have no idea. I swear."

Larkin started to speak, but the hospital room door opened. Larkin turned as Doyle entered, set his portfolio bag against the wall as the door clicked shut, and then approached Reynold's bedside. "Did you—"

Doyle lunged before Larkin could finish his thought. He grabbed the front of Reynold's hospital gown, tore a heart monitor free from his chest, the machine beeping erratically, and drew Reynold up so they were face-to-face. "She's a child," he shouted. "A fucking *child*, you disgusting pig!"

"Doyle!" Larkin grabbed his arm and yanked, but Doyle was a hell of a lot stronger than he looked.

Reynold was screaming.

The door was thrown open a second time, the uniformed officer putting a hand to her service weapon, then faltering as she took in the sight.

Larkin sidestepped, wrapped both arms around Doyle's chest, and yanked him backward so hard, so fast, they both tripped and stumbled into the wall on their left. Shoving Doyle off, Larkin turned, got in the path of the bed before Doyle could go at Reynold a second time, and shouted, "Get out of here."

"He's been abusing children his entire life."

"I know what he's done."

"I don't touch the kids," Reynold cried from the bed at Larkin's back.

"Shut up," Larkin ordered, turning his head long enough to address Reynold. He looked at Doyle again and pointed to the open door. "Get out."

"Evie—"

"Right the fuck now, Ira."

CHAPTER TWELVE

Larkin found his Audi parked on the third floor of the hospital's parking complex at West 165th Street.

More specifically, he found the Audi wedged between a matte black Hummer and silver Subaru Outback, with Doyle sitting on the concrete, back against the passenger door, knees drawn up and elbows resting atop. His portfolio bag lay discarded near the Audi's front bumper, like he'd chucked it upon reaching the vehicle and really didn't care how it landed.

Larkin's derbies grated against the uneven surface as he moved into the stall. He tugged his trouser legs up before crouching and lowering himself to the ground beside Doyle, their shoulders close but not touching. He stared at his vague, distorted outline bouncing back from the body of the minivan. Just a blob of ash-blond sitting atop of bigger blob of charcoal gray. The silence between them was punctuated only by the distant honking of rush-hour traffic on the street below and the occasional echo of a car doing loops throughout the complex, looking for that one available parking spot the garage employee swore was still available.

Doyle asked, "Is Reynold pressing charges?"

"I don't think so," Larkin answered. "I explained prison social hierarchies to him and where among inmates molesters found themselves. I told him I'd need his full and absolute cooperation if I was to put in any good word about keeping him isolated from the general population."

They were both quiet again.

From the street, someone yelled, "Hey, hey, hey, fuck you!"

Larkin closed his eyes.

—sandy-brown hair highlighted in gold, his freckled skin wet and sparkling like a hundred thousand diamonds, the stubble on his chin dark after a few days' growth, but it made his profile more handsome, more adult—

Larkin opened his eyes. The intruding and disjointed memories brought on from the tase were still behaving erratically, ballooning bigger and bigger like those toys that grew up to 300 percent their original size—just add water! He felt beaten down, wrung out, his inside glass and outside lead, but when he glanced sideways, it was Doyle sitting beside him.

Doyle.

Not Patrick.

A few unexpected tears slid down Larkin's cheeks and he hastily batted them away.

Doyle's mouth was clenched shut, the muscles in his jaw and neck pronounced, like he wanted to scream, needed to scream, but knew it'd fall on deaf ears, so what the hell was even the point? The moment was dragged out into the light, its soft underbelly a mark for violence in this cruel world. It was likely a matter of mere seconds before Doyle would inevitably curl into himself for protection, dig a hole to bury his shame and guilt, hiding everything under a smile of sunshine and jubilance up to heaven.

But right then, he just looked so… *sad.*

"Patrick," Larkin whispered.

Doyle turned his head.

Larkin blinked his wet eyes a few times. "My first boyfriend. His name was Patrick." He drew his hands back and forth over his knees. "He was murdered on August 2, 2002."

The hardness in Doyle's face, his eyes, diminished. "Why are you telling me?"

Larkin didn't blink, didn't look away. "My parents find my HSAM embarrassing. Dr. Myers finds it fascinating. Noah finds it exasperating. And none of them have wanted to hear me talk about Patrick. I know that everyone gets over their first love—like a rite of passage. But I can't. I won't. I wish I could, but my brain isn't…." A tear ran along the contour of Larkin's jaw and dripped off the tip of his chin. "In eighteen years, you were the first person who asked if I was okay. You were the first person to tell me I could talk about it, if I wanted—who didn't tell me to shut up. I know I'm not very good at expressing myself, so I don't think you have any idea what that meant to me."

Doyle swallowed, his Adam's apple working painfully. He took Larkin's hand, his own completely enveloping it. Doyle squeezed so hard that Larkin's knuckles popped. "Thank you for sharing that—for trusting me. And I know I said I could talk about her." Doyle's voice broke and he had to whisper the second part. "But I don't think I can right now."

"It wasn't meant to be a quid pro quo situation."

Doyle wiped his face with the heel of his hand, nodded, and leaned into Larkin for a hug. It lasted a long time—just the two of them, the cool concrete, the smell of motor oil, exhaust, and an urban summer. When Doyle finally pulled back, he said, "All these murdered kids… any one of them could've been me. It was dumb luck that kept me out of the hands of someone like Gary Reynold."

Larkin nodded.

"None of them deserved that."

Larkin answered, "Neither did you."

Doyle looked away, staring at the concrete as he struggled to collect himself.

But Larkin gently took his face between his hands, forcing Doyle to meet his own gaze, and those pyrite eyes, with a luster that shone right through the mourning veil, they touched the smoldering embers deep inside Larkin, stoking the single flame that had refused to snuff out. And this touch—this intimacy—between them, nothing compared, not even the pleasure and sensuality of sex.

"Mourning used to be a public ritual." Larkin drew his fingertips along Doyle's brow ridge, tracing the contours. "No one was ever alone. I care for you, Ira. And when you're ready—I'll listen."

Larkin parked in the school zone on the corner of West 181st and Bennett Avenue. He turned off the engine, set an NYPD parking permit on the dash, then looked at Doyle, silent in the passenger seat. He understood the unique and incomparable heartbreak of having lost the unwinnable battle against death. Larkin understood it so well that he'd made it his life's pursuit to seek justice in an unjust world. So he recognized, sympathized, with Camila Garcia's tragedy. He knew Doyle's sense of isolation and loneliness. But maybe Larkin was so surrounded with and so overwhelmed by death, had become so accustomed to compartmentalizing his thoughts and keeping the world at arm's length, that he'd not realized Marco's murder and Camila's sorrow were too relatable for Doyle.

Larkin didn't know the details of Abigail's passing, of

course. Hadn't asked about her since March 31, when it'd become apparent how *not okay* Doyle really was, but it was more the hurt and loss of a child in a general sense that was eating away at him. An association of Doyle's very own. An ever-constant reminder of the depression unto death that he'd survived seven years ago and kept living with ever since.

Had it been selfish of Larkin to seek Doyle's help on a case involving children?

"Why was Doyle assigned his current session."

And Craig Bailey, Doyle's supervisor and senior artist, had answered, "He always takes the cases involving children. Those are the worst ones, you know? But he always takes them."

Self-flagellation?

Self-destruction?

Or perhaps, like Larkin, Doyle sought a future for his victims that he'd been denied while growing up, that his own child had been denied as well.

Who are you hiding, Larkin wanted to ask. *Who betrayed your trust and broke your heart. Who made such a gentle man so angry inside.*

"Ira."

Doyle glanced over.

"I would like to preface this question with confirmation that I, in no way, think or feel you are incapable of doing your job."

He raised both eyebrows.

"Was it wrong of me to ask you to work this case."

Doyle was quiet. He took a deep breath in, slowly let it out. "I'm sorry about earlier. It was extremely unprofessional of me."

"I've gotten upset plenty of times during a case."

Doyle laughed dryly. "I'm sure you haven't tried to

assault a suspect."

"August 11, 2015, my first day working Cold Cases," Larkin began, "I was given a stack of twenty-two files and told to pick one. I chose Baby Hope. She was a nine-month-old found strangled to death and left in a burlesque theater restroom in Times Square, 1988. No security, no witnesses, no suspects—due to the transient lifestyle of the neighborhood at the time. I even had her exhumed from Potter's Field to take DNA samples. And on Tuesday, June 6, 2017, the results of that test came back. No matches with NCMEC or NamUs. No one missed her. No one even knew her real name. So I stepped out of the precinct, collected a tire iron from my car, and beat the shit out of a trash can on the street corner." Larkin looked out the windshield as he concluded, "I still haven't solved that case."

"You beat a trash can with a tire iron?"

"We're deviating from the point of my question."

Doyle took another calculated breath before shaking his head and saying, "It wasn't wrong of you, to ask for my help. I can handle this. And I've got your back."

"*That* I never had doubt of." Larkin left it at that, because throwing yourself into work was a necessity he knew all too well—manufactured distance from crushing emotions that offered the psyche a moment of respite. He gave Doyle a crooked smile, the expression never seeming to sit right on his face, then opened the driver's side door and climbed out of the Audi. Larkin buttoned his suit coat, watching over the roof as Doyle mirrored his motions. "Reynold wouldn't say where he hid the pictures he took of Megan, but if CSU hasn't found them yet, I'm certain we will."

"You think those are necessary clues?" Doyle asked, moving between bumpers before quickly crossing the street with Larkin.

"If we want the multitude of charges against Reynold to

stick, yes."

"But specifically regarding both subway murders—you think they're going to be at all relevant?"

Larkin considered the question. He'd given Doyle a brief, bare-bones account of his interview with Gary Reynold on their drive back to said man's apartment—from his claims of Marco unknowingly instituting a relationship between Reynold and this mysterious Archie Bunker, their anonymous method of buying and selling abusive material, all the way to Dicky's connection to St. Jude's kitchen and the Fifty-Seventh Street station, as well as the probability that they might have uncovered the identity of the man in the IKEA bag as that of Creepy Dicky.

But even with what Larkin had learned from his conversation with Reynold, he was still left with a multitude of unanswered questions: Who pushed Marco in front of an incoming Q train twenty-three years ago? Why had Archie suddenly ceased any and all communication—and before Larkin was ever put on his trail? If that John Doe in the IKEA tote was in fact Dicky, who killed him? What was their reason? Why had the photograph addressed to Larkin been left on his person?

It felt a little like a game of sudoku.

Larkin had, for over a month now, been watching Doyle work his way through a book of ever-increasingly difficult puzzles each morning. Doyle had an eye for detail, of course, but also the ability to comprehend the bigger picture. It was a particular kind discipline that made him so suited for forensic artwork. He understood how to capture unique elements when working on a composite sketch, but he managed his time and was mindful that his job was to construct an entire portrait and not to spend three hours capturing a certain glint a suspect had in their eyes.

Larkin had backseat-helped for a few puzzles. He'd

been overly confident while pointing to an empty square and explaining, based on the established results of the vertical column, the only possible answer was four, and Doyle would smile kindly, sweetly, drag his pen along the horizontal column that Larkin had overlooked, and point out that four was already in play. After Larkin had made the same mistake a few times, he stopped trying to beat Doyle at sudoku.

It wasn't that Larkin couldn't step away and take in the scene as a whole. It was only that by his very nature, he hyperfixated on the smallest details first. So the questions he had regarding their ongoing investigation were like his preoccupation with trying to fit that four into a box it wasn't meant to be in. Maybe by finding that *one right clue*, Doyle would be able to point out that the four was really a six and Larkin would be able to make all the remaining pieces fall into place.

"I think it would be irresponsible of us to write off anything as a potentially useful clue at this point," Larkin concluded.

They walked uptown on Bennett Avenue until reaching the congestion of police vehicles—two cruisers and a CSU van—and one irate civilian having a shouting match with a uniformed officer, claiming the NYPD gave his parked '90s Ford Festiva a fender bender, although Larkin was unsure of how the owner came to such a conclusion, considering the car was so banged up that it'd have been difficult to point out a bullet hole in its Surf Blue exterior. They flashed their badges to the second officer at the building's front door, made their way back across the lobby and down the basement stairs, only to be recognized by the female officer who'd originally run her sirens on Larkin for speeding.

"Detectives," she addressed, before giving Larkin a surprised once-over. "You're back."

Larkin figured she'd seen him taken out by EMTs nearly—he checked his watch—four hours ago. "Is CSU inside," he asked, motioning to the open door of the garden apartment just beyond.

She nodded, moved against the wall to allow them passage, and said with a nod of her chin, "Gloves and booties."

Larkin followed the motion to the left wall. Beside the sledgehammer were boxes of latex gloves and shoe covers. He collected the PPE, passed Doyle a set, and once Larkin had pulled the elastic polypropylene over his green derbies and slid the gloves on with a loud snap, he entered the apartment. "Cold Case Squad," he called loudly, so as not to startle whoever was working inside.

Neil Millett peered around the open door from inside the bedroom. He wore the same gloves and booties, but it was the first time Larkin had seen the CSU detective out of his shapeless PPE jumpsuit. He had a camera strap around his neck and wore a suit in a medium brown with a pale pink button-down and solid navy blue tie. The slim cut suited his tall, lean frame, and the color combinations, while on the tame side, Larkin thought, complemented his fair complexion and honey-colored hair. "Larkin. I'm flattered you requested *me* specifically to root around a pedo's desk drawers," he began in that ever-sardonic tone, underlain by only the faintest nasally quality. "But just so you know, I'm missing a drive-by shooting in East Harlem to be here."

"Our condolences," Doyle said from where he stood at Larkin's side.

Millett cracked a smile. "Kaltman got that assignment. Serves her right. She called out sick on the last full moon and I had to pull a thirty-hour shift. She wasn't even sick. She was in Vegas." Millett motioned to two evidence markers on the floor near their feet. "Be careful. I've got some taser darts and cast off over there."

"That's mine," Larkin stated.

"What?"

"Reynold tased me."

"Twice," Doyle added, raising two fingers. "I pulled out the darts before EMS arrived."

"You two are hard-core," Millett said.

Larkin plucked at his shirt and said with obvious disapproval, "It wasn't a teambuilding exercise, Millett. He ruined my shirt. This is Ralph Lauren."

"Gee, no Tom Ford?"

"Not on a detective's salary."

Millett didn't roll his eyes. He didn't have to. "Come in, then. But only to the bedroom threshold. I'm still working in here." He disappeared inside.

Larkin moved to stand obediently in the doorway and watched as Millett snapped a few photographs. "Anything of merit in his desk at the high school," he asked.

"Just the photographs you two found." Millett glanced over his shoulder. "Good investigating, by the way."

"I have an embarrassing number of commendations in regards to my investigative proficiency. I do not require further accolades."

"You can compliment me," Doyle said as he moved to stand behind Larkin. "I'm always grateful."

Larkin held up a hand, quickly saying, "That will not be necessary."

Millett shifted his line of sight to Doyle, just over Larkin's shoulder. He said matter-of-factly, "Your partner is giving me the evil eye."

"He's a bit territorial," Doyle replied.

"I most certainly am not," Larkin said, turning to address Doyle. "You're just flirting to get a rise out of me."

Millett raised both brows. "*Anyway….*"

"Have you found any photographs in the apartment,"

Larkin asked.

"Uh, you've seen the creep's walls, right? You'll need to be more specific."

"Photographs that are comparable to the death portraits he kept hidden at school. They'd have recently been taken in this apartment of a teenage girl with dyed red hair."

Millett gave a curt shake of his head before opening the closet door on their right. "Nothing like—*God*. It smells like piss in here."

"He kidnapped her," Doyle said somberly. "Kept her locked in the closet."

Larkin leaned into the room, attempting to look around the corner and into the closet. "Does Reynold own belts."

"He's got a few hanging up," Millett confirmed, still making a face. "Why?"

"Take them into evidence."

Doyle tugged Larkin back by the shoulder until the two of them were standing in the doorway, looking at each other. "You said Reynold's psychology wasn't that of a killer."

"He's not a man capable of premeditated murder, no. But someone strangled John Doe with an out-of-the-box weapon and locked him in a utility closet with a death portrait in his pocket. I can't rule out that Reynold perhaps panicked and killed out of self-preservation—especially if that individual turns out to be Dicky—who, from what it sounds like, would have rolled on Reynold for next to nothing."

"But why on Earth would Reynold leave that cryptic note asking for *you*?"

"I don't know," Larkin said with more force than what was typical of his discussions with Doyle. "But John Doe's murder is related to Marco Garcia's. It *has* to be."

"Hey," Millett cut in. "Mom and Dad."

Larkin and Doyle both turned toward Millett and stared.

A hint of a smirk flitted across Millett's expression as he pulled out a handful of belts from the closet, asking, "You found out who the human soup used to be?" He dropped the belts into a paper bag, crouched beside his kit, and began to fill out an evidence label.

Larkin answered stiffly, "Possibly."

In the brief silence, filled only by the scratch of Millett's pen and the radio of the officer just outside the front door, Larkin took in the bedroom again, now that he wasn't standing in the midst of a hostage situation. The mattress was still on the floor. The sheets were still mismatched. No headboard. No rugs. The nightstand held a thrift store lamp with a big, out-of-date lampshade and a single framed photo. There was a painted particleboard dresser in off-white to the left, with what appeared to be on its top, from afar, scratch-off tickets and a flashlight caddy with three AAA batteries still secured inside. Beside those was a black plastic box with no obvious door, handle, or lock so as to suggest its purpose.

"Where's the flashlight," Larkin asked.

Millett stood and looked in the direction Larkin was staring. "I haven't gotten to that side of—yeah sure, just come right in."

Larkin opened the top drawer of the dresser, carefully lifted several pairs of cheap tube socks, then found the small handheld flashlight. He unscrewed the back and dropped the contents into his hand.

"What is it?" Doyle asked, still standing in the doorway, like a man who knew how to follow simple requests.

"Heroin." Larkin set the small, plastic-wrapped capsules on the dresser alongside the flashlight.

"I've never seen a cop so disappointed in finding illegal drugs in a suspect's home," Millett said before returning to his investigation of the closet.

"So Reynold told the truth about intending to pay Dicky

with drugs. That doesn't help me." Larkin pushed his suit coat back, set his hands on his hips, and stared at the framed photo across the room. "The CDC developed a ten-item scale in which to measure Adverse Childhood Experiences, and a recent study concluded that male sexual offenders are three times more likely to have been sexually abused as children, twice as likely to have experienced physical abuse, and up to thirteen times more likely to have endured verbal abuse, when compared to the nonoffending male population. It was reported that in guilty offenders who claimed multiple victims who were one, strangers, and two, of a prepubescent age, they had ACE scores that mirrored those CDC statistics."

Millett was pushing clothes hangers along the rod as he said, mostly to himself, "I like to relax with a beer and campy horror films, myself, but I guess reading public health surveys is one way to induce sleep."

"Commentary is not necessary," Larkin remarked.

Doyle said, "I think a lot of people could claim to have had traumatic childhoods, though."

"The CDC's survey of seventeen thousand adults concluded that two-thirds have experienced at least one form of abuse or neglect while under the age of eighteen," Larkin said to Doyle.

"Exactly. But not all those eleven thousand adults turned into sexual predators. Experienced childhood trauma isn't anyone's fault, but the decision to enact abuse into adulthood is a clear and conscious decision they made. *That* has no excuse."

Larkin turned sideways, studying Doyle. "I agree. I'm only attempting to explain the uncomfortable positioning seen in the Reynold family photo."

Doyle raised his eyebrows and leaned to one side, as if to view the framed portrait from where he stood.

Larkin walked across the room, collected the picture

from the bedside table, and returned to his partner. He held it out: a snapshot from childhood—now discolored—a maternal figure standing at the base of a stoop, her arms crossed, a severe and hostile expression on her face. Beside her was a young Gary Reynold. He was clearly meant to be included in this family-of-two picture, but stood just far enough to the right that the distance between mother and son felt… awkward. Gary's brow was furrowed as he stared at the camera, one arm crossed over his front to hold the other, a fist clenched at his side.

"You think his mother abused him?" Doyle asked, looking up from the photo.

Larkin turned the frame around, undid the clasp, removed the cheap backing, and his stomach lurched like the floor had suddenly dropped out from under him. He sighed audibly, held up three portraits—all young, dead, redheaded girls posed provocatively on subway benches, two with crowns of what this time seemed to be geranium leaves—and said, "I think Gary's mommy issues are the least of his problems now."

Doyle's jaw worked, but he said nothing as he carefully collected the frame and photos from Larkin, handling them as if they were fragile, breakable—the only remains left of children who'd been deceived and degraded, but who deserved to have their likeness treated with love and protection.

"Seven unknowns," Larkin said, trying to modulate his voice to reflect the gentleness of Doyle's touch. "And still Marco to account for."

"You might want to make that eight unknowns," Millett broke in.

Both Larkin and Doyle turned toward him as he displayed in both hands a clear plastic bag tightly packed with gray granules.

"Are those cremated remains?" Doyle asked.

Millett nodded. "Seems to be."

Larkin tilted his head thoughtfully, then turned on his heel and studied the dresser a second time. He grabbed the plastic box on top, spun it, and revealed an identification tag stamped across the front.

LOUISE REYNOLD

03/22/1948 – 10/03/2012

Larkin picked up the box. It felt empty, but then something inside slid from one corner and thumped against the plastic. He held the box under one arm, wriggled the top free, and reached inside. He pulled out a disposable, Fujifilm camera, remaining photo count: zero.

CHAPTER THIRTEEN

After the walkthrough of Gary Reynold's apartment, Larkin returned to Precinct 19 to drop off his growing collection of death portraits, while Doyle picked up his own car and drove to 1PP. He'd not only needed to scan the composite sketch he'd worked on with Megan and submit it into evidence for Larkin's file, but Doyle had wanted to speak with Senior Artist Bailey about utilizing the unit's darkroom the next morning. Developing the photos on the Fujifilm disposable camera themselves would be a far quicker turnaround than sending it off to the lab to get around to in a few weeks, if not months, and Larkin wasn't surprised to learn that Doyle possessed the know-how in which to get the job done.

In high school, Larkin had taken a photography class for his required art credit, his thought process being he couldn't draw and he couldn't sculpt and he couldn't paint, but how difficult was it to point and click? But then the instructor had assigned the task of constructing a pinhole camera and developing their own snapshots. Larkin had taken the course with Patrick, when they'd still been *just friends*. They'd gone to the school's green roof with their cameras. The memory was from before the attack, before the HSAM, and it didn't resonate like his associations did now. In fact, Larkin wasn't even able to recall what Patrick had taken a picture of. But afterward, the other boy had stretched out on the grass and closed his eyes and looked a bit like a work of art himself, so Larkin had sat cross-legged beside him, opened the shutter on his camera, and waited as the photo paper was exposed to light.

When he'd developed the picture, it'd come out completely black.

His instructor had explained the camera likely suffered from light seepage.

Larkin had gotten a C- on the project.

So no, he wasn't surprised that someone who had two art degrees from renowned institutions, whose sketches could find missing people, whose sculptures could identify the nameless, whose paintings, Larkin had come to realize, were the very ones mounted to the walls of the apartment—the cityscapes he lost himself in, trying to count each and every pinprick of light illuminating the towers at night—he wasn't surprised at all that someone like Doyle could develop cheap camera film too.

It was 6:49 p.m. when Larkin unlocked 4A and stepped inside the dark, stuffy apartment. He shut the door, flipped the lock, and leaned back, closing his eyes. The walkup seemed to sigh around him, settling in for the evening as its tenants returned home, and Larkin wondered what kind of day Doyle's neighbors had lived. Had it been a day worth remembering—drinks at the neighborhood bar with friends to celebrate a raise, a promotion, an engagement—or had it been the kind of day that made you stand alone in the dark, following the calendar backward day-by-day as you tried to pin down that exact moment where your life went sideways?

Chaos theory stated that among the apparent randomness

of surrounding chaos and complexity was a pattern, interconnectedness, repetition. So where in Larkin's timeline had a butterfly flapped its wings too hard and disturbed the sensitive conditions that made up his life? And what outcome was he even questioning? His HSAM? His career choice? His failed marriage? His sleeplessness—the alarm clock numbers glowing 3:21 a.m. and Larkin acknowledging how easily, how quietly, he could slip away young, leave behind a handsome face, and people would politely remark: it's just *so tragic.*

Except when Larkin found himself standing in the bathroom, medicine cabinet open, tearing the contents out as he searched for the confiscated Xanax, craving the pills because the chemical high was better than feeling like the walking dead, a very small voice asked, Do you really want to *be* dead?

—Larkin vomiting on the bathroom floor, and when he sat up on his knees, Doyle stood before him in the same brown tweed suit he'd worn when they first met, offering a hand and glowing smile as he introduced himself: "Ira Doyle. It's a pleasure."—

Larkin slammed the cabinet shut on the still-jumbled associations. He stared at his reflection in the dark, illuminated only by light pollution filtering in through the small window to his left.

Do you really want to be dead?

"No...."

Larkin wasn't a religious man, he didn't subscribe to the concepts of a higher being, that he was a pawn in a game of fate—his story already predetermined and his self-will a concept in name only. But he also refused to believe that every misfortune, every injustice, every heartache was the product of unpredictability—that he was nothing more than meat meant to eat, fuck, and die. The answer was something in between, something nuanced, a sort of interconnectedness that lacked proper language.

Everett Larkin was a nobody.

But maybe everyone was a nobody.

And it was only in the exploration of one's self, the discovery of where one's heart lay beyond the veil, that we became *somebody*.

"Somebody," Larkin repeated aloud. He reached into his pocket, retrieved his cell, and placed a call. He remained in the dark bathroom as the line rang.

"Hey," Doyle answered, and he sounded very much like the man who'd nearly broken in two that afternoon.

"Hi."

"Everything okay?"

Larkin smiled. He absently shook his head, rubbed his temples, because of course Doyle, with so many arrows in his own back, tended to the well-being of another over himself. It was a common trait among those whose hearts were most bruised—to never want someone to hurt like they did. "No," Larkin answered simply. "Are you okay?"

The pause was profound.

Doyle echoed, "No."

A ghost of a laugh escaped Larkin. "I wish American social norms allowed for more honesty like this. Are you leaving soon."

"Yeah. I'm cleaning up the darkroom a little so it's actually usable tomorrow. You know what I just found in here?"

"What."

"A fruitcake. A whole fruitcake. I think it's from last year's holiday party."

Larkin smiled again. "I'm going to cook dinner."

"You are?"

"Don't sound so surprised."

"You don't cook, Evie."

Larkin didn't reply to that verifiable fact, and instead said, "In 2003, Jay Leno ate a bite of a 125-year-old fruitcake and didn't die. Toss the cake in the breakroom and come home."

Doyle's rich, top-shelf laugh seemed to reverberate off the walls of the darkroom. "I won't do that, but I'm on my way."

Larkin said goodbye, hung up, and went to the bedroom to strip out of the clothes that smelled of sweat, hospital antiseptic, and of neighborhood trash sitting curbside for morning pickup that he seemed to have collected on his walk from the Audi to Doyle's building. Larkin showered, dressed down in black jeans and a light summer flannel in shades of yellow, black, teal, and aquamarine, then flicked the fairy lights on in the main room. Larkin cuffed the sleeves at his elbows as he walked into the kitchen, where he then proceeded to dig through the cupboards and fridge before deciding—with the exception of no white wine, because Doyle didn't keep alcohol in the house—they had ingredients for making risotto. There were also scallops that hadn't been cooked yet, and a whole bag of spinach, because it had three times more calcium, iron, and potassium than leaf lettuce, and Doyle was more conscious of those things than Larkin was when they traded off on grocery duties.

He set out the ingredients, chopped shallots, and had just begun stirring stock into the rice when the door unlocked and swung open. Larkin met Doyle's expression, could see the fine lines of stress from maintaining the personal and private guilt that'd been threatening to overwhelm him all afternoon, but he also caught a spark, a glint, of joy in Doyle's eyes. Joy from simply seeing Larkin, even though it was—Larkin checked his watch—7:45 p.m. and they'd only been apart for an hour and ten minutes. Doyle's smile came out, like sunshine burning morning mist, and the lines in his face snapped like tension wire giving way.

"Smells good," he said, closing the door and propping his portfolio bag against the wall. "Risotto?"

"Yes."

"Do I have time to wash up?"

Larkin waved his free hand in a shooing motion, but did take a second look as Doyle stepped into the bedroom, tossed his tie, vest, and suit coat on the foot of the bed with his usual lack of concern for wrinkles, before unbuttoning his white shirt and pulling it from his shoulders. Larkin would have to thank whatever yoga guru taught Doyle the crane pose, because he might not have been a big, buff guy, but every muscle in Doyle's back and core were so defined that he could have been a living anatomical guide for medical students.

Doyle was in and out of the shower in a few minutes, rejoining Larkin in the same pair of relaxed, rolled-up jeans as yesterday and a plain black T-shirt. He grabbed a can of Coke from the fridge, poured a glass of water, and set the table with silverware and napkins. Doyle removed two bowls from the cupboard and offered them to Larkin, who plated the steaming risotto, plopped a few seared scallops on top, and added the spinach he'd just finished sautéing.

It was 8:02 p.m. when they sat down to eat.

Doyle popped the tab on his Coke, held the can up, and said, "Here's to your return to active duty."

Larkin tapped his glass. "A hell of a welcome back." He took a sip, put the glass down, and added, "Thank you for being there."

"You're welcome. Even though I doubt there was much assistance actually provided."

"That's ridiculous."

"It is?"

Larkin said, "Cold Cases often requires working alongside beat cops, detectives in other cities or states, and I've even worked with the FBI on a few occasions."

"Sounds like a lot of dick-measuring."

"Yes, and mine's the biggest."

Doyle clasped a hand over his mouth, but he snorted and a bit of Coke dribbled onto the tabletop. He grabbed his napkin to clean it.

"The point is," Larkin continued, letting a smile slip, "those were necessary partnerships. Yours is different. I *want* to work with you. You know things I don't. And—we balance each other out."

Doyle smiled as he wiped his fingers clean. "I think so too."

"But I don't want to talk about work or the case or anything like that."

"What do you want to talk about?"

Larkin took a bite of his dinner, shrugging.

Doyle tried the food and made a sound of delight. "Wow, this is really good."

"Thank you."

"Why don't you cook more?"

"I find it tedious." Larkin stabbed a scallop, brought it to his mouth, then lowered it before elaborating, "Maintaining defenses all day is exhausting. Having to walk a tightrope of engagement without becoming absorbed, in case the event turns south, because I don't want more negative associations. I have too many. So I suppose by the time I come home, and dinner needs to be cooked but I'm already so tired, and I look at the pile of ingredients and recipe directions… it becomes a sort of visual noise that's like… chewing on aluminum foil."

Doyle ate, listening to the explanation without interruption, then said at Larkin's conclusion, "The meditative qualities of cooking has the opposite effect on you."

"Yes. And in a twist of irony, I wanted to be a chef. I was accepted into culinary school upstate."

"Really?"

Larkin nodded. "I started college a year late because I was in the hospital. I went into psychology instead. Added a criminology major shortly after."

"Why?"

Larkin looked up, raising his eyebrows. "Why, what."

"Why psychology?"

Larkin chewed on his words for a moment, then said, "I don't think I can accurately describe the sensation of waking up and *thinking* differently than you did the day before. It's like you're a stranger to yourself. And no matter how hard I tried to be who I was before… he was gone. My memory and thought process is so hyperanalytical now, that it made sense to pursue an education that would help me understand all of the details I was memorizing." He shrugged, feeling a little self-conscious under Doyle's gaze. "That's all."

A loud silence settled between them.

Larkin asked, "What."

"I want to ask a question, but I'm concerned it'll prompt an association."

"About Patrick."

"Yes."

Larkin shook his head, looked at his bowl, and said very quietly, "You can ask."

"Did they catch the person who did it?"

"No."

Doyle reached across the table, wrapped his hand briefly around Larkin's left wrist, and gave it a squeeze. "I'm sorry."

"Tell me something about yourself. That I don't know yet."

Doyle let go, leaned back in his chair. "I'm not that interesting."

"You don't believe that."

Doyle smiled, his face—his entire body—lighting up. "I kept the very first voicemail you left me. I listen to it, sometimes. When I need to hear your voice. 'This is Detective Everett Larkin, Cold Case Squad. The time is 9:07.'"

Larkin tilted his head and asked, so curiously, so sincerely, "Why?"

Doyle set his fork down. He scratched at his stubble a moment. "Remember when you told me how it felt incredible to meet someone who understood your love language, even if it wasn't their own?"

"Of course."

"In the past, most guys have equated my need for touch with sex. Don't get me wrong, I love sex, but for me, touch isn't only about skin-on-skin. It's about the way someone smells. The way they sound. The way their smile makes me feel. When I listen to that voicemail, I feel... at home. *You* feel like home. And I think, if someone can make me that comfortable, they must understand my language pretty well too."

Larkin felt as if he was standing outside himself, watching a sort of belly-twisting vertigo effect take place—the kitchen, the apartment, the city shrinking out of view—the moment, the second, zooming in on him, closer and closer until *bam.* The beat that'd been building in Larkin's chest since Monday, March 30 at 9:44 a.m., dropped suddenly, and his spirit was flung free from his body—the sense of tipping backward in his chair, falling through the floor, the Earth, shooting through the cosmos before being blown apart into millions of pieces of stardust, scattered to the farthest reaches of the universe where time didn't exist and mourning wasn't a concept and there was nothing to latch onto but only the most naked of truths.

"Where your treasure is, there will your heart be also."

Could it be that in seeking himself, in pushing aside the veil, Larkin glimpsed a treasure that looked a little bit like calluses and cardamon and whiskey and pyrite? And that he wasn't a nobody—because on Wednesday, April 1, at 4:56 p.m., Doyle had kissed him and Larkin hadn't been gray, but was instead a rainbow. His treasure made him feel like a *somebody*. His treasure made him feel like this was a tried-and-true partnership.

In art and investigation.

In life and death.

In love.

Larkin's treasure was Ira Doyle.

And his heart had simply been waiting for his mind to catch up.

A knock at the front door brought Larkin back like the snap of a rubber band, his insides reverberating like kettledrums while he scrambled not to lose hold on all the profound sensations that'd accompanied his epiphany. Larkin watched Doyle push his chair back and stand.

"I'll get it. It's probably Mr. Gabel."

Humphrey Gabel, the clog-wearing octogenarian who lived above them in 5A, stopped by at least twice a week under the guise of updating Doyle on the comings and goings of the building, but Larkin suspected the truth of the matter was that the elderly man was lonely and Doyle had proven to be the only neighbor who'd ever given him the time of day.

Larkin scrubbed his face with both hands, listened to Doyle unlock and open the door—

But it wasn't Mr. Gabel who spoke—it was Noah Rider.

"What are you doing here?"

Larkin froze.

Doyle answered, polite but with a clear undertone of uncertainty, "I live here."

Larkin jerked his head in the direction of the door and quickly stood from the table.

Noah hesitantly entered the apartment at Doyle's offer, his eyes roaming the furniture, the walls, the things that humans accumulate like curious corvids, seeking what he knew, what was familiar, until his gaze came to a stop at Larkin. He'd gone home to change out of his school attire: dark rose chinos, a short-sleeve button-down with a light blue and white daisy pattern—one button appeared to be loose— and white sneakers. He looked so handsome, but then again, Noah was always handsome.

"Noah—" Larkin started.

Noah nodded, like the conversation had already been had and done. "You forgot, right?"

Larkin hastily fumbled his phone free from his pocket and pulled up his calendar of appointments. He scrolled down to the evening hours... it wasn't there. Skylight Lounge at 6:30 p.m., because Noah wanted to talk. He looked up. "I'm sorry."

"You left me waiting at the lounge—"

"You called me at work," Larkin cut in. "I was busy. I didn't have time to write it down. I'm sorry."

Noah picked up like Larkin had said nothing. "You left me waiting for nearly two goddamn hours. And when I come looking for you, you're having dinner with another man."

"There was no malicious intent. I forgot—"

"I forgot, I forgot, I forgot," Noah parroted with growing agitation. "You always fucking forget when it comes to me, Everett!"

"*Stop!*" Larkin shouted. "Stop talking down to me. Stop acting like I do this shit intentionally to get a fucking rise out of you. I have a traumatic brain injury, Noah, and you've known that for seven years. You know I have curious workarounds and strange habits and plenty of limitations and I'm doing the best I fucking can. I'm sorry I forgot to write down our dinner plans. I'm sorry I left you there alone. But screaming at me won't fix the problem!" Larkin's chest was heaving, his face felt flush.

Noah's own face was also blotchy, his model good looks replaced by offense and hurt and fury. "Whose apartment is this?"

Larkin narrowed his eyes. "What."

"You told me, when you moved out, that this was your new address," Noah said. "You told our *lawyers* this was your new address." He gestured wildly, viciously, at Doyle, who'd taken several steps into the living room and remained quiet throughout the verbal assault. "And yet *he* claims to live here."

Doyle said suddenly, "It's my apartment."

The stare Noah shot Doyle... if looks could kill.

But Doyle didn't shrink under the glower. "Larkin was on medical leave and in no position to deal with apartment hunting. I offered for him to stay as long as he needed."

"Out of the goodness of your heart?" Noah asked. "In a studio with one bed? Do you think I was born yesterday?"

Doyle raised his hands up in a defensive manner, but his voice was still a smoky calm as he said, "Noah, whatever you think is happening between us—we're friends. That's it."

"Sure," Noah answered mockingly. "Just fuck buddies, right?"

"No," Doyle said, more firmly. "We're not having—"

"He's *my* husband," Noah cried. "Not *yours*."

"Noah—" Larkin tried.

"You ruined my marriage!" Noah said accusingly, pointing a finger at Doyle.

Larkin stepped in between the two. "We ruined our marriage," he corrected, motioning between himself and Noah.

"Bullshit."

"You told me over and over that you understood," Larkin said. "But I think… a part of you… hoped all the weird shit I say and do wouldn't apply to you—would change *because* of you. And I think you've come to resent me and the fact that that isn't true."

"So now it's my fault?"

"No. I didn't say that," Larkin snapped. He took a deep breath, rubbed his eyes, and said, "You've underestimated your limitations when in a relationship with someone who's neurodivergent. I'm not blaming you for anything. I'm only trying to say that there's a disconnect between what you're capable of handling and what I'm capable of giving. It's not fair to either of us, and I've tried to tell you this a dozen times over the last fifty days. *It's not fair.*"

Noah's eyes shone with unfallen tears. He swallowed, sniffed loudly, and countered, "I really appreciate how you make me out to be stupid *and* heartless, Everett. Thank you."

"Jesus Christ."

"And don't think so highly of yourself," Noah continued, "because what you've been giving for the last year? Zero. Fucking zero."

"Great. I look forward to your list of grievances in court."

"Why wait? I can start now. You refuse to visit my parents with me."

"They don't want me around, Noah. They don't like me."

"How could they? They haven't seen their son-in-law

since our wedding. You don't listen when I talk to you."

"Sometimes your conversations are overwhelming."

"You hang up on me."

"I'm a detective. I can't keep taking personal—"

"You recently became a pill-popper."

"For my panic attacks." But Larkin's voice was growing quieter, weaker, like he was giving up, with every counter to Noah's attacks.

"You won't have sex with me."

"It's the Xanax."

"And—oh, that's right—you cheated on me." Noah smiled, but it was malicious, and pointed at Doyle. "With him. The guy you're apparently now living with, even though you wouldn't move in with me until we got engaged."

"All right," Doyle interrupted. He took Larkin by the elbow and gently steered him away while saying to Noah, "I think you need to take a breath—"

"Spare me the condescending attitude," Noah spat.

"I can't do this," Larkin said, heading toward the bathroom.

Doyle said to Noah, "I think you should go."

"I came to talk to my husband, not you."

"Be that as it may, you're in my home, and I'm telling you to leave. Evie, hang on—Noah, I'll ask if he can give you a call—"

Larkin shut the bathroom door, twisted the lock, and opened the medicine cabinet. He pushed Noah's and Doyle's voices out of his mind until they were muted, distorted, like he was listening to underwater recordings. The Xanax was still gone, of course, and there was no convenient way to get downstairs and retrieve the pills hidden in the Audi. So Larkin grabbed the ZzzQuil bottle, unscrewed the top, tossed aside the measuring cap, and brought it to his lips. He swallowed a mouthful of the berry-flavored medication, but it burned his sinuses, his throat, and he started coughing. Larkin scrambled to set the bottle on the edge of the sink, but it tipped over, purple antihistamine sloshing down the drain. He turned on the water, leaned down, and drank before coughing some more. It was only after Larkin had caught his breath that he registered the pounding on the door.

"Evie, open the door," Doyle ordered.

Larkin shut off the tap. He wiped his mouth. A cold sweat had broken out across his chest, his back, his underarms. His stomach twisted, and Larkin wondered if he was going to be sick. He leaned back against the sink, wrapped his arms around himself, and hunched forward.

"Answer me right now, or I'm unscrewing the doorknob."

Larkin slowly slid into a crouch against the sink cabinet. He drew his knees to his chest and started sobbing. "I can't do this anymore," he said again. "I can't—I can't live like this. I hate remembering useless, pointless information and forgetting what matters to everyone else. Who cares that the third button on Noah's shirt had a stray thread and is coming loose? I mean, *that's* what I focused on? *Who the fuck cares*! People think my memory is a gift, but I'm sitting on the bathroom floor and I can't stop crying and I miss Patrick and I miss Noah and I *hate* who I've become."

On the other side of the door, near the floor, like Doyle had sat down, he said, "I don't hate who you are."

"Then you're the stupidest fucking person on the planet, Ira." Larkin put a hand over his eyes as another sob tore out of him. "I love Noah and all I did was ruin his life."

There was a note of hesitation in Doyle's voice, but he asked, "Do you want me to go downstairs and see if I can catch him? Or—give me his number, and I'll call him for you."

Larkin tucked his face against his shoulder to awkwardly

wipe away snot and tears. He opened his mouth to speak, but the words crumpled like ash and he had to close it against another wave of cries threatening to come forward. He put a hand over his eyes again.

"People say things when they're scared or confused, and they usually aren't the right things to say," Doyle suggested.

"But he knows it cuts me to the bone. He knows I won't ever forget how it makes me feel. And it feels fucking awful, Ira. *Awful.* I'm one association away from crying in some other bathroom on a summer night, remembering what my soon-to-be ex-husband really thinks of me. And the worst part is, he's not even wrong. I've refused to visit my in-laws for the last two years, knowing it was making the rift between us worse. I do stop listening, then miss important details I should be writing down. I haven't been able to get an erection since January and I didn't tell Noah it was because of the Xanax—I just made it worse by taking more and more."

"Evie?"

"*What*," he snapped.

"You're not a cruel person. And I've never known you to make a decision without logical reasons to back it up. What you're saying—those are symptoms of a bigger problem."

Larkin snorted and wiped at his eyes. "If I'd just sucked it up and spent Christmas with his parents like Noah wanted—"

"But that's not Noah's choice to make," Doyle interrupted. "I know these are sensitive topics. They would be for any relationship. But the world wasn't designed with people like you in mind, and the only one who can advocate for your mental well-being is you. I know you speak in a very exacting manner, and that can come off as curt to some, but I... struggle to be entirely sympathetic to Noah's hurt when he's been made aware of your condition for a long time."

Larkin looked down, placed his bare left hand on the tile floor, spread his fingers, and dragged them back and forth against the lines of grout. "Do you—" He stopped, cleared his throat, and tried again. "Do you think people can love each other and still not be right for one another."

"Yeah."

"Do you think I'm blameless in this breakup."

"No. But I think you're ready to accept your faults and Noah isn't there yet."

Larkin said, "Maybe he loves what I represented. Not who I really am. At least, not anymore."

"Maybe."

"Have you been in love."

"Sure."

"How'd it end."

There was a pause before Doyle answered, "It hasn't started."

Larkin looked at the door. He didn't think, didn't calculate, merely moved on impulse, on instinct—shifting onto his knees, leaning forward to twist the thumb lock, and pulling the door open a crack.

Doyle sat sideways in the threshold, his back against the bookshelf. He raised his head, smiled softly, and said, "Hey."

"Hi."

"Are you coming out?"

"Have you ever had an epiphany."

Doyle raised an eyebrow but nodded and said, "Twice."

"How did they make you feel."

"At peace."

Larkin opened the door farther. "Mine made me feel happy." He knee-walked closer until he was right up against Doyle, taking his face into both hands. "And that made me realize the only happiness I've felt in a long time hasn't been in the moment, but through associations."

"Evie?"

"*Yes.*" And Larkin kissed Doyle, every emotion, every fear, every insecurity, ugly and raw and unrefined, all of it right there, in a single brush of lips on lips.

Take it or leave it.

Doyle took it. He wrapped his arms around Larkin and pressed their bodies together, holding like he'd been chasing night upon endless night and now, *now* he'd finally caught up to Larkin and only needed a moment to collect his breath. Doyle kissed Larkin fervently, but somehow it didn't lessen the moment, didn't reduce this profound comprehension they had of each other to something as mundane as the pursuit of physical pleasure, not after Larkin's admission of how numb he'd become toward sexual acts of any kind.

No.

Doyle kissed like they'd both been tumbling through the sky, careening toward Earth at breakneck speed, and finally, the gales—whipping them like ragdolls—threw Larkin and Doyle together. They both held on tight, and with that came a sudden and ethereal calm. The kiss was fear, relief, joy, uncertainty, beauty. It was day and night, the sun and moon, a promise to carry on just *one more time*, and the emotions you dared only feel when left in the safety of your own company.

The kiss… was love.

Larkin broke, leaned back, and opened his eyes, meeting Doyle's steady gaze. "Professionals or friends or something…. Is this the *something*?"

Doyle put a hand on Larkin's nape and drew them together again. "Yeah, it is."

CHAPTER FOURTEEN

It was 10:03 p.m. and Larkin lay in bed with a hand pressed to his forehead. Between the fight with Noah, all of it right there, sitting on the surface, still too painful to even look at from the corner of his eye, chugging ZzzQuil, and the subsequent meltdown, his headache was back in full force. He heard the fairy lights click off in the main room, and then the french doors opened.

"Can I have some Tylenol," Larkin asked.

"That depends on how much ZzzQuil you took." Doyle turned off the bedroom light.

Larkin could feel the glow from the touch lamp on the bedside table. "I wasn't measuring."

"Then, no." Doyle drew back the covers. He climbed into bed, his body a furnace as he draped himself over Larkin's chest.

Larkin moved his hand to Doyle's bare shoulder and drew it up and down his arm, fingertips skating along defined muscle, dark hair, encircling the occasional freckle. It was familiar, and somehow entirely new. Larkin's stomach fluttered when Doyle slid a hand underneath the ratty T-shirt he wore to bed.

"This okay?" Doyle asked, raising his head.

"I'm ticklish."

"Are you really?"

Larkin narrowed his eyes.

Doyle smirked but pulled his hand free. "I won't tell anyone."

"You better not."

Doyle propped himself up on his right arm. "Did you ever watch *Mister Rogers' Neighborhood*?"

"Of course."

"He talked a lot about love." Doyle rubbed his hand up and down Larkin's chest, a sort of wonder in his touch, like all this time he'd actually been holding back, and tonight he was touching—really touching—Larkin for the first time. "He said love is at the root of everything. Love or the lack of it."

"Are you looking to have a moral debate at ten at night."

Doyle said, "I don't want you using ZzzQuil anymore."

"What does OTC medication have to do with love," Larkin asked.

Doyle shook his head once. "Everything."

Larkin felt himself shrinking inward under Doyle's studious gaze. He'd never called out Larkin's behavior for what it was—he was addicted to pharmaceuticals, plain and simple—nor did he use derogatory terms that made the truth about himself all the more difficult to accept. Doyle hadn't brought up what had happened on Sunday, May 10, either. But he didn't have to. His actions had spoken louder than any sort of intervention.

—thunder boomed outside the bathroom window, so close, so loud, the walkup shaking and shivering from the onslaught of the summer storm, Larkin trying to silence

Patrick's screams, trying to silence the crack of his own skull that repeated over and over like a warped record, and Doyle finding him before he could asphyxiate on his own vomit—

Larkin shuddered and swallowed down the taste of bile and chemicals and artificial berry at the back of his throat. Doyle was still watching, waiting for a response. He said, "I don't have any more. I spilled it."

"Let's make that the last bottle, then." Doyle rolled over, tapped the lamp, and the room went dark. He settled onto his back, his knees cracking as he gave a languid stretch.

"Ira."

"Hmm?"

It was Larkin's turn to roll onto his side, and he leaned over Doyle, scrutinizing a face composed of gray shadows against a backdrop of black. "What do I smell like for you."

"What do you mean?"

"You said that touch was about more than skin-on-skin. I know my cologne has notes of almond, vanilla, lavender, and honey, but I think you meant something more conceptual and less literal."

Doyle laughed, and it held an air of self-consciousness to it. "You—it sounds so stupid—you smell kind of like nostalgia. Like when I could smell my grandmother's baking from out in the hall when I was a kid. A rare treat."

"So I'm… a homemade cookie." Larkin was thoughtful for a moment, noting that Doyle had once again slid his hand under the cotton shirt, but this time against Larkin's back, which was decidedly less ticklish. "And how does my smile make you feel. When I do smile, that is."

"You smile all the time."

"I don't, actually."

"You don't need to be smiling with your mouth to smile."

Larkin furrowed his brows and asked, "Do you know

what a smile is."

"You do it with your eyes. It's subtle, but I notice it. Like a glow that never gets snuffed out. It makes me happy."

"So I make you feel nostalgic, homey, and happy."

"I guess you do."

"That's very Live, Laugh, Love of you."

"You sonofabitch." Doyle laughed again, good naturedly as he grabbed the pillow out from under his head and whacked Larkin with it.

Larkin protested, then made a flustered noise when Doyle flipped him onto his back. "I think this constitutes as police brutality."

Doyle sat on Larkin's hips.

"Maybe not this part," Larkin amended.

"Report me, then."

"I'll let you off with a warning." Larkin touched Doyle's chest, pressing fingertips against muscle and dragging through well-groomed hair. "You're beautiful," he whispered. "I wish I didn't feel so physically numb."

Doyle leaned over Larkin, pressed their mouths together, and said against Larkin's lips, "It's not permanent. And the first step is talking to Dr. Meyers about changing your prescription."

Just the idea of no longer having access to Xanax, not even in his currently reduced state—read, his actual dosage—made Larkin's heart lurch against his rib cage. He didn't say anything, because he didn't trust what might come out, so he settled for a curt nod and a second kiss.

"Have you ever been in a darkroom?"

"I did complete the mandatory art credit in high school."

Doyle asked, presumably from the counter, although the room was pitch dark so Larkin couldn't say for sure where his partner was standing, "Did you pass?"

"That's a little presumptuous of you."

Doyle's chuckle filled the room like smoke billowing from a fire. A moment later, the safelight was flipped on, and his tall, lithe form was a shadowy silhouette highlighted in a harsh, red glow. "You have to load the film into the tank in complete darkness."

"I see," Larkin said from where he'd been leaning against the far wall, safely out of the way where Doyle wouldn't trip over him or where his charcoal suit—a favorite—wouldn't be in danger of getting splattered by bleach mixtures. "I made a pinhole camera."

Doyle glanced over his shoulder, smiling. He had his sleeves rolled back and was wearing the navy apron he'd grabbed from his office after they'd arrived at 1PP at 6:47 a.m. that morning. "Pinhole cameras are fun. I made one for Abigail." The statement had come so naturally that it not only surprised Larkin, but apparently Doyle as well. He returned his attention to mixing his developer. "She didn't really have the patience for it. All the photos came out blurry or black."

"Mine too."

Doyle moved with the film tank to the sink on his left and filled it with water. He returned it to the counter and set it aside before leaning back and crossing his arms. "I replaced them with some pictures I'd taken myself."

"Isn't that lying."

"Don't we already, when it comes to leaving quarters under pillows and letters from the North Pole?"

Larkin smiled and asked, very carefully, "Was she happy?"

Doyle nodded. He looked down, crossed one foot over the other, then cleared his throat and said, "We probably won't be able to enlarge and transfer the negatives to photo paper until tomorrow. Once the film is developed, it takes a few hours to dry, but at least we'll get a chance to see what's on the reel this morning."

"That's acceptable."

Doyle grabbed the tank and poured the water out. He checked the developing mixture with a thermometer, glanced at the public school-style clock on the wall, then poured the liquid into the tank. After securing the lid, he agitated the contents and kept doing so, thirty seconds for the first minute, then roughly ten seconds for each following minute, by Larkin's count. When a full eight minutes had passed, Doyle poured out the contents and refilled the tank with the bleach-fix concoction. He once again checked the clock before repeating the agitation process.

"Ira."

"Evie."

Larkin suppressed a second smile. "How is this going to work."

"The bleach? It dissolves the silver that's generated by the developmental process."

"Us," Larkin corrected. "I've never dated someone I worked with."

"Are we dating?"

Larkin blinked a few times. He pushed off the wall and stood straighter. "Wasn't that the implication behind 'something.'" He used air quotes.

Doyle picked up the tank and turned it again. "I don't want to rush you."

"I would say as much if you were."

"I know. But ending a marriage is a big deal. And you're still going through a lot. We don't have to call it dating."

"What would you suggest we call it."

"I don't know." Doyle concluded the agitation process and poured out the chemicals. He turned on the sink and let the running water funnel through the tank. He finally looked at Larkin again. "It could be casual."

"I don't do casual." Larkin studied Doyle for a moment. "Neither do you."

"How do you know?"

"You've entrusted me with your unlocked phone enough times over the last fifty-one days for me to know you don't have Grindr or Scruff or whatever the hookup app du jour is. You've never brought a man home since I've been staying with you, nor have you spent even one evening elsewhere that wasn't work."

"That makes me sound sad," Doyle said over the water.

"No. That wasn't what I meant to imply. I'm pointing out that your personal values don't align with the casual, nonexclusive, antirelationship sentiment that has come to dominate much of the LGBT community, making those of us wanting to settle down feel rather like outsiders." Larkin waved a hand and redirected himself. "Not that I'm suggesting we settle down. What I mean is, when I'm interested in a man, I commit myself entirely to him. And you do the same. So this, by its very definition, can't be casual."

Doyle turned off the tap. "I just want you to be safe, Evie. I don't ever want to be the cause of you getting hurt."

"Hurt is inevitable," Larkin answered. "Whether on purpose or by accident. It's best to acknowledge that in the beginning."

"That's rather pessimistic."

"Realistic," Larkin corrected.

Doyle set the tank on the counter and filled it with stabilizer solution.

"I know I'm a mess," Larkin said into the unsettled

silence. "I know that being caught in the middle of a divorce must be, at the very least, awkward for you. I know that my inability to never entirely be over men I've loved before meeting you will undoubtably cause upset. I know that I come with considerable baggage and that it can be, at times, too much. And if I've not successfully supplied enough reasons for you to doubt your interest in me...."

Doyle laughed, very quietly, under his breath while pouring out the final chemical. He turned around and studied Larkin in the otherworldly light.

"I'm not sure how easy it will be, given that we've set a precedent for working together professionally, but in eighteen years, I've never been happy having HSAM. Until now. Because I don't ever want to forget how you make me feel."

"That's arguably one of the most romantic things anyone's ever said to me."

"I have my moments," Larkin answered, his voice still its ever-consistent monotone.

Doyle wiped his hands on his apron as he approached Larkin. He leaned down and gave him a sweet and simple kiss. "Okay," he whispered.

"Okay yes, or okay no," Larkin asked, just as quiet.

Doyle smiled and kissed Larkin a second time. "Okay yes." He returned to the counter, spent a moment unfurling the film, giving it a final rinse in distilled water, and then flicking the regular overhead lights on. Doyle killed the safelight and asked, "Check that cabinet beside you for a magnifying glass?"

Larkin opened the doors of what turned out to be an entirely overstuffed storage locker. "I found the women's softball team jerseys they reported as missing last summer."

"There's also a twenty-four pack of salt and pepper shakers for the breakroom in there," Doyle said. "The magnifying glass should be on the second shelf from the bottom."

"Why isn't the salt and pepper in the breakroom," Larkin asked as he crouched and rummaged through a stack of unopened printing paper, photo paper, padded Flat Rate envelopes, loose binder clips, and a half-empty box of Lipton tea bags, which Larkin made a face at, before finding the magnifying glass pushed all the way to the back.

"I think they're being hidden. A detective in Major Cases comes down to the fifth floor to borrow our salt and he never returns it."

"Lieutenant Connor leaves aggressive Post-its on the fridge, and that seems to be enough when it comes to the protection of publicly traded condiments."

"I wouldn't exactly call the Forensic Artists Unit intimidating," Doyle answered.

Larkin made a sound in the back of his throat, something that had both a note of *obviously* and *you don't say?*, before standing in front of Doyle. Doyle held the strip up to the light and Larkin set the magnifying glass before each individual frame. Not only were the pictures thumbnail in size, but the coloring of the developed film was inverted and muted, with far less contrast than what the finished products would offer after printing. But Larkin didn't have the patience to wait until the film was ready for that process sometime tomorrow, so he squinted at the magnified images and waited as his brain broke down and processed all the pieces of the scene.

"You know what else Susan Sontag said about photography?" Doyle asked.

"What's that."

"That every picture is a memento mori. 'To take a photograph is to participate in another person's mortality.'"

"How do you think."

"Well, when you take a picture, you essentially steal a second of the sitter's life—freezing it for all time. And when they're gone, that image still remains. It is, for all intents and purposes, a memento of someone's death."

"That is a startlingly simplistic view on the subject matter."

"Isn't most philosophy rather simplistic, once you break it down?" Doyle countered.

Larkin took a small step to the right as he studied the next few negative frames. "Nothing is more corruptible than an artist," he quoted under his breath. "They're in service to the ascetic ideal—a conflict which wills itself to be *conflicting*. It is a will against the very life that has created him—the artist finds satisfaction in pain and ugliness."

"Nietzsche," Doyle answered.

Larkin glanced up, happy that he was not surprised. "Yes."

"Meanwhile, we keep looking at these 'aversions to life' because why?" Doyle emphasized by lightly shaking the film strip in his hands.

"We've become anesthetized to grotesque imagery."

"So we keep upping the ante?"

Larkin considered, then nodded. "Yes, exactly."

Doyle raised a thick eyebrow and asked with a sort of wry expression, "Then you consider a mourning portrait to be the artist's ultimate act against man? Or could it be paradoxical in that an artist finds satisfaction in the misfortune inherent in such photos *because* of the sense of peace they bring?"

Larkin frowned and lowered the magnifying glass. "Huh."

Doyle smiled.

Larkin checked his watch and said, "You're not to be trusted with philosophical conversations at 7:24 a.m."

Looking rather pleased, Doyle thrust his chin toward the film strip and asked, "What do you see?"

"Much of what we expected, per Ms. Flouride's testimony. We know, of course, the original artist—pseudonym, Archie Bunker—did not take these, and that Mr. Reynold has attempted to replicate the subject matter that arouses him by cutting corners. Namely, he did not commit murder. So while she's not dead in these pictures, he does have her posed oddly." Larkin shifted again to study the images farther along the strip. "Sitting on the floor with her legs splayed out and leaning back against the wall. There's a… broken doll quality to her positioning."

"Look dead," Doyle said without a flicker of the amusement he'd shown a moment before. "Hell of a stage direction."

"What Mr. Reynold did not replicate were any of the poses or tokens seen in the seven other portraits we've obtained. No clasped hands, no shoes, no flowers or leaves. Archie has very particular knowledge of postmortem photography and utilizes it in such a way that it's… natural."

"Overlooked in replication?" Doyle suggested.

"Yes. It's so subtle that I don't believe Mr. Reynold was aware of it as an element in the previous photographs he purchased." Larkin lowered the magnifying glass and stared at Doyle. "What does that tell us."

"Archie incorporates those details for himself, not his buyers," Doyle replied. He brought the film strip down, turned, and clipped it to a hanging rack to dry. "Where he learned the specifics of a relatively obscure and misunderstood moment within the history of Western photography could prove a vital clue in discovering his true identity."

Larkin put a hand to his own chest. "Tell me where I would learn about this."

"A misleading article written by a content creator at Buzzfeed?"

"Going right for the jugular, I see."

"Maybe I've been spending too much time with you."

"Hardly. You give off a sort of wallflower-meets-slacker vibe to strangers, which leads to incorrect assumptions being made regarding both your intelligence and professional qualifications. But since I've known you, you meet that speculation head-on with quiet but fierce jabs. My presence is irrelevant."

"A wallflower meets slacker?" Doyle repeated. "What am I, two-fifths of *The Breakfast Club*?"

Larkin's mouth twitched, but he kept his expression a careful neutral and replied, "I rest my case."

Doyle rolled his eyes.

Larkin asked, "Where would I learn about postmortem photography practices before the advent of digital media empires."

Doyle was thoughtful, taking a moment to clean the counter of his developing process. "Societies, libraries, college courses, museums or historic homes…."

Larkin shook his head absently. "That's still too many possibilities for narrowing down the most likely avenue of investigation. Pinning Archie's identity is what's going to lead to catching Marco's killer. It'll solve the current John Doe in the IKEA bag as well. I'm certain of that." Larkin pushed his suit coat back and set his hands on his hips. "The problem is, I have too much information that means nothing, in the grand scheme of two unknown identities."

"What would happen if the DB in the bag was identified first?" Doyle countered. "Would your thought process work in reverse?"

"In theory, I suppose it would."

Doyle opened the door to the darkroom and motioned for Larkin to follow. "Come on. You still haven't seen my composite sketch for Dicky."

Larkin stepped into the quiet hall—tired overheads and recirculated air still the same as before, although it was too early in the morning for the smell of last night's reheated dinner serving as today's lunch to waft out from the breakroom. Larkin followed Doyle back to his office, where Doyle untied his apron, tossed it onto the worktable, and then sat at his drafting desk. He pulled back the cover on the sketch pad, flipped a few pages, and stopped at the composite sketch Megan had assisted with.

The man she'd called Creepy Dicky appeared to be in his fifties, but looked exceptionally rough around the edges, like life had not been kind. He was white, with a large, sort of bulbous nose and gaunt face, a pinched expression around his eyes, with skin tags near his right eye, under his right ear, and down along the side of his neck. His hair was unkempt and sparse along the front, and Doyle had drawn his mouth partially open to reveal a missing incisor.

"I scanned and emailed you a copy last night, before I came home," Doyle said, glancing up at Larkin.

"Thank you," Larkin murmured, still staring at the drawing. "On the surface, he appears to match John Doe's characteristics."

"Did the ME mention John Doe having any drugs in his system? Megan was pretty insistent he was a habitual user, and Reynold claimed he was a heroin addict, right?"

"ME would have to run a test on hair follicles," Larkin answered. "He was found long after the window in which heroin would be detectable in urine or blood. But I'll call the OCME." He took out his phone, opened his calendar, and created a new list of to-dos for the case. "I'll check on the fingerprint status too. We only have a partial name and alias, but that's better than nothing. If he's got a long history of homelessness and drug use, someone on the force knows him."

"Someone at the MTA might too," Doyle pointed out. "Especially if he lives in the tunnels like the alleged kids at Fifty-Seventh."

Larkin nodded, still typing. "We'll be sure to ask Ms. Crowley and Mr. Armstrong at our appointment later today."

Doyle slid his index finger underneath the hair tie on Larkin's left wrist, not giving it a tug, but instead rubbing the pulse point.

Larkin glanced up from his phone screen.

A knock sounded from the partially opened door.

Doyle pulled his hand free and looked around Larkin. "Morning, Craig," he said as Senior Artist Bailey poked his head in.

Bailey hadn't changed from the last time Larkin had seen him in March. He was still thin, sporting that Tom Selleck mustache, wearing trousers that fit him like they'd been bought off the discount rack, and a tie more suitable for a school teacher than a detective—but Larkin decided, because Bailey was Doyle's immediate supervisor, he wouldn't say anything about the silliness of the Rubik's Cube pattern.

"Doyle, I'm so glad you're in. Larkin, it's been a minute!"

"Fifty-two days."

"I'm glad one of us is watching the calendar for more than just retirement," Bailey said.

"I have a minimum of twelve more years before retirement is even a consideration," Larkin answered. "Besides, to view my career as a means to a cushy end would be counterproductive and an insult to taxpayers."

Bailey didn't seem perturbed as he said, "Once you've hit thirty-three years on the force, you come find my grave and tell me you don't know the exact day you'll be retiring."

Larkin frowned, narrowed his eyes, and looked over his shoulder at Doyle.

Doyle nodded and answered Larkin's confused expression. "He's joking. Did you need something, Craig?"

"SVU's got a vic down at Presbyterian. Female student at Pace University left her campus residence to go on a jog a little over an hour ago, was grabbed from behind, dragged into that construction zone—you know the high rise I'm talking about?—and raped. Guy ran, but she says she got a good look at him. I know you're working with Cold Cases right now, but Loving called out sick and I've got a meeting with the brass upstairs."

Larkin turned to Doyle a second time. "I have plenty of phone calls to make."

"Are you sure?"

"An assault takes precedence."

Doyle stood from the desk, towering over Larkin in a single, fluid motion. "It should only be a few hours. I can meet up with you after I finish."

Larkin nodded.

Bailey gave a thumbs-up. "Thanks, Doyle." He stepped out of the threshold, leaving the door open.

Larkin started for the door too, but then Doyle called, "See you later, Butch."

Turning, Larkin watched Doyle shove supplies into his portfolio bag before offering a playful grin. And hesitantly, because nicknames, even in jest, always felt so odd to say, Larkin replied, "See you later, Sundance."

CHAPTER FIFTEEN

The atmosphere of Precinct 19 was typical of a weekday morning. Some beat cop had brewed a full pot of Maxwell House instead of Folgers, which Larkin could detect not only by the slight variance in the scent that lingered over the second-floor bullpen, but also because he'd reached the landing just as Jim Porter had finished shouting, "How can you mix the two up? It has a jingle, man! The best part of wakin' up is *Folgers* in your goddamn cup!"

"I don't believe that's word-for-word accurate," Larkin said as he took off his suit coat and draped it over the back of his chair.

Porter had growled at him in response.

Lieutenant Connor's door was closed—indicative of an in-progress meeting or subject-sensitive phone call, as he otherwise kept it open to keep an eye and ear on all the proceedings of his squad. Aiko Miyamoto sat at her desk across the bullpen, spinning back and forth in her chair while tossing a stress ball in the air and catching it as she spoke on the phone. Byron Ulmer was in the midst of ushering a middle-aged white woman into one of the interview rooms. She had short hair, upturned in the back and spiky from excessive hairspray no doubt, and she carried a massive purple purse on one shoulder that she kept adjusting. Her perfume was so persistent that Larkin could still smell it in her wake—cheap roses and baby powder.

Larkin began working: an email to the medical examiner, followed by a phone call with one of the former officers of the defunct New York Youth Empowerment Center, who claimed to not remember a part-time student mentor from twenty-three years ago, and my gosh, the boy was *murdered*? She had absolutely no recollection of this, and of course her thoughts and prayers were with the boy's family. Yes, of course, she'd be happy to give Larkin the telephone numbers of the other officers, although she doubted any of them would remember a Marco Garcia either, since their job did not often cross paths with those actually working *inside* the YEC. No, of course, they hadn't kept records about the students who attended the YEC—it would have been a breach of the trust they were building with street kids. And *of course* she wanted to assist the police in their investigation of these terrible tragedies, but for legal purposes, would absolutely require a warrant before dredging up employment records of former mentors.

"I have one more question," Larkin said.

"Yes, of course."

Larkin swore he could feel a new headache beginning to throb behind his left eye. "Can you recall—officer, mentor, anyone working under contract—who might have used the nickname Archie."

"I can't say I do."

"A second question, then. Anyone who was fired for misconduct."

"Oh my *gosh*, no."

Tapping his pen against the desktop in annoyance, Larkin said, "All right. Thank you for your time."

"Of course, Detective."

Larkin hung up. "Of course," he mimicked under his breath. He immediately wrote up a request for a search warrant, highlighting in particular that he sought the names and last known phone numbers and addresses of Youth Empowerment Center mentors who'd been employed during the same time period as Marco Garcia. Larkin had a growing niggling of doubt that this avenue, once approved by a judge—because Larkin was rarely denied search warrants—would yield anything of interest. It would make sense that Archie worked as a mentor—he'd have had unlimited access to at-risk children—but by having such a position, it also put him at the forefront of suspicion, and Archie had survived a long time without detection. He'd have been on the periphery. Someone who was always there but never seen.

That notion made the April Fools' letter all the more unsettling to Larkin.

Archie had been so prolific in his killings, but so careful as to avoid detection for a minimum of thirty-five years—a full ten years before Marco was ever tragically involved.

Why?

Why, after so long, had the subterfuge no longer satisfied him?

Why poke and prod at Larkin, specifically, when there were any number of decent detectives who could have taken a stab at this mystery?

Why endanger himself so boldly, so blatantly, knowing if he were caught, the only thing that would save him from certain death was the state's abolishment of the death penalty?

The more child victims Larkin uncovered, the more the scope of Archie's enterprise was revealed, the less he believed this was merely about a psychopath hungry for attention after over a quarter of a decade.

Something about this case wasn't *quite right*.

Lieutenant Connor opened his door, and the squeak

of hinges in need of lubrication snapped Larkin out of his concentration.

The cell sitting beside his computer mouse buzzed with an incoming text.

Larkin glanced at the screen.

Ira Doyle.

He opened the message. It was a gif of Lionel Richie, phone to his ear, with the caption: *Is it me you're looking for?* Underneath read: *Please consider checking on Noah today. I'll be there within the hour. xx*

That request immediately dredged up the night before— Noah shouting, Doyle trying to pacify, Larkin shutting himself in the bathroom, ZzzQuil burning, coughing, gagging, sobbing—

"Grim."

Larkin startled. His hold on the cell phone was sweaty. He set it down and looked toward Connor's open door. "Yes, sir."

Connor inclined his head inside before disappearing back into the office.

Larkin stood, smoothed his tie, and walked across the bullpen and into the room. He closed the door and took a seat in front of Connor's imposing desk. "I was at 1PP this morning," he explained without any prompting. "We found a disposable camera in the home of a suspect, so I opted to have Detective Doyle do the developing himself, rather than wait for the labs—"

Connor held up a big freckled hand. "I know you're working when you're not at your desk. This isn't about that."

Larkin crossed his legs and set his hands in his lap. "Okay."

Connor picked up a piece of paper from his desk and passed it over. "This fax came in shortly before you did."

Larkin accepted and studied the handwritten facsimile: *UMOS sexual misconduct. Everett Larkin, 19th Precinct. Ira Doyle, 1PP.*

That was it. No information as to its origin, as was the relative anonymity of faxes, and it wasn't addressed to anyone specific, nor had it been signed by the sender.

"What's this about, Grim?" Connor asked, his tone unusually subdued.

Larkin frowned slightly and shook his head. He was still studying the handwriting. "I'm not certain."

"Are you and da Vinci knocking boots or what?"

Larkin glanced up, raising one eyebrow. "No, we are not."

Connor waited.

"Detective Doyle and myself are… testing the waters, romantically, but this is an extremely new development. One I don't believe anyone could have proper notice of, which makes this fax hearsay and an obvious attempt at defamation of character. I like to entertain the notion that you know me well enough to believe I would never engage in inappropriate behavior such as this."

Connor leaned back in his chair and let out a heavy breath, like he'd been holding it. "I do know you well enough."

"The facts are," Larkin continued, "Detective Doyle and I do not have a supervisor-and-subordinate relationship on the force, which makes our decision to date within regulations."

"You're the first grade detective, not him," Connor pointed out.

"That might be true, but I'm still not his commanding officer. We don't work in the same squads, or even the same precincts. He's flown uptown due to the special circumstances regarding my caseload and that's all."

Connor chewed on his thumbnail a moment before

pointing to the memo. "Who'd be responsible for sending that?"

"I couldn't say without fear of false accusations."

"Grim."

"I don't know," Larkin repeated, a bit firmer. He looked at the paper once again. "UMOS—uniformed members of service—that's not an acronym well-known outside of the NYPD."

"You piss off another cop recently?"

"It's never my intention, but entirely within the realm of possibilities." Larkin studied the slant, the distinct tremor especially visible in the lowercase *e*'s and promptly stood from his chair. "I know this handwriting."

"What's—Grim, get your ass back in here!"

But Larkin was already in the bullpen. He ignored the sidelong look from Porter as he opened John Doe's accordion file, which he'd rubber-banded to Marco Garcia's, and removed the first piece of evidence that'd not only led to the correct conclusion that the DB in the IKEA bag could be tied to Marco's murder twenty-three years after the fact, but that both unsolved murders were no longer cold, due to the prompting of the April Fools' letter.

I HAVE A BETTER MEMENTO FOR YOU

The death portrait of the teenage girl, circa 1985.

Larkin turned it facedown on the desk and set the fax beside it just as Connor loomed over his shoulder. "This handwriting is quite distinct," he said before his lieutenant could speak. "See how it slants up and down—here and here—with this very consistent shake in certain letters—you'll see it especially in the curve of the lowercase *e*'s. It's identical to that seen on the back of this postmortem photograph."

"This writer have a stroke or get conked on the head?" Connor grumbled as he studied the two side-by-side.

Larkin winced. The first time he'd held a pen after August 2, 2002—his mother tried to convince him he was right-handed, but he knew, instinctually, she was lying—he couldn't remember how to write his name. He knew how to spell, hadn't forgotten the alphabet, but when his physical therapist helped him put pen to paper and asked he write his own name… nothing. It had been the first of many brain-to-body disconnects that'd forced Larkin to relearn a skill, and every time it'd been utterly *terrifying*.

"It's neither," Larkin said before clearing his throat. He forced himself to take a few deep breaths, in through the nose, out through the mouth, to slow his accelerating heart rate. "The writer has switched to their nondominant hand, is all—as a means of concealing handwriting that might otherwise be identifiable." Meeting Connor's forbidding expression, he said, "The perp—one makes the assumption for it to be this Archie Bunker character—has already established they know of me, have an interest in me." Larkin pointed to the death portrait and read aloud, "Deliver me to Detective Larkin."

Connor snatched the fax. He folded it in half, considering, before saying very quietly, "Just because they used a police acronym doesn't mean they're in uniform."

"This is true." Larkin added, keeping his voice low, "but the April Fools' letter had insider information—the *o*'s were created with the Department of Parks and Recreation logo. The media hadn't been privy to that detail."

Connor looked down at Larkin.

"This person is also responsible for the killings of these youth in the photographs I keep dredging up. Archie is either someone who knew Harry Regmore during his reign, or someone with access to insider information."

Connor's gaze shifted to the message on the back of the postmortem photograph. "He's taunting you."

"Challenging, I would say."

Connor's Irish complexion had grown flushed. "Killers like this goad law enforcement in order to feel something."

"Malignant narcissism," Larkin replied. "It provides a sense of superiority, of purpose."

"Yeah. And these taunts have a long history of turning into threats," Connor warned. "Against police officers, or against the public. How many photographs have you found so far?"

"Seven. But without a full confession from the perpetrator, it's impossible to say how many children have been killed between '85 and now. We have no bodies, no names. The database at the National Center for Missing and Exploited Children isn't helpful when the circumstances surrounding the disappearances were children running away of their own volition. And since he kills to essentially *fill requests*, victimology is problematic at best." Larkin continued, "Sir, when taking into account the Psychopathy Checklist, the array of possible serial murder motives, and the parasitic relation serial killers have with the media, this perpetrator is all over the map. For thirty-five years, this man known as Archie has been undoubtably using charm, manipulation, and intimidation tactics to satisfy his selfish desires. His interpersonal traits would suggest a grandiose sense of self-worth, and the way that Gary Reynold described him, Archie is *the* go-to man of this sexually deviant community. That would correlate with the lifestyle trait too, of attention-seeking—being the man all these scumbags look up to—"

"Attention-seeking is exactly my point," Connor interrupted. He held up the folded fax. "He's escalating."

"No, no, no. He's survived and thrived for thirty-five years. His affective traits would suggest no remorse, no guilt, but specifically, failure to accept responsibility. He wouldn't just…." Larkin struggled a moment to make sense of his thoughts, to put them in the right order. "By challenging me, he's admitting to murder. A lot of murder. Why would he do that. It's a red flag in the personality makeup of this man."

"Then what are you suggesting?" Connor countered.

"I don't know. There's something missing. *I've* missed something."

"You're a Cold Case detective," Connor said. "Not a behavioral analyst."

"But we can't ignore *who* Archie is," Larkin said, his voice rising, catching the interest of other detectives.

Larkin's desk phone began to ring.

"Your focus is the Garcia boy," Connor said. "And to find out what the fuck is going on with the DB from the subway. Don't get lost in all the FBI mumbo jumbo, Grim."

"The Psychopathy Checklist was an assessment tool designed by Dr. Hare, not the FBI."

Connor frowned. "Don't try to get the last word with me. I'm going to make some calls about this fax and run down the sender." He pointed to the still-ringing phone. "You answer your damn phone."

Larkin clenched his jaw, waited until Connor started for his office, then blindly grabbed the receiver. "What," he snapped.

"Uh... It's Millett with CSU. Is this a bad time?"

"Every time is a bad time," Larkin muttered.

"Aren't you chipper in the morning."

"What do you want."

"I think it's more what you want," Millett replied. "I got the test results back on Gary Reynold's belts that were taken into evidence. No joy. Only DNA found belonged to Gary Reynold. I went the extra step for you too, and asked the ME to compare them to the wound track on your DB in the IKEA bag—also not a match."

"So Gary Reynold didn't kill out of some sort of panicked, self-preservation."

"If he did, he tossed the evidence," Millett said. "Which is your problem, not mine."

"Your commitment to justice has been noted."

"Hey. Did *you* study physics and biochemistry and then take an unpaid internship position with the state police up in goddamn *Albany* just to get hands-on lab experience so you could spend your best years climbing into a manhole, waist-deep with rainwater runoff, motor oil, piss, used condoms, and more than one rat carcass?"

"No," Larkin said simply.

"Then shut up," Millett concluded.

"Thank you for your... informative call, Detective," Larkin said after a beat. He began to pull the phone away from his ear, then stopped. "Millett."

"Yeah?"

"On Monday, March 30, you asked if I was acquainted with Detective Doyle and suggested I speak with him regarding the death mask found in Madison Square Park."

"Uh, sure, that sounds right."

"Why."

"Why...?"

"Why did you immediately suggest Doyle."

"Because he's a forensic artist."

"Yes, he is. But how did you know Doyle would have such particular insight and knowledge into an obscure art form and no-longer-practiced mourning ritual."

"I've technically met him once before, prior to him joining the force. An ex of mine—let's just say they're into some of the more eclectic moments in history—runs an antique store, and one of my first times visiting the shop, Doyle was there. I don't think he remembers me from back then. It was nearly... seven years ago?"

"I don't see the correlation."

"Doyle was a museum curator. My ex was looking for direction regarding… what the hell was it… jet buttons or brooches or something equally not-interesting. Anyway. Doyle's quiet but he's hard to forget. A few years later, I was down at 1PP, for a meeting, I think, and I bumped into him. He'd just gotten promoted to detective and placed in the Forensic Artists Unit."

Hesitantly, because Larkin had the distinct and wholly accurate account of Doyle saying he'd once had lofty aspirations of a museum job, not that he did, in fact, have a museum job on his resumé, he asked, "Which museum?"

Millett hummed under his breath for a moment. "New York's Gilded Age Home of Art and Antiquities."

CHAPTER SIXTEEN

Ira Doyle had been a mystery all this time.

That's what Larkin thought as he stared at the museum's business page on Google. New York's Gilded Age Home of Art and Antiquities, the preserved nineteenth-century home of a well-to-do family, now open for educational tours, had a museum next door that specialized in local history, with a particular emphasis on the Gilded Age. Located on East Fourth, between Lafayette Street and Broadway, the museum was open Tuesday through Sunday, 10:00 a.m. to 5:00 p.m. Tickets could be purchased for the home, museum, or both—at a discount.

Doyle hadn't ever mentioned how many years he'd been a police officer, but then again, Larkin had never asked. He had assumed it was a career path Doyle chose relatively soon after grad school, when taking his choice of words into consideration.

Had Larkin been wrong?

Again?

It appeared so.

Larkin picked up the phone, dialed the museum's number,

and listened to it ring three times before a snooty-sounding older man answered. On impulse, Larkin lied. "My name is Everett Larkin. I'm a detective with the NYPD's Cold Case Squad. I'm doing some research in relation to a case and was told I might be able to speak with someone knowledgeable on postmortem photography."

The man said, "I do believe this is a first for us, here at the Gilded Age Home. We receive inquiries from all over the country about this and that, but in all my years as museum director, I can't ever remember the *police* making inquiries about our exhibits."

"Yes. Well. And your name is."

"Marcus Webster, sir."

"Mr. Webster, is there someone I can speak with."

"You can speak with me," Webster retorted in a hoity-toity tone of voice. "Although…." He faltered a moment. "I will admit, my knowledge is a bit on the general side. Damn. Of all times for such an inquiry…."

"Meaning," Larkin asked.

"Oh, it's nothing," Webster said automatically, but like someone who was going to explain exactly what they meant, regardless. "It's only, we had a curator who was fabulous, absolutely fabulous, with regard to some of the more, how shall I say this… *taboo* subjects in history. I'd suggest you speak with him, to be quite honest. But he's no longer with us at the museum."

"Does he have a name."

Webster laughed condescendingly. "Yes."

"I'm working a homicide, Mr. Webster," Larkin reminded. "My time and patience are both limited."

"Er, well, I don't have his contact information."

"I'm certain I can find it."

Webster made a sort of *harumph* sound, then said, "Mr. Ira

Doyle. That's I-R-A. Like I said, he did remarkable work over the years. Some of our most visited exhibits: Homosexuality in Gilded Age New York, Victorian sex and pornography—that was a very popular ticket as you might well imagine—and nineteenth-century death culture, which is why his name immediately sprang to mind." Webster sighed before adding, with what sounded to be authenticity, "We do miss him."

Before Larkin could even feel the question out, consider whether he wanted to know, *should* know, he asked, "Why is Mr. Doyle no longer an employee."

"Ah… he had a death in the family. The rest is… personal, I'm afraid."

"But you didn't hire him back."

"Pardon?"

Larkin's grip on the receiver tightened. He said in a clipped tone, "Mr. Doyle experienced a tragedy that is simply unfathomable to most in today's society, and your response to his needing time to cope with loss and subsequent grief was to fire him."

Webster blustered, "E-excuse me, *sir*, but we did not *fire* Mr. Doyle."

"No. Perhaps it all came down to your unwillingness to provide a paid leave of absence. Is that it. Maybe you firmly suggested he resign so that you might save face. You would not speak of your most skilled curator in the past tense otherwise." Larkin could feel his anger growing, unfurling, blossoming. "Thank you for your time, Mr. Webster." He slammed the phone down, turned away from his desktop in the computer chair, and leaned over on his knees. Larkin closed his eyes, pressed the heel of his hand against his forehead, and allowed himself to release pent-up rage through chest-heaving breaths.

They had told Larkin to shut up because people didn't want to know.

But Doyle?

They hadn't ever even listened to begin with.

"Larkin?"

Larkin raised his head and spun around. Doyle stood at the second-floor landing, the strap of his portfolio bag across his chest, a hesitant smile on his face. Larkin got to his feet, collected his suit coat from the back of his chair, and said, his voice almost steady, "Let's get a cup of coffee."

It was 10:14 a.m. and Larkin sat in a café named Coffee two blocks from his precinct. Technically, the business's official name was Sue's Coffee, but the "Sue" portion of the sign had apparently been damaged by scaffolding and the owner never replaced it, leading to the neighborhood's gentle shift from "Want to go to Sue's?" to "Want to go to Coffee?" over the decade that followed.

As far as sit-down establishments went, Coffee was one of the few locations that Larkin actually enjoyed and wasn't overwhelmed by. It was located in the basement level and patrons had to take stairs down from the street. It was extremely small, but without a sense of claustrophobia. The brick walls had been painted white, and funky but unassuming artwork hung from nails. The overhead lighting was warm and a mellow yellow. The speakers were always on, tuned to the kings and queens of blues and jazz, but the music was quiet, so one didn't feel like they were competing to be heard. What Larkin liked most about Coffee was the fact that they only had five seats—one barstool at the window, two single tables on the right, and one on the left just big enough for two.

Larkin studied Doyle as he placed their order at the counter. He wasn't above staring when it came to those shoulders, that trim waist, and an ass so fine even God would've said, "*Damn*." Doyle paid for the coffees, said something that made the girl behind the counter laugh and blush and probably fall in love that very second, then joined Larkin.

Doyle set two lattes on the table. His had a foam heart design on top. Larkin's was a tulip in theory, but in practice it looked more like a lumpy penis. Doyle sat before saying, "You look a little stressed-out."

"I'm always stressed-out."

"Do you need a Xanax?" Doyle shifted, putting a hand to his pocket for the daily pill box.

Larkin shook his head. He stared at the wall beside him, the rough edges, dips, and cracks in the painted brick for one, two, five seconds. He looked back at Doyle. "Yes."

Doyle retrieved the little box without comment, popped the top, and removed one of two pills. He set it into Larkin's extended hand before returning the box to his pocket.

Larkin dry-swallowed the Xanax.

"Evie?"

"I have to tell you something, but you're going to get angry with me and I don't want to carry that memory around."

"I'm not going to get angry," Doyle replied, his voice that ever-smooth and smoky heat.

"Yes, you will."

Doyle leaned forward, closing whatever distance between them that the table had provided. "Is it important that I know?"

Larkin nodded.

"Then if it's important, I can't be angry."

That made a certain amount of sense, and Doyle was, if anything, polar opposite of Noah when it came to action and reaction. But Larkin had been bruised and battered enough times, could dredge up any number of incidents where telling Noah something he had felt was important to their relationship ended up becoming an unforgettable association of humiliation or frustration, and Larkin was so afraid he was the common factor and that this—with Doyle—would turn out no different.

Doyle touched Larkin's wrist, gave the hair tie a few tugs.

"On April 1, while I was waiting to go into surgery, a letter was dropped off at the hospital."

"What kind of letter?"

Larkin retrieved his phone, opened his email, and spent a moment scrolling before he located the correspondence from the Bronx detectives who'd been assigned the case. They had provided a photo of the cut-and-pasted letters for Larkin's own record, as well as an update, which basically said they had jack shit to go on and to simply stay safe and vigilant. He offered Doyle the phone.

Doyle accepted, studied the body of the email, the attached photo, his thick brows drawing together. He'd finished after a full minute—he must have, since the email was brief and Doyle was a relatively fast reader—but he hadn't looked up from the screen.

Larkin tilted his head, caught the absent flicker of Doyle's eyes roaming the screen, staring right through it, as he must have been considering what to say. Larkin felt like he was going to be sick. He stood up.

Without looking, Doyle reached a hand out, not touching Larkin's arm, but hovering very close to it. "Please sit."

Larkin slowly sank back into the chair. He rubbed his sweaty palms against his trouser legs. "Don't yell."

At that, Doyle looked up. "I will never raise my voice to you. Okay?"

"Okay."

Doyle pushed the phone across the tabletop. It bumped Larkin's latte and coffee sloshed over the rim. "Why didn't you tell me about this? Why didn't you tell me yesterday, when I *asked* if there was something more going on?"

Larkin turned off the screen before pocketing the cell. He absently drew his index finger back and forth through the spilled coffee. "I didn't know how. At first I—I didn't have the spoons to even think about it. Then the boys in the Bronx had no leads. And seeing as I was unable to make sense of its meaning, I suppose I didn't want to… worry you unduly."

Doyle sighed. He leaned back in his chair, crossed his arms, and stretched his long legs out to the side of Larkin's seat. "But you know it's related to these cases we're working now. I mean—right? That subway token?"

Larkin nodded. He tugged a napkin free from the dispenser and sopped up the sticky mess. "In the beginning, I believed it to be a direct message from Marco's killer."

"Maybe from Archie?"

"Yes."

"So we're considering that pig responsible for everything?"

"It makes the most sense. I believe that on the night of May 19, 1997, Marco saw something, and he was murdered to keep it secret. I believe what he saw involved Archie and these children." Larkin finally looked up. Doyle didn't seem… angry, per se, but he was definitely tense, despite the boneless way he had of sitting. "I'm now uncertain that the April Fools' letter is actually from our perpetrator."

"Why?" Doyle asked warily.

So Larkin told him.

Amid the somber and raw genius of Bessie Smith on the overhead speakers, the steam and frothing milk at the cappuccino machine behind the counter, and the quiet *click, click, click* of the single other patron typing on their laptop, Larkin told Doyle about the fax. He told Doyle about its anonymity, its veiled threat against their careers, the usage of police department lingo, and how, short of a professional handwriting analyst to confirm his claim, Larkin believed the sender to be the same individual who'd scribbled on the back of the first postmortem photograph.

Doyle was leaning forward again, elbow on the tabletop, hand rubbing his ever-present stubble. He asked, when Larkin had finished, "What did your lieutenant say?"

"A lot of things."

"About the fax—*us*."

Larkin answered, "Lieutenant Connor is a decent man who is also very aware of what a discrimination lawsuit would entail for the department."

"You're brutal," Doyle said with a hint of amusement.

"Thank you."

Doyle picked up his mug and took a sip of the cooled-down coffee. He licked foam from his lips before saying, "Look, Evie… I'm not happy you hid this."

"I didn't hide it."

"You did. Because you had an opportunity to explain it all yesterday, and you chose not to. That being said, I understand your thought process as to why. I'm still not happy, but I get it. But going forward, can we just… *not*? We have to be a team from the onset or this won't work."

"Out-in-the-field, rule four: Always tell the truth."

"I think it's rule five."

"The driving one doesn't count."

Doyle took another sip of the latte. "Have you considered two perps?"

"What."

Doyle shrugged. "You're trying to assign these correspondences to Archie, but by your own assessment, they don't fit into his personality. Connor might see it as escalation, and maybe, if Archie was relatively new at this kill-and-photograph initiative, but he's not. That first photo you obtained is from the '80s. He's been doing this as long as *you've* been alive. It doesn't make sense, purely from a survival point of view, that he'd suddenly take chances like reaching out to you—by name—*three* times. One of which was before Regmore's arrest even hit the evening news. How'd he know who you were?"

"I don't know."

"It sounds like two conflicting behaviors."

Larkin considered this. "If that was the case, what is the end goal of the individual behind the correspondence. To put me on the path of arresting Marco's killer, or to harass me."

"I have no idea," Doyle answered. "Any logic behind the motive is lost to me, but it'd explain the inherent dichotomy seen in both cases and the available clues."

"You're very smart," Larkin murmured, almost absently, as he turned the concept over in his mind.

"I know."

Larkin looked at Doyle a second time. He was sporting that trademark smile. And maybe it was the Xanax kicking in, but he asked suddenly, "Why didn't you tell me you used to curate exhibits on death culture."

Doyle's expression skittered and dropped like a skipping stone succumbing to gravity. "What?"

"I called the Gilded Age Home," Larkin said.

Doyle stared for a long minute before scrubbing his face with both hands.

"Your inability to fold and put away clean laundry notwithstanding, you're nothing short of perfect, Ira. But sometimes I also feel like you're a complete mystery. I asked Neil Millett with CSU why he'd recommended you by name in March. He said he'd first met you when you worked at the museum."

"Jesus," Doyle muttered under his breath, shaking his head.

"I'm sorry," Larkin said. "I didn't mean to pry. Not—not entirely."

"I didn't mention it because it was a long time ago and the museum and I didn't part ways on the best terms."

"Because of Abigail."

Doyle looked like he'd aged a decade in a matter of seconds. He said, "Because I'm a recovering alcoholic, Evie. I made some really bad decisions, and they cost me."

Larkin blinked.

Doyle's self-admission of having abused gin.

His religious zeal when it came to maintaining an exercise routine.

His insistence on remaining busy even in his downtime.

The ever-constant, alcohol-free home.

Doyle pinched the bridge of his nose. "I'm six years sober. I should have told you sooner."

"There isn't a rulebook in place for these sorts of conversations," Larkin said, as gently as he could manage. He reached, awkwardly took Doyle's free hand, and gave it a quick squeeze while hoping his default of touch aversion wasn't painfully obvious at that moment. Because Doyle needed comfort, and Doyle's love language was touch.

Doyle returned the squeeze, and there was a certain amount of fear in his expression as he lowered his hand from his face. So much of Doyle's life was being dredged up that he was clearly struggling with those long-buried truths now being laid out in the sun for even Larkin—*especially Larkin*—to see. "I hope this hasn't changed the opinion you had of me."

Larkin said, simply, "Never."

"So the murder weapon wasn't a belt either," Doyle said, following Larkin up the stairs to the second floor of Precinct 19.

Larkin had informed Doyle that not only had no DNA been recovered from Reynold's belts, but that none had matched the wound pattern, leaving them with yet another dead end in the ongoing mystery surrounding the body in the tote bag. Upon reaching his desk, Larkin retrieved the autopsy report and accompanying photos belonging to John Doe that he'd printed the day before, and held up one that showed the distinct and consistent pattern around the side of the neck.

"It looks like a belt," he said with only the smallest hint of protest in his tone.

"It'd be a pretty big belt," Doyle said, placing his thumb and index finger to the photo, then mimicking the relative size by placing his fingers to his own neck.

"Wide belts are back in vogue."

"Says who?"

"Fashion," Larkin said with a shrug.

Doyle crossed his arms, still studying the grim autopsy photo. "Maybe that's what it is—some kind of high fashion chain belt. Although then you need to take into consideration the mindset of someone who'd yank off their thousand-dollar Gucci belt to use as a weapon."

"You also make the assumption that someone who wears a thousand-dollar Gucci belt would be an active patron of the subway."

"Good point."

But the concept, however flawed, gave Larkin an idea. He looked across the room—Miyamoto's desk was empty. "Stay here," he said to Doyle before walking toward the breakroom. Larkin poked his head around the corner, then stepped inside. "Miyamoto."

She turned from the counter with a start, finger in her mouth as she was in the midst of shoving half a donut in. "*Whu*?" she asked around dough and cream.

"I see you found the donut I left you."

Miyamoto wiped some of the cake batter from the corner of her lips. "Fank yoo," she replied.

Larkin moved toward her, extending the photograph. "You wear an appropriately alternative wardrobe in your off-hours. Do you know of any belts or accessories that would match this wound pattern."

Miyamoto took one look at the photo, groaned around the donut in her mouth, and dropped the other half of the Krispy Kreme confection back into the box Doyle had brought Larkin yesterday. "Thanks for ruining a perfectly intimate moment with fat and carbs and sugar, Larkin."

"You can continue after answering my question."

"The moment's lost." She snatched the picture, giving Larkin a dirty look as she did. Miyamoto shifted her posture, putting her weight on her left leg and jutting a hip out. "Might be a bullet belt."

Larkin cocked his head. "Like a… a bandolier."

Heavy footsteps entered from behind, and Ulmer muttered, as he bullied his way to the fridge Larkin and Miyamoto stood by, "Moto and the Homo." He grabbed the coffee creamer from the top shelf, shut the door, and poured some into a mug from the cupboard.

"Give it a rest, Ulmer," Miyamoto grumbled.

Larkin said, completely straight-faced, "You're much more afraid of us than we are of you. Have you considered standing perfectly still. Perhaps our vision is based on movement."

Miyamoto pointed at Larkin and countered, "I thought

you were supposed to play dead around gays? Lie down on your belly? Spread your legs?"

"That's an open invitation to attack," Larkin corrected.

"Got it, got it. *Oh*! Ulmer, have you tried discharging your guts out your anus? Like a sea cucumber?"

Ulmer slammed his mug down on the counter, turned, and said to Larkin, "I hear you and your artist buddy are butt-fucking."

Larkin didn't react, but asked, in the same monotone, "Have I mistaken a high school locker room for Precinct 19."

Miyamoto asked Larkin, "For real? Did you forget you're married?"

Larkin met her surprise, briefly raised his left hand and tapped his bare ring finger with his thumb, then shoved his hand into his pocket.

"Oh shit, man, I'm sorry," she said.

"I'm not."

"You were busy on medical leave."

"Yes, I try to plan my soul-crushing breakups accordingly."

Miyamoto snorted and shoved Larkin with her elbow.

Larkin looked at Ulmer, who was glowering. "You saw the fax."

"The entire squad uses that machine," he retorted.

Larkin glanced at Miyamoto from the corner of his eye. "It's a bandolier," he asked again.

She seemed to recall herself, returned the autopsy photo, and said, "Not a real one. It's a dummy belt—the bullets can't be fired. Totally harmless and part of the punk aesthetic since forever. Even this new generation of pop-punk fetuses wear them, but kids these days, they've got no clue. They think it's all about *the style*." Miyamoto tapped the side of her head as she said, "Punk is a mentality, not a look. Be yourself and fuck the rest." She left the breakroom.

"Touching," Ulmer said into the quiet.

Larkin stared, unblinking, at Ulmer. "I don't care what you say about me."

"No? Good. I've got plenty to say."

"But if you try to tarnish Doyle's reputation simply due to his general proximity to me, I will take off my badge, and I won't regret what I do in the moment that follows."

"Are you threatening me?"

"Absolutely." Larkin walked to the door.

"Grim."

He turned in the threshold.

"You think you're so goddamn smart."

"I don't think—I know."

Ulmer smiled a nasty, vicious kind of smile. "Moto's dusty pussy will take any attention it can get, even if it's from an uptight prissy fag, and you might have fooled Connor into thinking you walk on water with those mental card tricks you perform, but I know you're teetering. Aren't you? Just one well-timed breakdown away from jumping in front of a bus." He winked. "Good luck, pal."

Larkin hesitated a fraction of a second, then left the room. He strode quickly through the bullpen, conversations, ringing phones, shuffling paper, all of it falling back, further and further until it registered like static found in between radio stations. Larkin ignored Doyle standing to one side and speaking into the desk phone receiver, and opened the top drawer where he kept his office supplies. He reached for an unassuming 2x3 envelope, the sort used for evidence collection at crime scenes, but also for hiding Xanax from his too-vigilant—partner? friend? romantically interested party? *Boyfriend?*

The envelope was empty.

Larkin watched Ulmer sit down at his desk with his

coffee, meet Larkin's stare from across the room, and then begin typing on his computer.

Larkin quietly shut the drawer and put his hands on the desktop.

"Grim!" Connor shouted through his open door.

"What."

"December 27, 2006."

"Wednesday," Larkin answered automatically.

"Thank you," Connor called back.

"Larkin."

"What." Larkin looked up.

Doyle had a hand over the speaker of the phone. "The ME has an ID for John Doe."

CHAPTER SEVENTEEN

John Doe's identity hadn't been that of Creepy Dicky.

Dr. Baxter had been insistent on the matter. "I understand that this composite sketch matches the general description I provided, Detective, but do you know how many white males between the ages of fifty and sixty live in Manhattan?"

"The 2016 census estimates that specific demographic to be a population of a little over 170,000."

"Cool," Baxter remarked, in a tone that suggested he felt Larkin's answer held no particular merit to the conversation. "But of those 170,000 old white guys, this isn't the one you're hoping for. For starters, he's not missing an incisor. And secondly, even with the level of decomp we were dealing with, there'd be evidence of a habitual user. I'm telling you—this guy wasn't homeless, he wasn't an addict, and he took decent care of himself."

"My mood has been steadily going downhill this morning," Larkin warned.

"Yeah? Well, I'm about to turn that frown upside down. Your vic is Alfred Niederman of 189 Elizabeth Street. His prints came back—he did some time in '84 for abusing a corpse in a funeral home."

Larkin had glanced up at Doyle at that point, asking warily into the phone, "What exactly did he do to the corpse."

"He was caught undressing and posing the body."

"Jesus Christ."

"You're welcome," Baxter had answered in a singsong voice before hanging up.

And that was how Larkin and Doyle found themselves on the corner of Elizabeth and Grand at exactly 11:40 a.m. Larkin slapped his permit on the dash. He'd made a clear "no parking zone" a parking spot, as the streets of Chinatown were much smaller and more heavily congested than what was north of Fourteenth Street, and he wasn't in the business of circling the neighborhood until a spot opened up.

"The only online presence for an Alfred Niederman that I can find is an obit for a ninety-four-year-old in Colorado," Doyle began, shutting the passenger door and following Larkin to the sidewalk, all while still scrolling on his phone. "There's also an HVAC repair company owned and operated by an *Alfonso* Niederman in Jersey City, and a single Facebook profile under that name, but no photos or family details. He began studying photography at Parsons School of Design in 1983 and is a fan of *Diners, Drive-Ins, and Dives*. No posting history."

"Photography," Larkin echoed, hands in his pockets as he skirted an overflowing trash can on the corner. Someone had piled household garbage beside it: a CD/cassette boombox missing one detachable speaker, the brush nozzle attachment to a handheld vacuum, and a window AC unit with a note taped to it: *I'm fucked, don't take me home.* "I do not make assumptions, nor jump to conclusions that are unfounded, but what the hell."

"And you know what else," Doyle began, "Niederman working even a brief stint at a funeral parlor could have been enough to obtain some of the education shown in the postmortem photographs. A good mortician knows their mourning history."

"So he went from posing bodies for wakes to posing bodies for pornography. Fantastic."

"Once is chance, twice is coincidence, three time's a pattern," Doyle answered.

Larkin glanced up. "It's funny. Sometimes I think you read my mind."

"Wouldn't that be something? I'll bet it's full of daydreams not suitable for all ages. Me, naked, with a pocket square on my crotch—for propriety's sake—lying on a bed of DD5 forms with a sultry, come-hither expression."

Larkin stopped walking.

Doyle stopped too and turned to look back.

"Have you worn my pocket squares on your crotch. Because these are silk." Larkin put a hand to his breast pocket in emphasis.

"No," Doyle said, a mischievous smile growing to encompass his entire face. "But now you can't stop thinking about it, can you?"

"You're unbelievable."

"Evie, you don't know the half of it."

Larkin was absolutely not blushing as he bullied past Doyle and took point once again. They crossed the street, passing lost tourists traveling in packs three across, produce vendors lined along the sidewalks with handwritten signs in Chinese and piles of fresh lychee, dragon fruit, cherries, apples, and longan set out on makeshift tables, and one poor bastard fighting to get the only available Citi Bike, clearly stuck, released from the dock. They walked by a tea museum, two local pharmacies, a bakery, and one hole-in-the-wall shop still selling knickknacks from Chinese New Year, before coming to a stop outside the unassuming front door of 189.

A Chinese man, maybe in his forties, bald or purposefully shaven, it was difficult to say, wearing chic tea shade glasses, a salmon-colored polo, and khakis, stood to the side of the door. He looked both Larkin and Doyle over before saying, "You must be the cops?"

"Yes, I believe we spoke on the phone," Larkin said, offering his badge before a quick handshake. "Detective Everett Larkin. This is my partner, Ira Doyle."

The man nodded, looked at Doyle as he flashed his own badge, and introduced himself. "Dan Chen. Al was one of the tenants that came when I bought the building… geez… at least ten years ago." He returned his attention to Larkin. "He's really dead?"

"That's correct," Larkin answered. "And you had no reason to be suspicious of his absence."

"You're asking? No. I mean, I'm not friends with my tenants. The only time I really hear from them is if something breaks—which they rarely report anyway—and when the rent's due first of the month. I suppose, if you guys hadn't shown up today, I'd have eventually reported him missing come June when I had no rent check."

"May we see Mr. Niederman's apartment."

"Sure." Dan tapped a code on the door panel and the locks buzzed open.

Larkin and Doyle followed Dan into the vestibule and up the stairs.

Doyle asked, bringing up the rear, "Did Mr. Niederman live alone?"

"Yup," Dan called over the creaking of the stairs. "Pretty sure he was a confirmed bachelor."

"Mr. Niederman was homosexual," Larkin asked.

Dan stopped at the landing of the second floor and turned

to look down at the two still on the stairs. "What? No, no. I meant, like, literally. Al was definitely into women. I've had enough casual conversations with him over the years to know that much. But he was… kind of socially awkward, you know? I guess he never found the right socially awkward lady to play house with." He motioned them to follow him to the end of the hall. Dan removed a set of keys from his pocket, unlocked the door to 2D, and pushed it open.

Larkin took out a pair of latex gloves from his pocket, with Doyle doing the same, and said, "If you will remain in the hall, Mr. Chen."

Dan blinked owlishly, glanced into the apartment, then back to Larkin. "Is it a crime scene or something?"

"Mr. Niederman's death is being investigated as a homicide. Everything is a potential clue." Larkin stepped into the studio.

Upon first glance, the apartment was incredibly unassuming—bland, even. There was little, if no, personality, polar opposite when compared to the *home* Doyle had turned his own studio into. There was an antique range and fridge to Larkin's right, a generic storebought rack with various pots and pans stacked on its shelves, with a sink and counter just large enough for a coffee pot on the left. A shower curtain and bath mat were visible beyond the sink, and Larkin glanced into the nook to confirm, yes, the shower was in the kitchen. A window stood across from it with a view of the second-floor apartments of the building on the opposite side of Elizabeth Street, where tenants had likely been subjected to a wet and naked Niederman, fresh from the shower, on more than one occasion. Around the corner was a twin-sized bed, neatly made, a floor lamp and oscillating fan, both turned off, and a half-full garment rack pushed against the wall.

"Nothing like exfoliating in the same room you brew your morning joe," Doyle said at Larkin's back.

Dan replied from the doorway, "It's an old building."

"How much was Niederman paying?" Doyle asked.

"Eighteen hundred a month."

"What did he do for a living?"

"He worked for one of those janitorial cleaning services," Dan said. "The sort that clean the big Midtown offices after hours."

"And he had no problem making rent?" Doyle asked.

"He was never late," Dan confirmed, a shrug in his voice.

Larkin tuned out after he heard Doyle ask about obtaining any employment information Dan might have had. He didn't have to babysit his partner—Doyle was a competent investigator. Crouching beside the garment rack, Larkin picked up a pair of brand-new, heavy-duty, black rubber-soled shoes with orthotic inserts—the exact sort of shoe he expected someone who was on their feet all day to own. Larkin put the pair back where he found them. There was a distinct empty spot between the new shoes and a pair of beaten-up sneakers, where a third pair of shoes should have been. He stood and carefully shifted the hangers, noting several pairs of polyester-blend black trousers, the same V-neck shirt in four different shades of gray, and half a dozen industrial uniforms toward the end. Larkin removed a hanger and studied the bright blue shirt with a logo in the shape of a mop and bucket and the company name embroidered underneath: Shine & Sparkle Cleaning.

"Shine and Sparkle Cleaning," Larkin called from the bedroom area.

Doyle appeared around the corner.

Larkin held up the shirt. "This explains why he'd been partially undressed." He returned the uniform to the rack and pointed to the floor. "Missing shoes."

Doyle removed his cell from his pocket and started

typing. He put it to his ear a moment later and said, "May I speak with Alfred Niederman's manager? Yes, you can tell her that Detective Ira Doyle, with the NYPD, is on the phone."

Larkin stared at the strip plug on the floor that both the fan and lamp were using. There was a third cable plugged in as well, but it went in the opposite direction, disappearing around the far side of the bed. Larkin followed it, finding it attached to a black modem on the floor. A router was plugged into the top socket in the wall outlet beside it. Larkin took a second inventory of the bedroom, but it was as sparse as a military barrack.

Doyle lowered the phone from his mouth and asked quietly, "What're you looking for?"

"There's a Wi-Fi setup and it's on," Larkin explained. "Where's Niederman's computer, tablet, smartphone."

Doyle raised his brows and turned in a slow circle.

Larkin brushed past him, stopped, and stared at the door beside the shower. He'd missed it entirely upon first inspection, due to the curious angle of the studio layout and the fact that the door had no trim and was painted the same off-white as the walls. "What's this door," he asked.

Dan said, still standing in the threshold, "Toilet."

"Why is there a padlock on it."

"Come again?"

Larkin tugged on the lock in question. Generic store-brand hardware. "Doyle."

"I'm on the phone."

"I need you to break into another lock."

"Can I put you on hold for a moment? Thank you." Doyle tapped the phone's screen and then approached Larkin. "I'm on the phone," he said again.

Larkin tugged on the lock as he met Doyle's eyes.

"Do you know how much more difficult it is to pick a padlock?"

"You're very capable."

"Thank you." Doyle looked over Larkin's shoulder and toward Dan. "Do you have bolt cutters in the building?"

Dan studied the two curiously but nodded. "Got some tools in the basement. Give me a second."

Doyle glanced at Larkin after Dan's steps receded into the stairwell. "I don't carry extra paperclips on me."

"I'm mildly disappointed."

"You get a thrill out of me breaking the law?"

"It's not breaking the law when you have explicit permission," Larkin corrected. He asked, as Doyle started to raise his phone, "Can you break out of handcuffs."

At that, Doyle leaned forward and braced one gloved hand on his thigh as he let out a breathy laugh. "In this situation, did *you* put me in the handcuffs? Because if that's the case, why would I *want* to break free?"

Larkin turned toward the open door so Doyle couldn't see his smile.

Dan Chen returned approximately four minutes later, slightly out of breath but wielding bolt cutters, just as Doyle wrapped up a conversation with Martha Russell, Niederman's manager at Shine & Sparkle.

"She's emailing me his full employment history and his calendar for the last thirty days," Doyle explained, pocketing the phone. "Apparently he's worked for them the better part of twenty years and a lot of businesses have come and gone in that time."

"Terrific," Larkin muttered, taking the bolt cutters from Dan. "Any of note."

"Lots of mom-and-pop and drugstores, but he's been mostly relegated to offices the last decade."

"Mom-and-pop, as well as drugstores, could explain his early access to photo minilabs." Larkin got the blades around the shackle of the lock and pressed down hard. It took another attempt and a few seconds more than Larkin would have liked in front of an audience, but the case-hardened steel finally snapped in two. He handed Doyle the cutters.

"Aren't you butch," Doyle said quietly.

Larkin worked the broken lock free and opened the door. The room was barely big enough for the toilet that it housed—let alone a person in need of it. Larkin flicked the light switch. Nothing. He held up his cell, the flashlight app illuminating the DIY darkroom Niederman had constructed around the toilet: walls painted black, shelving installed overhead, a sort of impromptu table that, once standing inside the room, could be extended from the wall, jugs of chemical developers shoved behind the toilet, and a hanging rack with strips of dried negatives, now curled, still tacked and waiting for his return. The silver case of Niederman's MacBook gleamed from a shelf as Larkin passed the light over it.

"And this might explain the lack of lab-printed data on the backs of some of the more recent photos," Larkin muttered. He stepped into the cramped space and asked, "How long should film be hung for."

"No more than a day," Doyle answered. "It definitely shouldn't be stored like this—you get those permanent curls in the film."

Larkin gently lifted one of the negatives, held it against the white of his latex glove, and shined light on it. He didn't even need details for the murky image to make sense. The geometry of the photograph was enough. "Dead children."

Doyle swore under his breath.

"He developed these before going on the hunt again," Larkin theorized. "He stood here on Sunday, May 10, and developed two rolls of film—twenty-seven photos each of two more dead and posed children—then he hung the rolls to dry, shut the door, and walked to Second Avenue to catch the F in the evening hours. He got off at Fifty-Seventh Street. He's hunting for Reynold's fourteen-year-old redhead. Something goes wrong. He's found dead nine days later, with evidence of an unknown person of interest requesting my presence on the case." Larkin lowered his phone and turned to stare at Doyle. "Archie Bunker, aka Alfred Niederman, has been supplementing his income since the '80s by selling pornographic and necrophilic images to a closeknit community of sexual predators. He murdered these children." Larkin furrowed his brow and asked, "So who murdered Alfred Niederman?"

CHAPTER EIGHTEEN

There was a parking ticket under the windshield wiper of the Audi.

Larkin grabbed it before sliding behind the wheel. He crumpled the orange notification and tossed it into the backseat.

Doyle glanced over his shoulder from the passenger seat before saying, "I think you have to pay that."

Larkin turned the ignition, but didn't move to take the car out of Park. He stared out the front, saying, "The one viable suspect we had in Marco's murder, the only person who could potentially provide the truth of the matter, has been dead himself this entire investigation."

"Maybe."

"That wasn't a statement open to further discussion. Alfred Niederman killed Marco Garcia. Marco worked with at-risk youth. He walked them to the Fifty-Seventh Street station every night. Marco somehow came into possession of Johnny Doe's death portrait a week before his murder, which means he knew something of what was going on. Marco was aware of and suspicious of someone or something the night of May 19, 1997, or he wouldn't have gone down to the platform. Niederman was hunting. Niederman killed Marco for catching him in the act."

"It's extremely plausible," Doyle answered, slow and even. "But without evidence or sworn testimony—"

"Marco's been dead for twenty-three fucking years," Larkin snapped. He turned the ignition off and looked at Doyle. "What am I supposed to tell his mother. 'I know you were desperate for some kind of closure, some sort of reprieve, but there will be no justice, no peace, no silence. I let you down. I told you I wouldn't, but I did. And now, if you'll excuse me, the department wants to pin another goddamn medal on my uniform.'"

"You're not going to say any of that," Doyle replied. "Because you're not done working this case. We still have multiple avenues of investigation to explore."

Larkin shook his head.

"Yes, we do," Doyle insisted. "CSU's taken Niederman's computer into evidence and they're going to pore through it. Don't forget that he had a business card for St. Jude's Mission in his pocket and Reynold claimed Dicky was a frequent guest of the church's meal program. We've also got the MTA staff who—what? What's wrong?"

Larkin had his head on the steering wheel. "I need a Xanax."

"You had one a few hours ago."

Larkin gripped the wheel.

Doyle put a hand between Larkin's shoulder blades and gently rubbed up and down. "I know you're upset. I am too. I'm trying really, really hard to not be happy this guy's dead."

"It's not that. Not only that," Larkin whispered. "I want to be high so badly, I feel like all my seams are unraveling and I'm splitting in two and I'm going to fucking die. What the fuck is the point in taking antianxiety medication if all it does is give me crippling anxiety when I'm not high as a goddamn kite." Larkin sniffed and wiped his face. "I can't think, I can't *function*, without medication. But it's—like—" He took a strangled breath, forehead still pressed to the steering wheel. "I have to pick between feeling too much or feeling nothing at all and I hate it."

Doyle's hand moved to Larkin's shoulder and forced him to sit back. "Take a deep breath. Another one. Evie, I can't and won't ever know what living with your level of HSAM is like. Honestly, I can barely fathom it. But the fact that you're trying to find ways to make it work says an awful lot about your unwillingness to give up. Xanax is the wrong course of treatment for you. Okay? It's that simple. And coming down from an addiction is really hard. That much I *do* know." He curled his hand around Larkin's nape and gave a gentle squeeze. "But I'm going to help you, and we're going to get you on the right meds so you stop feeling like this."

"Like what."

Doyle considered for a moment and then suggested, "Hollow."

Larkin swallowed that dose of bitter reality and it hurt like hell. He reached for the center console, opened it, lifted the false bottom, and retrieved the 2x3 envelope. He put it in Doyle's hand, closed the console, and stared out the front windshield again. He listened to Doyle open the envelope.

"Okay" was all Doyle said.

Larkin glanced sideways when he heard the distinct shake and slide of a pill falling free. "What're you doing."

"I'm giving you one. You've been taking so much for so long that part of your anxiety right now is actually withdrawal symptoms." Doyle offered it. "You can't cold turkey this medication. So take it, and tonight, once you're home, call Dr. Meyers and talk to her about tapering off your prescription."

Larkin took the Xanax with a shaky hand and dry-swallowed it. "You could've had the whole world."

"I don't want the world. I want you."

"But I don't deserve you," Larkin murmured.

Doyle leaned back in his own seat. "Believe me, I'm the lucky one."

"How can you say that with a straight face."

Doyle met Larkin's stare. "The poor kid with no dad, an absent mom, who spent most of his childhood in more trouble than not?"

"Look at you now."

"*Yeah...* I lost my daughter and became an alcoholic," Doyle stated without any sort of inflection, but the pyrite in his eyes burned bright. He reached for Larkin's hand. "I feel like I've gotten a second chance with one of the smartest men I've ever met. And the kindest. And the gentlest. With a wicked sense of humor that he pretends to not have and who's so handsome that he takes my breath away when he walks into a room. How could I *not* be lucky?"

Larkin felt guilty that Doyle's admission of—call it what it was, for God's sake—of love made him immediately think of Noah, but his poor, abused brain couldn't help but compare and contrast situations, people, relationships, as a means of self-preservation, and Larkin could not pull up a single moment in his Rolodex where Noah's words made him feel happy.

Like *this*.

Like he was at the bottom of that deep, dark hole and *finally* looked up.

It was jubilance up to heaven.

And it was incredible.

"Sometimes you make my brain turn off," Larkin said. "No one has ever made me feel that sense of... clarity. And I can focus on just one thought, and it's always, you are such a good man."

Doyle whispered, "I really want to kiss you."

Larkin leaned over the center, grabbed Doyle by the back of his head, and brought their mouths together. Doyle made a sound that began in surprise and ended in pleasure. He tasted warm and a little sweet and citrusy, like sunshine and lemon candy. His soft lips were at delightful odds with the scrape of his whiskers, and the way Doyle melted into the seat, encouraging and relishing in the control Larkin asserted, that was icing atop an already-perfect cake.

Larkin broke the kiss first, and he drew the tip of his tongue over Doyle's mouth before pulling back.

Doyle stared at him, his chest rising and falling out of sync. "You have permission to kiss me like that, literally, whenever you want. I'm talking Mets at the World Series, bases loaded at the bottom of the ninth, and if you want to kiss me, I've already forgotten what baseball is."

Larkin smiled.

Doyle gave the hair tie around Larkin's wrist a tug.

"Yeah," he answered, before starting the engine.

It was 1:22 p.m. when Larkin parked on the corner of Sixty-Second and Lexington. St. Jude's Church was a gothic revival structure heralding from 1842, with original stone walls, a seventy-foot spire, and later incorporated Tiffany stained glass—all information that Larkin possessed because he'd been married here on Saturday, March 12, 2016, and prior to reserving space for the ceremony, he and Noah had been given an *expansive* and *passionate* tour by the building manager.

Larkin shut the driver's side door before he pointed to a

newer addition built toward the rear of the church. "That's the community hall where they hold meal services." He pocketed his keys before adding stiffly, "I was married here."

Doyle met his gaze. "Really?"

"'Til death do us part."

Larkin said, "They're welcoming of LGBT, and it was a concession to my in-laws, who'd have no part in their son's marriage if it didn't take place in a church."

The afternoon sun bore down overhead as they crossed the street. It was nothing like the oppressive heat that made a steel-and-concrete jungle absolutely unbearable during the months of July and August, but it was enough to remind Larkin he was very fair-skinned and hadn't ever known a tan. He passed the church proper and led the way to the front doors of the community hall. To the left was a wall-mounted sign that displayed a welcome message, a relatable Bible verse, and the days and times the kitchen was open to those in need. Larkin grabbed the handle, pulled the door open, and motioned Doyle to step inside.

The hall was brightly lit with fluorescent overheads and full of foldable round tables that reminded Larkin of high school cafeterias, although these were covered with blue dining cloths. The room was still busy with guests of nearly every age and ethnicity: single mothers with children too young for school; the elderly in sweaters and light coats, despite the warm summer day; a table of troublemaking-looking teenagers wearing an abundance of torn jeans and black, their alternative hair likely styled with office supplies versus costly product, as well as a table of men who'd isolated themselves from the rest of the crowd—Larkin suspected they were the ones who spent actual nights on the street. A buffet on the left side of the hall was staffed by several individuals wearing aprons and hairnets, dishing out a lunch of baked chicken and rice, a side of mixed vegetables, and fresh fruit—Bosc pears, by the looks of them. The commotion of dozens of conversations—English, Spanish, Chinese, Urdu, and Larkin was pretty sure he picked up some Greek and Polish too—seemed to vibrate the room, but the second dose of Xanax was keeping the noise to a manageable level.

Barely, anyway.

Larkin headed toward the buffet and said to an older woman with graying locs, "I'm looking for whoever might be in charge."

She pushed a pair of glasses up the bridge of her nose with a knuckle. "And who might you be?"

Larkin retrieved his badge and quickly, discreetly, flashed his identification, as he didn't want to unsettle any of the guests by his presence. "Detective Everett Larkin, Cold Case Squad."

The woman shared a slightly suspicious look with the tall, gangly man at her side who'd been serving rice, and then she pointed a gloved hand across the dining hall and said, "Noel Hernandez is the operations manager for the kitchen."

Larkin turned on his heel and looked in the direction she pointed just as the man in question, who appeared to be making the rounds and checking on some of the seniors scattered throughout the hall, glanced their direction. From the corner of Larkin's eye, the woman was waving Hernandez over, which he acknowledged and began to weave through the tables toward them.

Noel Hernandez was Larkin's age and roughly the same height and build. His dark brown, almost black hair was styled in an edgy undercut, and he wore his facial hair in a short, well-groomed boxed beard. Hernandez had on a pair of gray trousers and an almost saffron-colored button-down— no tie. "Welcome to St. Jude's Mission," he said with a big smile. "Can I help you gentlemen?"

Larkin once again removed his badge. "Detective Everett Larkin, Cold Case Squad. My partner, Ira Doyle. May we speak with you somewhere private."

"What's this about?"

"If we can take this elsewhere," Larkin said again.

"Sure… okay." His tone was still polite, despite his obvious confusion.

Hernandez led the way through a pair of swinging doors and into a kitchen that smelled overwhelmingly like the canned mixed vegetables being served, grease, and dish soap. On Larkin's right, an industrial dishwasher roared and a high-powered spray hose competed for attention as a short, chubby man loosened food debris from massive baking sheets. A woman in chef whites was loudly discussing tomorrow's menu with two prep cooks, and on the far left, near a walk-in fridge, a petite woman dropped an armful of pots and pans.

Larkin visibly jumped.

"Somewhere a bit quieter?" Doyle called, touching Larkin's elbow discreetly.

Hernandez headed toward a back door and outside into a narrow alleyway—a gate on the right led to the sidewalk, and the left appeared to access the churchyard. They were shaded by an ancient-looking dogwood, its white flowers still clinging to branches in late May. The kitchen access door closed behind Doyle and the grounds were suddenly still, serene, like the hustle and bustle of the city that'd grown up around St. Jude's couldn't penetrate its invisible force field.

Larkin took a slow breath.

The street gate groaned loudly before slamming shut. All three turned.

"What're you doing, Courtney?" Hernandez asked.

A young woman—maybe a college student volunteering in her free time—startled and squeaked. "Oh! I'm—uh—taking out the trash."

"That's Nate's job," Hernandez replied.

"I was just helping."

"All right. Go help inside, please." He waited until she'd scurried past them and disappeared through the door, before saying, "Another vape break. These kids think just because it tastes like mango, it ain't gonna kill them…. Anyway, what can I help the boys in blue with? You'll have to forgive me, I don't have much time—we serve between five and eight hundred meals a day. We're pretty busy here."

"I understand, Mr. Hernandez," Larkin answered. "How long have you worked for St. Jude's Mission."

He laughed, and it had an airy, carefree sense about it. "Am I under investigation? Our food is donated by neighboring restaurants, stores, and upstate farms. I assure you, we're not stealing our chicken and rice."

"I suspected no such thing," Larkin replied. "I'm merely establishing basic personal information relevant to my interview."

Hernandez gave Larkin a skeptical once-over. "I've been the operations manager for three years. Before that, I worked as a line cook for the kitchen. And before that, prep. Before that? Dishes. St. Jude's is very important to me. I want to return the kindness the church showed me as a boy."

"You were a guest," Larkin asked.

"That's what I said."

Doyle eased into the conversation by saying, "Sometimes it all comes down to that one person who won't look the other way."

The tightness around Hernandez's eyes softened. "Yes, exactly." He uncrossed his arms, the defensiveness of his posture melting away as he tucked his hands into his pockets. "You have some firsthand experience in that, Detective?"

"Couch-surfed for a time," Doyle answered.

"You look like you've done all right for yourself."

"I'm trying." And just like that, Doyle had connected on the intimate human level that Larkin hated, *loathed* most about the job. Doyle had shown his underbelly, his weakness and trauma, so that Larkin didn't have to. So that they didn't lose this interview.

Seizing the opportunity to begin anew, Larkin asked, "Are you familiar with your guests on any personal level."

Hernandez shrugged. "We provide for anyone who walks through our doors. We don't ask their names, their employment status, or where they live. It's dehumanizing—to force someone to prove they need a helping hand. Suffice it to say, lining up outside our doors at noon every day but Sunday is enough of a burden on one's pride." He looked at Doyle before adding, "But I speak with our guests. I ask how they are, how the food is, if there's anything I can grab for them, and after a while, yeah. I know their names. I know how far they travel to sit down and eat here. I know about their two jobs and the one-room apartment and Mamá is feeding her family at St. Jude's this week because it was either groceries or new shoes for the school year."

Doyle looked at Larkin.

It was obvious—painfully so—who Hernandez wished to speak with, so Larkin nodded in suggestion for Doyle to take point.

Doyle asked, "Do you know an individual who might go by the name Dicky?"

Helpfully, Larkin raised his cell phone and showed Hernandez their composite sketch.

Hernandez looked at the screen and nodded. "Sure. I've known Dicky a long time. Since I was a troublemaker myself."

"Does he visit St. Jude's?"

Again, Hernandez nodded. "He does."

"When was the last time you saw him?" Doyle continued.

"I see *a lot* of people, Detective."

"Please do your best to approximate," Larkin interjected.

Hernandez shot him an annoyed look. "I don't know. A week ago? Two weeks? Something like that."

"You don't serve meals on what days," Larkin asked.

"Only Sunday," Hernandez confirmed.

"We're trying to pinpoint the last time Dicky was seen," Doyle explained. "Any details you can provide would be helpful."

"Not this week," Hernandez said. "That I'm confident of." He smoothed his beard a few times, gaze focusing somewhere over Doyle's left shoulder as he thought back. "Come to think of it, maybe not last week either…."

"So prior to the weekend of May 9 and 10," Larkin asked.

"That sounds about right. Dicky doesn't come every day to begin with, so it's not strange to only see him once or twice a week."

"Except it's been thirteen days," Larkin said.

Hernandez frowned at him. "I guess it has been. Is he in trouble?"

"We'd like to speak with him," Doyle answered.

"I can't help you there. Look, I'm trying to be cooperative. What's going on? You said you were Cold Cases?"

"That's correct," Larkin said. "I'm looking into the unsolved murder of Marco Garcia. He was—"

"*Marco?*"

Larkin cocked his head at the swift and sudden change in Hernandez's tone. "That's correct. He was a part-time mentor at the Youth Empowerment Center."

Hernandez motioned in a distracted manner toward the south as he said, "The YEC over on Fifty-Fifth. His poor mother. I had no idea it was still unsolved."

"How was it you came to know Marco?" Doyle asked.

Hernandez quickly wiped his face with the back of his hand. "I was a student at the YEC. From… I can't remember when I started going, but I didn't stay long… before junior high, anyway. Me and my best friend, Jay, we started hanging out there after hearing from some kids on the street that it was pretty chill. They served meals, which is what got us there, honestly. Jay and I liked the gym too, but I remember we were still dumb little shits and the high school boys monopolized that room. One day, we said, 'Fuck, we're already here, let's hang out in the art room. We don't have to do nothing if it's lame.' That's how we met Marco. He was cool, you know? Older than us, but not an 'adult' who wouldn't understand us kids and the kind of shit we dealt with. Real trustworthy."

"Do you know what happened to him?" Doyle pressed.

Hernandez took a deep breath, then licked his lips. "Someone pushed him in front of a train."

Larkin watched Hernandez's face carefully, asking, "Is that before or after you stopped attending the Center."

"I stopped after that. Wasn't the same without Marco and Jay."

Doyle picked up on that before Larkin could open his mouth. "What happened to Jay?"

A stray tear rolled down Hernandez's cheek and into his beard. "Someone killed him, man. He wasn't even thirteen. And then when Marco—all I could think was, I'm next. So I left. Never went back to the YEC."

"What was Jay's last name," Larkin asked, watching from the corner of his eye as Doyle retrieved his notepad. "Was his murder solved."

"Come on. A black boy from the projects? Do you *think* it was solved?" Hernandez shot back.

"No," Larkin admitted. "Probably not."

Hernandez took a big breath, his cheeks puffing as he let the air out. "Last name was Gibson. Joshua Gibson. He always went by Jay. Look, it would have been impossible to solve anyway."

"Why."

"There was no body."

Confused, Doyle asked, "Then how did you know Jay was killed?"

But Larkin looked at his phone again, hastily scrolled through the files and scanned evidence, then pulled up a photograph—the one he'd found wedged in between the pages of *Hamlet*. He turned his phone toward Hernandez and spoke over the two. "Is this Jay Gibson."

Hernandez glanced from Doyle to the phone, and then paled.

Doyle automatically reached for him. "Do you need to sit down?"

"No, I'm—where did you get that?"

"Is this Jay Gibson," Larkin asked a second time.

"Yes, yes, yes. But where did you find that picture?"

"Among Marco's personal effects." Larkin lowered his cell. "You gave Marco that photograph, didn't you. At first, Jay disappeared. And then you found yourself in possession of that picture. When you realized he wasn't asleep, you went to Marco for help. You trusted him. Marco told you he'd take care of it, didn't he."

Hernandez doubled over, his hands on his knees. "*Fucking hell….*"

Doyle patted his shoulder a few times, instructing Hernandez to take deep breaths—in through the nose, out through the mouth.

Larkin squatted down in order to meet Hernandez's torn expression. "How did you get the photograph."

"I found it," he whispered. "Jay'd been gone a few days. His mother didn't have a phone—too expensive—so I couldn't call him. Waited outside his school, outside his building, but he was nowhere. Checked with some of the boys at—" He faltered, backtracked, reworked what he'd been about to admit, "Some other street kids, but they hadn't seen him." Hernandez slowly straightened his posture, although he was still looking decidedly gray. "At the YEC, I didn't want to take any classes that night, so I snuck into the janitor's closet to smoke a joint. There was a windbreaker hanging on the back of the door, so I checked the pockets for cash. Found some developed pictures—remember the paper envelopes they used to come in? They were all of Jay. I freaked. I mean, I lost it. I remember puking into the mop bucket. I took one of the pictures and I found Marco and I told him. I told him everything I knew, and he promised he'd do something about it." More tears welled in Hernandez's eyes. "I killed Marco, didn't I?"

Larkin narrowed his eyes. "No. You did not."

"I didn't trust the police. But if I'd told them instead… Marco was just a fucking kid. What was I thinking?"

"You were not responsible for Marco Garcia's death," Larkin reiterated. "Alfred Niederman was."

That's when Hernandez's expression did something… *strange*. His brows rose and his eyes grew, like in surprise, but then the rounded, geometric shapes in his face elongated, drew out. Surprise transitioned to its close and often mistaken for cousin: fear.

Emotion was present in a situation Larkin had expected it to be devoid.

And he'd caught it.

"Do you know Alfred Niederman."

Hernandez wiped his mouth and shook his head. "No. I—I don't know the name."

"Mr. Hernandez," Larkin said, "Marco Garcia has never gotten justice. Jay Gibson has never gotten justice. Six more victims, and these consist only of those whose photographic evidence we've obtained, have never gotten justice. Do not lie to me. Not now. Not about this."

"I'm not lying," Hernandez protested. "Look, I'm sorry, but I've got a kitchen to run and people to take care of. If you're trying to find out what happened to that Niederman guy, look at Dicky." He pushed between Larkin and Doyle and started for the door.

Larkin turned. "Who said anything about Niederman being dead."

Hernandez stopped, looking over his shoulder. "I assumed. You were asking about Dicky's whereabouts and you're trying to solve old murders."

"I don't believe you," Larkin said simply.

"That's on you, Detective. If you want anything else from me, you'll need a warrant, and I'll be asking for a lawyer." Hernandez stepped through the kitchen door, and it banged shut behind him.

A warm breeze picked up, scattering loose white petals into the manicured lawn.

"He's lying," Larkin said.

"Yeah," Doyle answered.

"He was smoking in the janitor's closet," Larkin continued. "Logically, the windbreaker belonged to the janitor."

"Archie Bunker worked at the YEC the same time as Marco," Doyle said, picking up the train of thought. "Archie is Niederman."

"And Niederman worked for a custodial service," Larkin concluded. "Goddamn it. *There's* my proof he murdered Marco. After his students had boarded the downtown Q on the evening of May 19, Marco confronted Niederman about the death portrait of Jay Gibson. The one witness on the platform said Marco had been arguing with a man in a 'utility uniform.'" Larkin spread his arms out to either side. "Coveralls. I'll bet Niederman's uniform used to be coveralls back then."

Doyle was still staring at the kitchen door. He bit on his thumbnail, chewed it for three, five, seven seconds, then said, "You think Hernandez killed Niederman? Some sort of revenge for what happened to his best friend twenty-three years ago?"

"The business card in Niederman's pocket puts him in Hernandez's direct orbit."

Doyle retrieved his cell and scrolled through recent calls. "I'll ask Niederman's manager if she can confirm over the phone his employment at the Center in '97." He put the phone to his ear.

Larkin unbuttoned his suit coat and rested his hands on his hips. He pushed Doyle's whiskey voice to the back of his consciousness, letting it ebb and flow like the tides. Smooth. Soothing. A constant murmur that he could latch onto, the sort of white noise people used to help them fall asleep—a psychological addiction to a rich baritone. Larkin turned his face, closed his eyes, and soaked up the kisses of sunshine that peered through the boughs of the dogwood. He spun his mental Rolodex and let it stop on Niederman.

A lesser man would wrap the investigation here.

Let Niederman's death succumb to and wallow in the same inactivity, the same injustice that had been served to his victims all these years.

Because who the fuck cared that a child molester and murderer was offed?

It was justice in its own right—a betterment for all of society.

But Everett Larkin had sworn an oath to uphold the constitutions of the United States and the state of New York to the best of his ability, and to allow vigilantism, to turn a blind eye to a perpetrated crime—*to murder*—was detrimental to his skills, his pride, his self-worth, and made him no better than the one who'd killed Niederman. That person was to be tried in a court of law by a jury of their peers, no matter what Larkin thought.

Besides, to investigate Niederman in death was to investigate Niederman in life, which would aid Larkin in identifying all of those lost children. And when justice was served and one by one their cases closed, he could shuttle those forgotten names and forgotten souls onto somewhere better. Where they would be remembered for who they were and not what they had become.

Reynold had claimed that Dicky, a longtime homeless man, had been someone Niederman had known since the community of pedophiles had interacted with each other on now-defunct internet forums. Hernandez had further confirmed this as fact when he claimed to have known Dicky since he was a kid—when both Jay and Marco were still alive.

Fast forward twenty-three years.

Alfred Niederman was murdered Sunday, May 10.

His body was discovered on Tuesday, May 19.

Megan had maintained she, and other youths who squatted at the Fifty-Seventh Street station, had last seen Dicky on Friday, which, because she'd been kidnapped Monday, May 18, would make his last appearance in the tunnels Friday, May 15. A full week after Hernandez had last seen him at St. Jude's Mission.

Megan's explanation that Reynold had learned of her through Dicky, that Dicky would sell out anyone for a hit, had erroneously led Larkin to believing that Dicky had been the DB in the IKEA tote—that he'd been a sort of loose end. And yet, Hernandez's story was that he hadn't known Niederman—but he deduced this stranger was dead, and that if the police wanted a suspect, they ought to question Dicky.

Almost like—

Larkin whispered, "You hadn't planned the murder."

It'd been heat-of-the-moment self-defense. Nothing more.

"I know how to look out for myself."

Except someone else *had* had intentions when they went to the station that night. That's when you were recognized.

"Punk is a mentality, not a look."

Because you visited St. Jude's regularly—just as the generation of misfits before you had.

"—look at Dicky."

Dicky was the perfect scapegoat—another unwanted outcast of society.

Larkin opened his eyes. "But you didn't prepare your alibis together. Who would think to do that, when neither of you are killers by nature…."

"Larkin!"

Larkin startled and looked at Doyle.

"It's the hospital," Doyle said, waving his phone like he'd been trying to get Larkin's attention for a hot minute. "They're saying Megan's not in her room."

"How'd she get around the officer on door duty."

"The idiot took a bathroom break before he was relieved. She must have slipped out then."

"When was the shift change."

"Quarter to one."

Larkin pulled back the sleeve of his suit coat. It was 1:45 p.m.

"I'm sure she skipped because she doesn't want her legal guardian knowing of her whereabouts, but I *told* her—"

"I know where she's going," Larkin said, running for the iron gate that opened onto the street.

"I'll call you back," Doyle said into the phone before rushing after Larkin. "What do you mean, you know where she's going? To Penn Station—Amtrak?"

"Fifty-Seventh Street," Larkin corrected. He yanked the gate open, an obnoxious clamor nearly drowning his voice out as he added, "She's going to kill Dicky."

CHAPTER NINETEEN

The F at Fifty-Seventh Street was only nine blocks from St. Jude's, but in order to head downtown, they'd first have to hook a right and drive uptown simply to turn around, because Larkin had parked on the east side of the street, opposite the church. Combined with the usual nightmare that was Midtown traffic, it'd take at least fifteen minutes to reach the station.

It was easier to run.

And because Larkin and Doyle were both runners— pedestrians and red lights taken into account—they were able to reach the subway in under seven minutes.

Coming to the corner of West Fifty-Seventh and Sixth Avenue, Larkin shot across the sidewalk as the blinking red hand turned solid. He skirted around a bicycle coming up the bike lane, and at the last second, dodged left to avoid a mommy jogger and her double-wide stroller, instead hurtling the ledger bar of the scaffolding that covered the block. Larkin rushed down the stairs of the subway station as a mass of bodies was exiting. He barked NYPD at the assholes trying to come up on his right, forcing them back into the throng of people.

Larkin burst into the station proper, taking a deep breath as he surveyed the redesign he'd visited two days ago and reorienting himself. Larkin had actively avoided riding the subway since college—his HSAM being so sensitive to sound associations and stimulation overloads—and he could think of literally no greater Hell on Earth than being stuck in a packed car during rush hour, idling in the tunnel because of train traffic, the swell of bodies pressing in on him, the hum of the AC, the *pop*, *pop*, *pop* of chewing gum, bells and chimes of Candy Crush being played at full volume, a baby kicking and screaming in their stroller, fresh-from-college finance bros discussing the faults of the working class and whether Tom was going to bring coke to the party tonight in the same breath of conversation, and then the doors between cars opening and a dance team comes in with their speaker at full volume, screaming, "Do you know what time it is?" Larkin shuddered. Yes, he was a New Yorker who had to read the subway signs, seeming to lack that intuitive knowledge about the system that most riders possessed, but it was better than the alternative.

Doyle came to a stop at his side. He asked, only slightly out of breath in the way of a runner with exceptional stamina, "Which side was Marco on?"

"Uptown. The north end."

"We need to get them to hold the trains."

Doyle left Larkin, approaching the bullet-proof ticket booth, where the attendee inside was chatting through her microphone to a track employee—a young black man in steel-toed boots, jeans, a long-sleeve shirt and reflective safety vest, with a hard hat tucked under one arm and a utility belt with a radio strapped around his waist. Doyle butted into their conversation by flashing his badge, and something he said sparked recognition in the track worker's face, who offered a hand and appeared to be introducing himself.

The two returned to Larkin's side, with Doyle saying,

"Larkin, this is Demetrius Armstrong. He reported the DB on Tuesday."

"Mr. Armstrong," Larkin said, quickly shaking his hand. "Everett Larkin, Cold Case Squad."

"Yeah, hey," Armstrong replied. He had a light-up-the-room smile like Doyle. "You guys are a little early. My boss isn't going to be here for about another hour, and I was about to clock-out for lunch—"

"Change of plans, Mr. Armstrong," Larkin interrupted. "We need to go into the uptown tunnel."

"You need to go... *in* the tunnel?"

"Yes. At once. Immediately."

"Uh... yeah, I don't... having workers on the tracks disrupts train schedules. It's gotta be planned in advance. Ms. Crowley might be able to organize getting you in the tunnel between midnight and five o'clock," Armstrong suggested.

"No," Larkin said flatly.

Doyle stepped in to explain, "There's a population of runaways and homeless who have set up a sort of camp somewhere between here and Sixty-Third and Lex. A teen girl among them is wanted for murder, and we believe she returned to this station less than an hour ago."

Larkin added, "I have probable cause that she intends to kill another individual who's currently hiding in the system. Now, please pretend this situation is a track fire."

"The number-one rule on the tracks is, *do not* touch the third rail," Armstrong warned, turning the beam of his flashlight on the raised and covered rail. "My dad worked for the Transit Authority in the '80s. He told me he saw a guy step on the track and explode. Arms and legs literally shot off his core like missiles."

"Noted," Doyle said from the rear.

It'd taken longer than Larkin preferred to get to the platform and actually climb down the access stairs into the tunnel proper, but Armstrong didn't have the sort of authority they'd needed, which required a phone call to Ms. Crowley, the station manager, which turned into a conversation with the Command Center, who then of course looped Lieutenant Connor in on the request, before approval was given to reroute uptown F trains onto the E line from West Fourth due to "police activity."

Larkin and Doyle had left behind their suit coats in exchange for the same orange safety vest that Armstrong wore, and with pistols drawn and kept at low-ready, proceeded into the tunnel that'd been in twenty-four-hour continuous use for a hundred years. The garbage that'd settled on the tracks was the usual sort—empty soda bottles, napkins, candy wrappers, one uncapped and used needle, and a crust of pizza being hauled into the shadows by a rodent of unusual size. Maintenance lights, their bulbs grimy with dirt and soot and God only knew what else, did little to brighten beyond the immediate steps in front of them, while their flashlights illuminated years of graffiti along the walls. Most of the tags were sloppy, the artist's name indecipherable, but there were one or two, the deeper they moved uptown, that Larkin almost dared to consider art.

Illegal, certainly, but a sort of beautiful and gritty urban art nonetheless.

"You know," Armstrong said from ahead of Larkin, "I'm not surprised to hear there's an encampment in this tunnel."

"Why do you say that."

"Well, most folks don't realize it, but the reason the subway tunnels are different sizes and connect at certain stops but not others is because, prior to the MTA, the subway was run by three companies—all with their own plans and schematics. That's to say, this F train is the IND and it can't run on the original IRT lines because they're too narrow. So the MTA has all these workarounds. In fact, my pop told me stories about starting his patrol in one neighborhood and coming out in a completely different precinct, just by walking underground. MTA didn't even have complete schematics of their own system in the '80s—that's why they've got half-finished tracks, tunnels that lead nowhere, abandoned lines discovered during construction…. I wouldn't be at all surprised if they still didn't know about some of what's down here. That's what makes it a haven for the mole people."

"Mole people," Larkin repeated.

"You're not supposed to call 'em that," Armstrong replied. "But some embrace the term."

"Why do you know this," Larkin asked.

Armstrong laughed cheerfully and said, "I'm a bit of a train geek. Me and my dad have been going to conventions every year since I was waist-high. We love it. Everyone's got a thing, you know?"

"I suppose so."

"Anyway," he continued, "The Q was suspended in the late '90s for track repairs, and Fifty-Seventh was the final stop. It was a convenient station to hop the tracks and head uptown to the BMT line at Sixty-Third. That was used to store non–rush-hour trains until the Second Avenue Q line finally opened a few years ago." Armstrong stopped walking, turned, and cast his flashlight on Larkin and Doyle. "All it'd take is one person trying to keep off the grid to discover the relative seclusion of those tracks, and *bam*, encampment."

Armstrong began walking again, the scuff and crunch of his boots echoing off the arched walls and rounded ceiling.

"That wouldn't be the case anymore, though," Doyle called. "Right? Because of the new Q line?"

"Lots of nooks and crannies to hide in, Detective. Pop

once found an access point some kids were using. They called it 'The Hole,' and that's exactly what it was."

The air was growing more humid and stagnant the deeper they walked, and perspiration prickled under Larkin's arms, beads of sweat following the curve of his spine. He noted that the accumulated garbage, due to either obnoxious riders purposefully tossing it onto the tracks or the rush of wind that followed trains entering and exiting stations picking up loose debris, was thinning considerably, making the refuse that *was* present stand out in a more blatant manner.

As they turned a corner, the space around them opened suddenly, making for more than enough clearance on either side of the track so they no longer had to walk along the rails and sleepers. "We're underneath Central Park now," Armstrong explained.

Doyle made a sudden hushing sound. He had a finger to his lips when Larkin turned around. He pointed toward the right. "Hear that?"

Larkin listened. It took a moment for the echo of their steps to recede from memory and the uncanny silence of the underground to come in like a rogue wave, but then he heard it.

A distant, but consistent *ting, ting, ting*.

Metal on metal.

He raised an eyebrow in question.

Doyle murmured, "Someone knows we're coming. They're warning others in the area."

Armstrong turned his flashlight on the far wall, panning back and forth until pausing at an access door covered in grime. It'd practically blended into the darkness, save for the doorknob that was shiny from constant use.

"Where's that door lead?" Doyle asked, keeping his voice low.

Armstrong shrugged. "Could be a utility room, cable room, maybe a shortcut between tracks. The Q, N, R runs this way too." Armstrong stepped carefully as he made his way toward the door, so as to avoid making noise that'd echo and mark their position. He grabbed the handle and gave the door a hard yank.

Someone shouted—a roar of unbridled rage and fury— metal *thwack*ed flesh and bone, and Armstrong was flung off his feet. His flashlight somersaulted through the air, illuminating the blade of a shovel, fresh blood glistening on its tip, and Armstrong's boots as he fell backward, and then the light dropped to the gravel at the same time something *crack*ed and Armstrong cried out in distress.

—*Boom. Squish. Crack.*—

In the doorway stood a stranger, his details scant in the haphazard glows of their flashlight beams: torn plaid pants, jean jacket, maybe a studded belt. He wielded the shovel, likely stolen from an MTA worksite, like a baseball bat.

Larkin froze in terror.

His fear was so unchecked, he imagined his expression comically grotesque in its inhumanness.

Because that monster, that ogre, that devil, stalked Larkin in that place where sleep and wake met and nightmares were real and that *crack, crack, crack* of his skull under the force of a baseball bat repeated forevermore.

"Drop it and put your hands up!" Doyle shouted.

Larkin snapped free from the choke hold of shock, of horror—Doyle's voice an anchor to reality, a reminder that nightmares were only dreams shrouded in a black cloak and memories were only receipts of the past and that Larkin wasn't prey, that he was *safe*.

The man—boy, Larkin thought upon second glance— disappeared through to wherever the open door led.

Larkin swore, holstered his weapon, and crouched beside

Armstrong. The man's nose was clearly broken, his cheek sliced open, with blood all over his face, but when Larkin reached under his head, he pulled his hand back with a start to see it covered in dark, warm blood. He grabbed his own fallen flashlight to see Armstrong had hit his head on one of the track fastenings.

"Larkin!"

"I'm right behind you," Larkin shouted, already stepping around Armstrong, reaching under his arms, and heaving the bigger-built man into a sitting position. He couldn't leave Armstrong lying right beside the track—God forbid an unanticipated train pass through and immediately kill him. Larkin turned, his derbies scraping loudly as he dug his heels into the ballast and gravel, dragging Armstrong toward the wall for safety. He couldn't linger, not even to check Armstrong's vitals, because Doyle was already through the door and *he* was the priority.

Larkin drew his SIG P226, moved to the door, and made a quick check of the situation. Doyle stood at the edge of the walkway, looking down—onto a lower-level track, perhaps—bare cables and supports running overhead. Larkin slipped through the doorway in time to make out Doyle's next words:

"Megan, listen to me. I know you're scared. It's okay to be scared. But violence is always a choice, and you can choose, right now, to let him go."

Larkin wiped his bloody hand on his trouser leg before adjusting his grip on the pistol and edging forward. He looked over the embankment to see an abandoned and flooded system. The MTA pumped nearly fourteen million gallons of water from their active tracks *daily*—Larkin supposed an unused tunnel was the least of their concerns. But standing in the calf-high water was Megan Flouride, dressed in the same clothes she'd been wearing when they rescued her from Reynold's apartment. She stood behind an older, gaunt man on his knees in the muck, with one arm wrapped around his neck and, in her other hand, what looked like a heavy-duty plastic knife, like those that would have been served with her hospital meals, carved into a deadly point. The man was alive, but bleeding from a neck wound. He was struggling to bat her away, but he looked so high, it was amazing he was even conscious.

"Megan," Doyle tried again.

"*No!*" She pointed the homemade weapon in Larkin's direction before pressing it to Dicky's neck, tears and snot streaming down her face as she screamed, "Make him go away or I'll do it! I'll fuckin' stab this motherfuckin' junkie right now."

"Larkin," Doyle said calmly. "Take a few steps back."

Larkin hesitated, then did as asked, instead taking the rear in order to search up and down the walkway for wherever Megan's hired muscle had disappeared.

"It's just you and me," Doyle insisted.

Megan's voice was hysterical as she said, "I didn't mean to do it! That sick old fuck's been around before. My friends would disappear, and we'd all think, I guess they went home. I guess they found a place to crash. Maybe they made enough money trickin' to *get out.* But—but—he *killed* them! I know, because he came that night, and I was alone on the platform. He tried—he tried—" Megan couldn't finish the sentence as she began sobbing.

"You defended yourself?" Doyle asked, and Larkin could hear a tremor intermixed with his words.

"*Yeah,*" she cried, sounding so very small.

"What happened?"

"He p-put his hands around my neck, but Tony showed me how to get away."

"Is Tony your friend with the shovel?"

Megan's response must have been physical because Larkin didn't hear her reply.

"We know someone put a belt around Alfred Niederman's neck," Doyle said. "We know that's how he died. And we know it was a bullet belt. Maybe something you'd like wearing."

"He tried to kill me!" Megan protested.

"How'd he end up in the bag, Megan?"

Larkin could hear a struggle, hear water splashing.

"Megan," Doyle tried again. "Put the weapon down and talk to me. Will you do that for me?"

She sniffled, coughed, and spit before saying, "He's still up there with you, isn't he?"

"Don't worry about Detective Larkin."

Megan's voice was quieter, like her adrenaline was beginning to wane, and she said, "Mr. Hernandez found the bag in one of the trash cans on the platform. He helped me drag the body into the utility room because it'd been left unlocked."

"You called Noel Hernandez for help?"

"He was just *there*," Megan insisted. "He saw everything, but he promised I wouldn't get in trouble because that old bitch was a bad guy. Mr. Hernandez swore he was—that he got what was comin' to him. So he helped me hide the body, then told me to just go. Don't come around St. Jude's anymore, don't stay in the city. *Go!*"

"But you didn't have the money," Doyle concluded.

Megan's whine preceded another volley of tears. "Mr. Hernandez threw my belt away—so no one would find DNA, he said. And that dude—Gary—had a taser, so I couldn't...."

"What happened was self-defense," Doyle explained. "But this, what you're doing with Dicky, isn't the same thing. Megan, if you kill him, you will go to jail. Don't do that.

Don't risk your entire life for this."

"I have to!"

"No, you don't," Doyle insisted.

"He'll just sell us out for more drugs. That's what happened. He tells old guys where we hang out for some dope, then they come down here—try to touch us...." She faltered, then said in a false bravado, like she was not only trying to convince Doyle, but herself, "I have to do this."

"*Megan*!"

Dicky gurgled.

Megan screamed, so high-pitched that it could have shattered glass.

Larkin ran to the edge of the walkway in time to see her, her hands and T-shirt bloody, fling the knife and Dicky aside before she took off running through the filthy water.

"*Jesus Christ*," Larkin swore, holstering his pistol a second time before jumping onto the submerged tracks. He splashed through the water and grabbed the homeless man, his body odor and unwashed clothes ripe enough to make Larkin's eyes water. He heard a scramble of boots on gravel, then a second door, toward the south, open and shut. "Go after her!" he called up to Doyle.

Doyle was gone in an instant, chasing Megan into the dark via this different route, but ultimately in the direction from which they'd come.

Larkin dragged Dicky toward a sort of elevated nook built into the wall underneath the walkway. There was a mattress, duffle bag, camping stove with a pot, and something that might have been SpaghettiOs inside, all neatly tucked away, where no MTA employee would ever know to look, unless they climbed down into the sewage themselves. He heaved Dicky up, pushing his bloody, sodden body onto the mattress before shucking off his safety vest. Larkin ripped the material until it was a long, reflective strip, and wound it around Dicky's neck, knotting it tightly enough to put pressure on the wound—he didn't think Megan had nicked an artery, there wasn't enough blood—but not so much so that Dicky would choke.

"Give me your hand," Larkin demanded, taking Dicky's hand and making him press it over the knot. "Hold it like this. Keep putting pressure on it so you don't bleed out."

"...*Hurts*...," Dicky croaked.

"Shut up. I'm going to call for help. Don't even think about dying." Larkin checked his phone, the screen a beacon in the dark, musty tunnel, but he wasn't at all surprised to see No Service load in the top left corner. Shoving it back in his pocket, Larkin hoisted himself out of the track bed and onto the walkway. His derbies squelched as he ran through the first still-open door, returning to Armstrong. Larkin got down on one knee, noting the bubbly, wheezy breaths the man was taking through his broken nose. He grabbed the two-way radio off Armstrong's belt, pressed down on the side button, and said, "This is Everett Larkin with the NYPD. I'm in the uptown F tunnel with Demetrius Armstrong of the MTA, somewhere underneath Central Park, and I need two buses ASAP. I've got head trauma and a knife—"

Larkin's breath *whoosh*ed out of his lungs in a sudden rush as something hard and heavy slammed into his back. He dropped the radio and collapsed forward. He felt paralyzed, gulping for air like a landed fish. A boot came down on his back, holding him pinned, while a hand dug the SIG from his holster. Larkin coughed reflexively, his body doing whatever it could to kickstart his lungs. The pistol slid free, the boot lifted, and Larkin was able to roll onto his back.

The same boy—maybe this was Tony—dropped the shovel in favor of the gun. It was clear he'd never held a pistol before, was surprised by its weight and unsure how to grasp it. "Leave Megan alone, and I won't have to shoot you, pig."

Larkin didn't move.

Didn't twitch.

Didn't blink.

The radio crackled with a response to Larkin's request, asking for clarification, confirmation, location, *anything*.

Tony took a few steps backward, using the track on his left side to keep in a straight line. He was still awkwardly pointing the SIG in Larkin's general direction, likely to hit anything and everything, from the ceiling to Larkin's forehead, if he pulled the trigger. "Don't move," he said again. Then he turned and bolted for Fifty-Seventh Street.

Larkin watched the teenage boy's dark outline become lost to the blackness, nothing but his silhouette bouncing along the walls in disproportionate shapes as he raced past bare bulbs. His back twinged painfully as Larkin eased onto his knees, and he gasped once getting to his feet, but he grabbed the shovel and, fueled by undiluted adrenaline and rage, ran after Tony.

Because that little shitweasel was armed and was going to take Doyle by surprise.

Larkin kept along the wall, not only to reduce his visibility, but to avoid kicking up gravel and garbage and immediately warn Tony that he was being followed. Larkin could shoot *himself* after letting a teenager get the upper hand, but luck was on his side in that Tony was ultimately a dumbass kid, shit-scared, and running like being followed wasn't even a thought in his pretty little head.

As Larkin rounded the corner, light came into view—like finding the pot of gold at the end of a rainbow. He could make Megan out in the far distance, pulling herself up from the track bed, clinging to the platform floor, swinging a leg up, and rolling to safety. She'd had enough of a lead on Doyle, familiar with every possible shortcut that'd put distance between them, that Larkin could make out Doyle's figure walking into the artificial light, like he'd thought he'd lost her, until he spotted Megan standing on the platform and hurried toward her.

Tony was nearing the access stairs and gate that kept the general public from exploring the active tunnels, and when he spotted Doyle out in the open, he shouted Megan's name and threw the gun at her. Larkin didn't wait to see if she caught the weapon. He charged at breakneck speed toward Tony, barreled into the teen with his left shoulder, and sent him sprawling onto the steep steps.

Tony cried out, "Oh my God, you broke my fucking ribs!"

Larkin ignored the crocodile tears, retrieved the handcuffs from his back pocket, bent over Tony, and cuffed one wrist. He attached the other to the gate so that Tony couldn't run and was forced to cower on the stairs. "I'll be right back to Mirandize you, you *sonofabitch*." Larkin grabbed the shovel he'd dropped in the scrabble, then got close to Tony's face and whispered, "Not a peep, or you and me are going to have a come to Jesus. And if your gal pal shoots my partner, you'll be dealing with the bad cop and *only* the bad cop." Larkin narrowed his gray eyes and nearly growled, "Got it."

Tony's eyes were so wide, they were nearly bulging. He nodded, panicked little breaths escaping from between his lips in a near whistle.

Larkin moved around him, quietly creeping up the steps and easing himself over the gate. The platform was empty, as it'd been roped off from upstairs, and Megan stood alone toward the middle, gun shaking wildly in her hands as she pointed it at Doyle. He stood in the middle of the open tracks, both hands raised in the air. Larkin could pick up the deep cadence of Doyle speaking, but wasn't able to make out the individual words. He moved on the balls of his feet at an angle, his back to the downtown tracks as he gave Megan a wide berth so as to sneak up behind her.

"Stop it!" Megan cried. "Just *stop*. You're from the street. You get it. Why're you actin' like this, Ira?"

"I'm a police officer," Doyle corrected. "And I want to help you. We can still make smart choices. Right now, you can decide to put that gun down, and we can walk away from this."

"You'll come after me," Megan retorted. "I just want to go to Montana. Let me go to Montana."

"You can't go to Montana if you shoot me."

The gun wavered, began to point toward the floor, but then Megan squared her shoulders and raised it again. She awkwardly yanked the hammer back with both thumbs.

"Megan—" Doyle started.

A train that hadn't gotten the fucking message about reroutes, its headlights bright as it rounded the tunnel corner from the south, laid on its deafening horn when the conductor saw Doyle. The brakes engaged and metal screeched against metal.

Larkin spun the shovel in one hand, held the handle tight, and slammed it into the back of Megan's knee. She screamed, fell, and the gun went off, a round firing into the white subway tiles above Doyle's head. Larkin grabbed the pistol from Megan, who now lay on the ground, cradling her leg. He holstered the weapon and bent over as Doyle was trying to hoist himself up onto the chest-high platform.

The train laid on the horn again.

Sparks shot up in a spray of bright white and blue as the wheels grated against the rails.

Larkin shouted, "*Ira!*" He grabbed Doyle's hand with his left, but the weakened, post-surgery muscles were close to giving out, the soles of his shoes were skidding along the tactile caution strip as Doyle's heavier weight overpowered him, and Larkin blindly reached for, caught, and hauled Doyle up by the back of his belt just as he slipped and crashed backward onto the platform.

The train zoomed past them and came to an emergency stop half a dozen yards ahead. Heat and wind rushed onto the platform a second later. A silence settled over the station.

Larkin was shaking underneath Doyle, who lay sprawled atop him. He yanked his arms free, grabbed Doyle's face in both hands, and asked, "Is all of you here?"

Doyle looked over his shoulder, like he actually had to confirm both legs were attached by sight and not feel alone, then said with an equally shaky voice, "Looks like it. Thanks."

Larkin wrapped his arms around Doyle's neck and began to cry.

Out of fear?

Relief?

Larkin didn't know.

He didn't care.

CHAPTER TWENTY

Larkin considered, for precisely four seconds, to take up cigarette smoking.

In reality, he was certain he merely wanted something to do with his restless fingers as he listened to the phone ring against his ear.

It was Friday, May 22, 4:24 p.m., and Larkin sat on the rooftop of Doyle's building, his back against the surrounding ledge and a warm breeze mussing his ash-blond hair.

One more ring and it'd click over to voice—

"Hello, Detective," Camila answered.

Larkin hadn't considered the possibility that Camila might have actually saved his contact information in her address book, and was thrown off balance by not having the upper hand with his usual *This is Detective Everett Larkin, Cold Case Squad.* He struggled for the proper introduction but ended up simply saying, "Hi."

Neither of them spoke for a moment, and when they did, it was over each other.

"I wanted to tell you—"

"I saw you on TV."

"I'm sorry," Larkin said. "You go."

"On TV yesterday," Camila reiterated after a brief hesitation. "At the subway station."

"Yes."

"The news said you caught a child molester."

"It's a bit more complicated than that."

"Will you tell me?"

Larkin intended to say, *I'm sorry but the investigation is still ongoing. I'm sorry, but I can't divulge certain details of the case yet. I'm sorry. I'm sorry. I'm sorry.*

Instead, he told Camila everything. He told her that twenty-three years ago, a twelve-year-old Noel Hernandez confided in his trustworthy mentor at the YEC that he'd found photographs of his best friend, dead and in compromising positions, in the janitor's closet. He told Camila that Marco Garcia promised to take care of the situation, and when he'd approached Alfred Niederman with the story Hernandez shared, Niederman panicked and shoved Marco in front of an incoming Q train. He told Camila that Niederman never stopped his abuse, and for another two decades, floated from job to job, through his company like a toxic cloud of exploitation and death, always on the hunt for whatever suited his fancy—be it access to early photo labs, before he was forced to build his own darkroom and learn the art, or access to the children themselves.

He told Camila that a whole new generation of runaways was being subjected to Niederman's sadistic pleasures, that they'd become accessible due to a homeless man who'd never gotten the help he needed and who Niederman kept strung out on heroin. He told Camila about Hernandez's wild and unfounded claim, after he'd been arrested for aiding and abetting second-degree murder, that he'd received an anonymous letter at the church one afternoon with proof of where Niederman could be found, and that the sender would "leave it up to you to do with this information what you will." How Hernandez had sent Dicky on his way with extra food from the pantry, if in return Dicky would give Niederman his card, because Hernandez wanted to finish the business he never could as a kid.

He'd wanted to kill Niederman.

And Larkin told Camila how Megan had been in the wrong place at the wrong time, and the fourteen-year-old had managed to strangle Niederman the same instant Hernandez came looking around the station, sick of waiting for Niederman to show his face at St. Jude's, and how, together, they'd hidden his body but failed to come up with one shared alibi—leading to Larkin's breakthrough on the case.

Larkin was quiet afterward. The wind was still blowing, and he imagined Camila listening to the static over the other end.

"My son's murderer will never go to trial," Camila said, very quietly.

"I'll see that he's found guilty."

"He's dead, Detective."

"Posthumously."

"What will it matter?"

Larkin closed his eyes. "Maybe it's the kind of ending where you decide whether you want something out of it."

"I'm tired, Mr. Larkin," she answered, using Larkin's name instead of his title, for the first time. "I don't think I have the energy. It's like fighting the inevitable. The sun will always set. The tides will always wash out. And Marco will always be gone."

Larkin swallowed.

"Do you think it's wrong of me to be happy that man is dead?"

"I think we all grieve differently, and our solace is just as unique."

"Come now. Be honest. Jesus will judge me, not you."

Larkin let out a breath of a laugh as he opened his eyes again. "No. I don't think it's wrong. I think it's human—to hate. The capacity is in us, after all, or such a word wouldn't exist in our vocabulary. But I think, to love, is far greater."

"I cannot love that man, Mr. Larkin."

"Love can be interpreted in so many ways, Ms. Garcia."

"That girl—she will go to court?"

"Yes. She has to."

"I would like to be there. I think I should be there. I think people should know what he did to my son and so many other babies, before they judge her too harshly. Will you see that this happens for me?"

"I will."

"Detective?"

"Yes."

"Every night, I say a prayer for Marco. It helps me dream of him. But last night, I had a dream about a white boy. With green eyes. What color eyes did your Patrick have?"

Larkin's heart felt as if it'd seized in his throat, but somehow, he managed to whisper, "Green."

Camila made a sort of knowing sound before saying, "I think, maybe you are right... about love."

Larkin ended the call. He took a moment to add a reminder to his calendar about seeing Camila included in Megan's court proceedings. After, he slowly got to his feet, walked across the pea gravel, and pulled open the roof access door. He took the stairs slowly, quietly, stepping past Mr. Gabel's door and heading down to the fourth floor. Larkin opened 4A, entered the studio apartment with its fairy lights and chugging window unit and the treasure of his heart standing at the kitchen counter.

Doyle looked up from chopping carrots. "How'd it go?"

Larkin shut the door, strode across the room, took Doyle by the hips, and kissed his mouth firmly, deeply.

Doyle awkwardly dropped the knife onto the cutting board, ignoring it as it bounced and fell into the sink with a loud clatter while he draped his arms over Larkin's shoulders.

Larkin slipped his tongue free before opening his eyes.

Doyle said, "That was some phone call."

"We haven't had a first date."

"No, we haven't."

"I think we should."

"What'd you have in mind?" Doyle asked.

"Do you like night drives."

The intercom buzzed before Doyle could answer.

Larkin released him.

Doyle walked to the speaker box on the wall beside the front door, pressed the microphone, and said, "Yes?"

"It's Noah. Rider. Everett's—uh—could I come up for a second? To speak with him?"

Doyle looked over his shoulder.

Larkin sighed but nodded. "Sooner rather than later, I guess."

Doyle pressed the door lock, held it down for a few seconds, then let go. He said, while waiting at the front door, "I'd love to go on a night drive."

"Okay."

"But we have to invoke out-in-the-field rule four."

Larkin crossed his arms and asked, "Always tell the truth."

"That's rule five."

"I'm not letting you drive."

Doyle grinned when there was a quiet knock. "We'll see." He opened the front door.

Noah stood in the doorway, still dressed in the business casual he wore to school. He held a white envelope in one hand. "I'm sorry, I don't even want to be here, but I think it's important."

"Come in," Doyle said, politely ushering Noah inside.

Larkin still stood at the counter. "I meant to call you yesterday," he said as Noah walked toward him. "I got caught up."

"I saw the news." Noah thrust the white envelope out. "This was in our—my—mailbox when I got home from work. I opened it… but it's meant for you."

Larkin uncrossed his arms and hesitantly took the offering. It was greeting-card size. No name, no mailing address, no stamps marking it as having traveled through the USPS. "What is it."

"Just look at it," Noah said.

Larkin held the envelope by one corner and carefully wriggled free the folded cardstock from within. He opened it to reveal cut-out magazine letters, pasted together to form new words:

SHAME ON YOU, LARKIN

The *s* had clearly been cut from an advertisement for the New York City subway—its font highly recognizable.

TO IGNORE MY MEMENTO

The death portrait of the unknown girl? Or the message scrawled on the back?

"WHAT THEY ARE, SO SHALL WE BE"

In the crease of the letter was a ticket stub, like those for Broadway theatres in the 1980s.

COME FIND ME

Everett Larkin and Ira Doyle return in:

Broadway Butchery
(Memento Mori: Book Three)

C.S. Poe is an author of gay mystery, romance, and speculative fiction. She is a Lambda Literary and two-time EPIC award finalist, and FAPA, Indie, and two-time e-Lit award winner.

She resides in New York City, but has also called Key West and Ibaraki, Japan, home. She loves Romanticism artwork, Gilded Age New York, the films of Buster Keaton, coffee in the morning and whiskey in the evening, true crime, and cats. She's rescued two cats—Milo and Kasper do their best to distract her from work on a daily basis.

C.S. is an alumna of the School of Visual Arts.

Her debut novel, *The Mystery of Nevermore*, was published 2016.

cspoe.com

ALSO BY C.S. POE

An Auden & O'Callaghan Mystery
(co-written with Gregory Ashe)
A Friend in the Dark
A Friend in the Fire

NOVELS:
Southernmost Murder

NOVELLAS:
11:59

SHORT STORIES:
Love in 24 Frames
That Turtle Story
New Game, Start
Love Has No Expiration

Visit cspoe.com for the latest book releases, titles in audio, and available foreign translations.

Join C.S. Poe's mailing list for advance excerpts and cover art of upcoming books, exclusive sales, convention appearances, and more!
bit.ly/CSPoeNewsletter

Printed in Great Britain
by Amazon